Payal Dhar (she/they) writes books for middle-grade and young adult readers. They have been writing stories since they were seven years old. Unfortunately, no one will ever know what was in them because her dog ate everything. They write on a computer these days, and hope they'll never cross paths with a Pting. She is the author of *There's a Ghost in My PC*, *Hit for a Six* and *It Has No Name*, among others, and has also co-edited *Eat the Sky, Drink the Ocean*, a unique YA feminist anthology.

In their day job, Payal is a freelance journalist on science, technology and society. If you'd like to get in touch, especially to recommend good books, you can do so at: payaldhar.com.

In the series

The Prophecy: Sands of Time, Book 1

SANDS *of* TIME

BOOK TWO

THE KEY

PAYAL DHAR

Speaking Tiger

YOUNG ADULT

Content warning:
The Key is an exciting, drama-filled fantasy adventure novel, with danger lurking around unknown corners, and twists when you least expect them. But it also has some elements that may not be suitable for some readers. The story mentions suicide and suicidal thoughts among teens. Please read with care.

SPEAKING TIGER PUBLISHING PVT. LTD
125A, Ground Floor, Shahpur Jat,
Near Asiad Village, New Delhi 110049

An earlier version of this work was first published by Young Zubaan in 2007

This edition published in paperback by Speaking Tiger Books in 2023

ISBN: 978-93-5447-518-4
eISBN: 978-93-5447-513-9

10 9 8 7 6 5 4 3 2 1

Typeset in Adobe Garamond Pro by Jojy Philip
Printed at HT Media Ltd, Greater Noida

CONTENTS

1

LEV WANTS ANSWERS

The worst thing was, there was no pain. In fact, there were no words for the horrible, discomfiting wrongness of that—that mangled, lacerated mess that was once his right hand, the stench of blood and flesh, and yet not to feel the agony that should be there. There were times when Yazid wondered if he was actually dead.

This perpetual darkness, the gnaw of hunger, the hard ground digging into his back. And the bone-chilling cold—if this was hell, then everyone had been wrong about it.

Where else would he be headed, though, if not to hell?

Then came the fevers that indeed did feel like fire, followed by chills that left him shaking until exhaustion overcame consciousness. He lost count of things like night and day, pain and discomfort, hunger and thirst, hot and cold.

The days—weeks? months?—rolled into each other. Yazid dreamt of home, family, his favourite sister, of hot food and soft beds. Sometimes there was a voice, someone touching him, moving him, feeding him. Sometimes he thought it was his mother and it gave him comfort. Other times, he fought against whoever it was, because he knew he had to.

One day, there were more voices, and it didn't seem like a dream. Loud, clamouring ones; soft, prodding ones. He was lifted up and carried out into light so bright that his eyes burnt. The hard, cold ground gave way to yielding warmth. Gentle hands tended to him. A new, soft voice talked to him in words he didn't know, but he understood that it was telling him he was safe. New sensations assailed him as well—pleasant smells, welcome warmth, and soothing comfort.

Maybe, just maybe, he *was* going to be all right. Maybe he *was* alive. Maybe he *would* have a chance at redemption.

Then he was alone and it was dark again. For a while, this felt like a different sort of darkness—a tender one, filled with kindness, that embraced him rather than devoured.

A shadow rose from this soft darkness, and as his vision cleared and the face came into focus, Yazid's body chilled again.

'We are safe now,' said Kilyana quietly.

That's when he knew that he, at least, wasn't.

~

'The Warriors of the Shadow were an anarchist group that eschewed the leadership of the High Council. The history of their origins is sketchily documented. It is said that they existed for over two thousand years till they were destroyed by the High Council's intervention during the Kendark Civil War in 1995.'

Half a dozen senior Preferred drank in every word, half in disbelief that the much-feared-and-speculated-upon Warriors were finally being talked about.

'I must impress upon you that this is a classified subject,' Halvard Tamati continued, 'that we are only talking about right now under a special dispensation.'

To make his point, he held up an electronic document filled with tiny text. On top lay the High Council logo of an hourglass and the words, 'May the Sands of Time keep the ground beneath your feet' in dancing Proto letters. At the bottom of the document were a number of seals and signatures—confirmation from the highest powers-that-be allowing them this limited freedom.

'According to Law 241A of the Laws of the High Council, discussion and speculation about the Warriors is a crime,' Tamati went on. 'Back until the twentieth century, when the Warriors were rampant, they put the very future of the worlds at stake. As an organization, as an ideology, the Warriors sought to bring down and control the Sands of Time. It is the duty of every Halvard, serving and future, therefore, to ensure that they never rise again.'[1]

Lev wished he had a way of quelling the sick fluttering in his stomach. His advanced Guiding companions—Rehan, Valerie, Mingmei, Owen and Za-Ab—listened with rapt attention, while he fidgeted.[2]

---

[1] The Sands of Time is a giant hourglass filled with a mysterious sand-like material, whose flow corresponds to the flow of time. It is housed in a secure chamber inside the Halvard Castle. We don't know much about the Sands, except that if it stops or is interrupted, time will unravel. It is the job of Halvard, like Tamati, to make sure it runs smoothly. Halvard-in-training, like Lev and his classmates, are called Preferred.

[2] Lev's frustration stemmed from the fact that he knew far more than what Tamati was telling them. Last year, he and Maya had

'Halvard,' he said, raising a hand finally, 'you refer to them in past tense.'

'Of course,' said Tamati. 'Didn't I state that they were wiped out in Kendark?'

Next to Lev, he felt Za-Ab shifting, staring at him, then raising his hand and speaking with his hands and fingers, 'Are we sure of that?'

'Are you questioning the High Council's official records?' Tamati responded.

'No, Halvard! I just wondered—'

'Before I continue,' said Tamati, pinning Za-Ab with a severe glance, and then taking in the rest of the class, 'I must reiterate, yet again, that this is classified information. You are not permitted to discuss this outside of the classroom, even amongst yourselves. But at another level, as Halvard of tomorrow, it is imperative that you know your history.'

Lev started to raise his hand again, but Val got in first.

'But I don't understand. You say the Warriors no longer exist. If so, the danger is past. Why, then, is it a classified subject?'

Tamati nodded. 'A very good question. You see, ever since the Warriors were officially destroyed, petty criminal groups have attempted to gain notoriety by professing affiliation to their ideology.'

'But surely,' put in Lev, 'we should know as much as possible about anyone who rejects the leadership of the High Council?'

---

tumbled headlong into a 2,000-year-old secret of the Warriors—the Aidiyar Prophecy—a carefully planned conspiracy to take control of the Sands of Time. And the Warriors were willing to kill for it.

Their Guide instructor nodded. 'That might be one way of looking at it. On the other hand, it could also result in unnecessary speculation, and encourage unsavoury elements. That itself would be harmful to the Sands of Time.'

'What about these "unsavoury elements", then?' Even the usually quiet Owen spoke up. 'Who are they? Terrorists? Can we talk about them?'

'Recall that no era of human civilization has ever been free of crime.' Tamati said. 'Are they terrorists, you ask?' He shrugged. 'Troublemakers would be a better term—no proof of any organization or philosophy. You might want to study the official crime statistics for the latest figures.'

'I still don't understand,' said Rehan, or Ray, as everyone called him. Odd that it had taken him this long to enter the discussion—he was usually the most vocal of the lot. 'Why does the High Council have to be all cloak-and-dagger about it, especially if the Warriors are finished? There's worse stuff in Roz, isn't there?'[3]

'You do not have the security clearance for me to go any deeper into that side of the discussion with you.'

'Isn't that contradictory, Halvard? Didn't you just say our primary responsibility is to deal with threats to the Sands?'

---

[3] Roz is short for Amrozan, which is the Proto word for our world. There is another alternate world called Olaman, or Lam, where the Sands of Time is housed, where the Halvard Castle is, and where Preferred are trained. Halvard and Preferred can travel between the worlds via the Portal Road. Roz and Lam are also connected by the Sands of Time, but there isn't enough space in this book to explain exactly how. If you're interested, you could look up a book about Thandolwethusian mathematics in the Castle library. Oh wait…

A slow anger was building up inside Lev. So this was how the High Council 'dealt' with the Warriors? By pretending they were history, and sidestepping any direct questions?

At least Tamati was right about one thing—they were dangerous. Lev had a scar running down the middle of his torso as evidence of that.[4]

'How are we supposed to protect the Sands without full knowledge of the Warriors' ideology?' he asked, interrupting whatever Tamati was saying in response to Ray. 'And if they were indeed destroyed, what do the High Councillor's Elite Guards do?'

'The Elite Guards,' said Tamati in a tone one would take with an argumentative ten-year-old, 'are tasked with rooting out any individual or group that profess to defy the High Council's law. If you are really interested, there is a very lucid account of the defeat of the Warriors called *The Call of the Dark*.'

'But that's just a Halvard's journal about the Kendark War,' Za-Ab protested. 'Not an authenticated historical account. Where can I find a political history of Kendark? Background information on what exactly happened there, before and after the uprising?'

'For that,' said Tamati, 'you would need to be Z-level security cleared, I am afraid.'

Lev gritted his teeth in frustration. Halvard Tamati moved on to telling the class about the Kendark Civil War a quarter of a century ago, when the still autonomous

---

[4] Remember the earlier footnote about the Warriors being willing to kill to protect their Prophecy? While Lev had survived the attempted murder, the scar running down his body reminded him of it every day.

mountain city had been taken over by the Warriors. It was a rather glorified account of how the High Council had sent in Halvard to intervene on behalf of the city, with very little information about the Warriors themselves. He also did not mention that in return for their intervention, the High Council had done exactly what the Warriors had wanted to do—annex Kendark.

But nobody pointed it out. Everyone was restless, not just Lev, dissatisfied, for once, with their lesson.

'Halvard Tamati,' Lev said abruptly, interrupting the instructor again. 'What about assassins? What do we know about them? They were trained by the Warriors to kill, weren't they? Rumours say they still exist.'

A variety of expressions crossed the Halvard's face—like he was trying all of them out before deciding which one would do. Surprise, irritation, anger. He finally laughed, but it was forced. 'Assassins are just stories. When I was a child, my mother used to tell me, "Eat your greens or the assassins will come and get you!"'

Lev clenched his fists till his knuckles were white.

An almost impossibly tall man stood at Chiyo's door. For a second or two, she stared wordlessly at him. Noah, with his fair skin and white-blond hair, could look like death incarnate at the best of times. Right now, though, he was the most welcoming sight she had had in weeks.

She broke into a grin. 'You, Halvard, are a sight for sore eyes.'

Noah's mouth twitched—about as much of a smile as she'd get from him. 'You look like you've seen a ghost.'

'You have to admit, you are pretty ghostly. How are you?'

'I'm well, thank you. You? And Lev?'

'We're okay, I suppose.'

Chiyo beckoned him inside and he settled cross-legged on one of her floor cushions, while she made tea for them. She took longer over it than she had to. There was so much to say and none of it easy.

'It is good to see you…a relief actually,' she said finally, bringing over tea and a plate of rice crackers. 'I can feel my shoulders relaxing—I didn't even know how on edge I was.'

'For that, I apologize,' said Noah. 'It was not your burden to carry.'

'It is a collective burden, Noah, even those of us who don't know of it. But I only meant that it was lonely. More so for Lev.'

Noah nodded. 'It was. For us too.'

'And Maya? How is she?'

Noah's eyes flickered to the floor. That little movement said more than words would.

She sighed. 'You haven't been in touch, have you?'

'No. I needed the distance. No amount of blocking would have kept from her what the poison did to me.'[5, 6]

That was to be expected. 'But she is okay?'

---

[5] To control the Sands, the Warriors needed an object called the Key of Chaos hidden in a remote region of Lam. Maya and Lev, along with their Watchers (Noah and Chiyo respectively), had gone in pursuit of the Key to keep the Warriors from getting it. In the ensuing showdown, Noah had been shot by a poisoned bolt. He would have died, had it not been for some desperate first-aid from Maya.

[6] Blocking is something Watchers can do to limit what their Preferred know about them.

'Physically, yes. But she's not been having an easy time.'

'It's not your fault. You did the right thing. You're no good to her if you're not a hundred per cent.'

'Yes, I know that. Theoretically.'

Rice crackers crunched in the silence between them. Then Chiyo asked, 'When are you getting her back?'

'Soon.'

'Good. Lev will be pleased.'

Noah drank his tea in more silence, but his unease remained palpable.

'Spit it out.'

'Well, I…don't know how to say this, but both Maya and I…we appreciate your support, yours and Lev's. But I will—we will—completely understand if you should want to distance yourself. The repercussions and consequences could be disastrous.'

'Noah—'

'Wait, let me finish, please. With Nira's help, I have been looking closely at the Prophecy. If our reading is right, the Key gives its holder a lot of power. I'm not sure what that power is, but it is likely to be very important to the Warriors. As a Watcher, I can understand if you wanted to keep Lev at a distance, and I know Maya will understand too. Eventually.'[7]

---

[7] The Prophecy details how a Halvard of exceptional strength will use the Key to control the Sands of Time. According to the Warriors' calculations, one of these people could have been Lev, the other Yazid. Fortunately for the Warriors, Yazid's Watcher (Kilyana) was already one of them, so they handpicked thirteen-year-old Yazid as the future Shadow, the wielder of the Key. This also meant that, to make sure Lev didn't emerge as a future threat, they wanted him

Chiyo stared at his unreadable face for a while, nonplussed, but she had learnt to read some of his quirks over the dozen or so years she'd known him.

'It changes nothing,' she said finally. 'You and Maya stood by us when the situation was reversed. But this is not about paying back that debt—it's about friendship, loyalty, and most of all, doing what's right. I do trust you, Noah, and even Maya. It is just the power the Key gives her that I am wary of. Our Preferred may not understand the nuances of that, but you and I, we have to.'

Noah gave a slight nod. 'Thank you. And Yazid? Any news of him?'

Chiyo's exhale whistled through her teeth. That was a whole different burden. 'No. I feel responsible...I should have done something.'[8]

'Regrets,' said Noah quietly. 'They never do us any good.'

---

gone. So they had tried to kill him. Remember the scar? However, when it came to the final showdown, it was Maya, not Lev or Yazid, who had been able to claim the Key.

[8] Chiyo had been the first to suspect that Yazid's Watcher had been manipulating him, but for many complicated reasons, she had continued to give her the benefit of the doubt until it had been too late. Grown-ups make bad decisions sometimes, even Watchers.

2

MAYA DROPS A BOMBSHELL

Maya woke with a start, heart in mouth, drenched in sweat.

She was used to this; so much so, she'd stopped wondering what had woken her. That was her new thing these days—lying awake at night, staring at the darkness.

She reached for her phone. The time blinked on the screen: 4:56 a.m.

That much-coveted smartphone had been a late birthday gift, not just in honour of turning thirteen, but also a gesture of appeasement from her parents. *Please stay,* was the unspoken message. *Don't go away again to unknown worlds we neither understand, nor want to. Please be normal.*

She picked up her phone and unlocked it, opening the app that collected news alerts from around the world—from pandemic updates to what was happening in Palestine, Syria, Ukraine, Kashmir, about floods in Brazil and Australia, snowstorms in America, student protests in her own state in India.

It was a simple little tool she had put together to filter the news using some specific parameters. She wanted the news behind the news. She wanted, no, she *needed*, the proof that she knew was around somewhere that the Warriors were behind most—if not all—of the unrest in the world, whether it was natural or being done by humans.

She needed proof that all this was not because of her.

Or maybe that would just prove it *was* because of her.

She kicked off the covers tangled around her legs and padded to the kitchen to get some water. There was a bottle on her bedside table, but these nighttime wanderings too were a recent habit.

The glass shook in her hand, and she set it down after a sip or two. She opened the door to the balcony and stepped out. She hugged herself against the cool breeze, leaning her head against the grille that rose up to the ceiling. She closed her eyes and breathed deeply, reaching for her Spirit and allowing her heightened senses to take her further away.[9]

An autorickshaw with a bad silencer sputtered down the road. A dog barked somewhere. There was a sudden tinkling of prayer bells in the neighbourhood. Birds had begun to chirp. As muted sounds of azaan from the neighbourhood mosque started up, Maya opened her eyes. Why couldn't she concentrate today?

---

[9] Spirit is that mysterious force inside all of us that sometimes makes us do surprising things that we didn't think we were capable of—like running really fast when we're scared, or solving a complicated problem when we're concentrating really hard. Halvard and Halvard-to-be have more Spirit than us ordinary folk, and they can harness it at will.

As a matter of habit, she pressed her nose against the grille and tried to peer into the flat underneath the one she lived in. For the past two months it had remained lifeless. No light shone under the door, no sound came from inside, no one answered if you rang the bell. Maya had made some surreptitious enquiries and discovered that Noah's rent and maintenance bills were paid up for the year.

Every day when she passed it, she looked with numbing sadness at the advertisement pamphlets that littered the ground-level balcony, damp, dusty, some faded beyond recognition.

Somewhere deep down, Maya knew Noah wasn't coming back. The burden of being Watcher to someone who would destroy the worlds was too much. While she understood that Noah wouldn't—maybe shouldn't—come back, part of her hated him for deserting her. Yet another part loved him enough to want to spare him being part of the terrible Prophecy.

But she couldn't go on like this. Her head felt like it was going to burst—not from pain, but from a weird sensation of being too full, as thoughts tumbled and wrestled for space. Her limbs clamoured to move, refusing to stay still. Even without Spirit, she could hear the blood swishing around inside her head. Her skin felt too small to contain her.

Then, a light snapped on in the window below.

Relief almost took her legs out from under her. Another few seconds passed before Maya remembered she could move. She ran into the house and grabbed her phone.

Shit! I don't have his number!

But there was the building intercom. Tiptoeing into the hall, she picked up the landline receiver and dialled the number for his flat. Her heart was beating so wildly, she hoped it wouldn't fly out of her chest.

'Hello?'

That voice, with the odd clipped accent that had become so familiar, had her tongue-tied for a second. 'N-Noah…it's me.' She added, just in case: 'Maya.'

'I know,' he replied, a smile in his voice. 'Go to the Portal Road. I'll join you there.'

~

It was surreal, to see him before her, in person. She held her breath, worried that if she moved, he might disappear.

Then he held out his arms and an unseen force propelled Maya into them. He hugged her back tightly.

'I'm sorry it took so long,' he said at last.

Maya let him go and looked around the Portal Road, a circular path along the edge of a bowl-shaped green, about the size of a small stadium, the whole thing suspended in a mist of emptiness. The Portal Road was the only way to travel between Olaman, where the Halvard Castle was, and Amrozan, her 'reality'.

Maya stayed silent.

'You didn't think I would come back, did you?' Noah asked.

She stared fiercely at the ground, willing the tears not to fall. Instead, she poured her rage into her words.

'How dare you leave me like this? For all this time, and not a word! I *know* you were sick, but the Warriors—this pandemic, floods, everything! I—'

'I'm back now. I'm not going anywhere.'

'You'd better not. Even if someone chops off your head, you can't leave me like this again!'

'I won't. I promise.'

Maya rubbed the back of her hand across her face, waving away the snow-white handkerchief she was being offered. 'Were you very sick? Why were you so hazy?'

'Because I was far away. I had to recover the slow way, and I didn't want it affecting you.'

'Are you okay now?'

'I am, yes.'

'Is Lev all right? Have you met him?'

'I have. He's fine, can't wait to see you.'

'And Yazid?'

'No news, I'm sorry.'

Maya sighed. 'That's not good, is it?'

Noah grimaced and shook his head.

Despite the mixed news, she already felt lighter, and was fairly sure it wasn't Noah's doing. She studied him carefully.

He remained inscrutable as ever, impossible to tell with a glance that his a'fin—that is, Maya herself—was prophesied to be a very dangerous Halvard who could destroy the fabric of time.[10] Or that he had just recovered from a long and difficult illness after being infected by a poison bolt. She took in his ice-sculpture looks, down to his almost white hair, now slightly longer than the usual severe crop, curling at the edges. The only colour that pierced his face were his eyes, incongruously bright, like jewels.

---

[10] There are two kinds of Watcher–Halvard (or Watcher–Preferred, in this case) pairs, a'fin and a'lef. A'fin, or Linked, pairs have certain advantages, such as, mirroring each other's consciousnesses, knowing when the other is hurt, being able to draw strength from each other, and so on. A'lef pairs are unLinked. They are rarer than Linked pairs.

They sat on the inner edge of the road, on the grass that covered the dip in the bowl.

'I've been following the news. So much is going wrong. All this makes it easier for the Shadow, doesn't it?'

Easier for ME. Easier for me to destroy everything.

'Oh, Maya—'

'That's okay, it's the truth.' She wished her voice remained steady when she said that.

'We could have met here on the Portal Road, you know,' she said after a long silence. 'We could have met regularly, and I didn't have to spend two months thinking you'd never come back.'

'That would have been…difficult,' said Noah.

The indignation went out of her like air from a balloon. It had been hard for him too.

'If you had any sense,' she said brutally, 'you *wouldn't* have come back.'

'I am your Watcher. I will always come back.'

'But I might be evil and destroy the Sands of Time, the worlds.'

'Only if you choose.'

'You keep saying that it's a choice, but you can't be sure, can you?'

'I believe it. You'd know if I wasn't telling the truth, wouldn't you?'

He was right. She didn't have anything to say to that.

Finally, Noah asked, 'Do you think you're ready to come back to the Castle and resume your training?'

'Yes, please. Roz will kill me otherwise. When can we start? Today?'

'In a day or two. We've had a long break, so I'll have to work out a new schedule for you. You will also need a Healer's evaluation. Do you want me to talk to your parents?'

'Do we have to tell them?'

'Now that they know, I'd feel better if we weren't going behind their backs. Let me speak to them.'

'No, I'll handle it. They already hate you and think you're…never mind, I'll handle it. But Noah, what are we going to do about the Warriors and the Key?'

'As long as we have the Key with us, the Warriors are powerless, the Prophecy is powerless.'

'Hmm. I guess you're right.' She pushed herself to her feet. 'I need to get back, before Amma's Zoom yoga. By the way, I have a mobile now.'

'Good. Give me the number. I'll text you about when we can return to the Castle.'

'Please don't text, Noah. Not even old people text these days. WhatsApp me.'

'Noted.'

'Oh wait, before I go, you should have this back.' She reached under the neck of her T-shirt, and pulled something out and over her head. She took one of Noah's hands and put it there. 'Here. I kept it safe for you, like you asked.'

Noah looked at it for a few seconds: a dark thread with a silver pendant in the shape of a chess knight. It had belonged to his daughter.

'I think you should keep it,' he said. He put it back around Maya's neck. 'It's yours now.'

~

Maya picked out the peanuts from her plate of poha, arranging them in a neat curve along the edge of her plate.

Next to her, Manan kept himself from collapsing on his geography textbook by propping his head up with both hands, his breakfast forgotten next to him. Across the table, Amma was typing on her laptop, a deep frown on her face. She stopped to sip her coffee and take a bite of her muesli now and again. Meanwhile, Appa was pretending to attend an online departmental meeting, his mic on mute and video off.

They are so normal that I feel almost normal myself.

And she was going to destroy the illusion in a minute.

A second.

Now—

'I'm going back,' Maya announced. 'To the Halvard Castle. With Noah.'

For a moment or two, nothing happened. Time itself might have stopped in that complete silence, a pause button on reality. In those brief seconds, Maya believed that it would all be okay.

Then, the edges of reality joined up again, and time resumed its march.

Her parents exchanged a look, their faces crumpling. Even Manan gave a sharp gasp.

Maya watched them all in turn. She wished she could make it easier for them, or at least not be the cause of all the pain. The knowledge—albeit knowledge they only half believed—that their thirteen-year-old had strange powers that gave her access to an alternate world was not an easy one to carry. Or that everything they took for granted about existence, about the past, present and future of humankind, of what they thought of as reality, was a reflection of what happened in a parallel world.

So they had done the only thing they could—tried desperately to pretend that it had all been a bad dream and that everything was now normal.

A loud *ding-ding* made them all jump—someone's mobile.

'Maya,' Amma began uneasily. 'Look—'

'Please, Amma,' interrupted Maya. 'I have to go, with your permission or without it. I'd rather go with it.'

3

YAZID CAN'T BELIEVE HIS EARS

A couple of days after Noah's return, in the early hours of the morning, Maya came back to the Eternal City for the first time in two months. It was afternoon in Lam—this time difference had enabled her to keep her initial training a secret from her parents. She had been able to slip away and train for a couple of hours with no one being any the wiser.

'Why do I need a Healer's evaluation?' Maya asked. 'Is it because of the pandemic?'

'It's routine—you need to have one every year.'

'And who's my Healer?'

Please say it's Stephen!

'It's Stephen for now.' *Yes!* 'But only because of the… situation with your age. I'm guessing you'll eventually be assigned to Eidora, who's my Healer.'

'Why can't Stephen continue to be my Healer?'

'He's much too senior to be dealing with lowly Preferred.' It was delivered in a deadpan tone but Maya knew he was teasing. She rolled her eyes.

The evaluation was uneventful—standing for a few minutes inside a chamber called a scanner while it bleeped and blinked at her, then spewed out a screenful of readings that Stephen studied. He then pronounced her 'disgustingly healthy' and summarily dismissed her.

'When can I go find Lev?' she asked Noah as they exited the Dispensary.

He checked his watch. 'In another fifteen minutes or so, I'd guess. Chiyo said he goes swimming after his classes.'

They decided to wait by the lake, the one behind the Castle that Maya had discovered last year. They walked around the main section of the Castle, through the lawns, and up a damp, leaf-covered path through the trees. The trees kept out the wind, but it was appreciably colder than the last time she'd been here. Crossing a small courtyard surrounded by hedges, they went up the steps cut into the mountainside.

'It's freezing,' she said, tucking her hands into the pockets of her fleece-lined windcheater that Noah had given her. 'Does it snow here?'

'No chance. It's at least twelve degrees today, very far from freezing,' said Noah. 'But I should have got you a hat and some gloves. Shall we go back and get them?'

'No, it's fine.' She blew into the air. 'Look, I'm breathing clouds.'

'Fascinating.'

They walked up the hill, and Maya gasped as the wind stung her cheeks. She put her face up to the sky and inhaled deeply, the strong smell of pine welcoming her back.

She laughed. 'I'm turning into ice and yet I love it. Am I getting hypothermia?'

That made Noah laugh too. He put a hand on her head and out of nowhere, a welcome warmth spread through her.

'Whoa! What's that?'

'A perk of Spirit.'

They stopped in the middle of the stone-and-wood walkway that spanned the lake. Maya clutched the side and peered at the water underneath. 'I'm glad to be back. I missed being here, and…everything here.'

'Everything here missed you too,' said Noah mildly.

'What? You say such weird things sometimes.' She stared at the rippling surface of the lake. 'It's funny, but in spite of everything, I feel I belong here.'

'Of course you do. You and I and Lev and Chiyo are having a little meeting tomorrow. I will catch you up on all that I've found.'

Maya nodded. 'Lev's not really got anyone, has he?' she said, talking more to herself than anything. She'd spent a lot of time thinking about this. 'His father died and then this thing about the Prophecy happened. I can't really know what he feels, but even for someone like me, I feel that he is the only friend I have, and I have an entire family and all back home. He doesn't.'

Noah leaned against one of the pillars along the walkway, studying her. There was a time when his piercing gaze would have unnerved Maya.

'What? Why are you staring at me?'

'I know that sometimes you worry about having an evil side because of the Prophecy. But I want you to remember that I think—I *know*—here and here,' he tapped his head first and then his chest, 'that you are all right.'

'Su-ure.' She stretched the word out. 'You are my Watcher, you have to say that.'

'Evil people don't worry about their friends.'

'Oh.' She was quiet for a while. 'Noah?'

'Yes?'

'If you ever think or get even a teeny little inkling that I might be dangerous to Lev, will you take me away?'

'I promise,' said Noah, pressing his right fist to his heart. That was his Watcher's pledge, and not given lightly.

'Thank you.' A gust of biting wind blew across the lake and Maya's teeth gave a little chatter. 'What's the time?'

Noah checked again and nodded.

She ran all the way.

~

Yazid watched Kilyana put the radio together again that night. Was it finally going to work? He wasn't sure which eventuality would be better—being stuck here with this outlier community that followed neither High Council nor Warriors, or going back to civilization and home.

Kilyana's frustration was muted tonight. Yazid presumed that meant she was concentrating. She had patched the transmitter with components from her old comms receiver, everything held together with tape, and had somehow procured a thick coil of wire for an antenna. The battery was a problem because they didn't have the right kind of charger. It had taken her a while, but she'd managed to rig it up to charge using Spirit. It worked, but only gave a few minutes of power at a time.

Yazid sat cross-legged on the bed, drawing unending parallel lines on a piece of paper, pretending to be absorbed in his work. Of course, Kilyana would know in an instant if she turned her attention to him that his mind was elsewhere, but she was too engrossed in the radio.

He was getting stronger by the day, slowly regaining the use of his hand, now a rather grotesque pink in colour, with dead skin peeling off in patches. He still struggled to hold the pencil steady, but at least it was less uncomfortable now. The folk here may not have indoor plumbing, but they were definitely skilled healers—small h, of course.

Maybe soon he would regain his power of speech as well.

The radio gave a sort of cough and he jumped. Even Kilyana jerked back in surprise. Then she darted forward, jammed the earpiece into her ear and picked up the mic.

'Councillor?' she spoke, hunching over the mic. 'It is I, Kilyana.'

The pencil fell out of Yazid's hand. *Councillor?* A buzzing filled his ear. The Warriors had people on the *High Council*?

Of course they did. Who was he kidding?

He had to pull himself back together and focus again. Kilyana had turned away from him, and he had to strain to hear.

'I haven't much time, Councillor. It has taken me long to get this radio going and the battery will run out soon. Yazid injured himself in his attempt to get the Key. He nearly didn't survive.'

A pause while the Councillor must have been talking.

'Yes, he is recovering. But he doesn't have the Key.'

Pause.

'Not just yet, no.'

Pause.

'It's not a game. Before I tell you anything, I need a promise from you. I need your promise that we have immunity.'

Pause. Then Kilyana laughed.

'Lev? Lev doesn't have the Key, Councillor.'

Then she flung the earpiece away from her with a curse. Yazid flinched. He was back at his writing by the time she turned to look at him, but he knew she knew that he had seen and heard everything.

~

Taxing physical tasks were a comfort these days. Like holding your breath for countless laps of the pool, until your chest wanted to burst. Lev was starting to revel in pushing his endurance to newer limits.

Chiyo wasn't best pleased about it. 'It feels like you're punishing yourself,' she had said once.

'I want to feel strong,' he had replied.

'Not all strength is physical, and not all of your strength is in you,' had been her cryptic reply. 'Don't hurt yourself,' she'd added, leaving the rest of it unsaid: *Or else, I will have to intervene.*

Lev came up with a gasp, lungs screaming, gulping in delicious air. He flipped over on to his back, waiting to catch his breath, squinting at the lights on the ceiling of the pool complex. This was one of the most peaceful parts of his day, when the pool was deserted except for the life guard. As his breathing slowed, he closed his eyes, focusing on the gentle bobbing sensation.

When he opened his eyes, he saw a figure standing at the edge of the pool. For a moment, he thought he was dreaming. Then he remembered. He swam to it, and in one sweeping motion, hauled himself out of the pool and engulfed Maya in a crushing hug.

Maya hugged him back fiercely, and then pushed him away. 'You're dripping on me.'

'Sorry.' He pulled off his cap and goggles and continued to stare at her. 'You're really back.'

'I'm really back,' she said, intently brushing water droplets off her bulky jacket. She wouldn't look at him.

Just as well—Lev turned away and picked up his towel from the rail, wiping his face before draping it around his shoulders

'It's great to have you back.'

'It's great to be back. How are you?'

'Good. You?'

'Okay, I guess. Roz sucks big time right now.'

'Tell me about it.'

~

The awkwardness slipped away as quickly as it had manifested, and Maya studied Lev carefully. In these last few weeks, she had discovered to her alarm that she could no longer picture him in her mind's eye. But before she could drink in every bit of his face, her eyes went straight to the neckline of his swimming costume, to the tip of the scar that ran down his body.

'Does it hurt anymore?'

He shook his head.

'Good.' She looked him up and down with a frown. 'You seem different. I can't… Wait—' She reached out and squeezed his arm experimentally. 'Oh my god, you've grown muscles over your bones! You're not skinny any more.'

'Did you just retrospectively body-shame me?' Lev squinted at her.

Maya punched him lightly on his arm. 'Looks like you've learnt some big words too.'

He nodded towards the changing rooms, and they proceeded towards it. 'You're different too. You're taller—and your hair is longer.'

'Am I taller? That is good news.' She wished she'd stop growing horizontally too, but somehow it bothered her less these days.

I guess I have bigger things to worry about.

After Lev had changed, the two Preferred left the pool complex and ventured into the lawns. They walked through the gardens in silence, until they arrived at a point where the trees parted to give a view of the mountains. Not that there was much of a view tonight. It was moonless and cloudy. Even the stars were hidden.

Maya would have loved to make her way down and sit by the smooth, rounded rocks on the banks of the Mishaera river that ran through the forest. Instead, she closed her eyes and, with practised ease, emptied her mind. In this state of total concentration, she was aware of her Spirit. She let it fill her.

The river crashed over the rocks so loudly, that she might have been right next to it. Her clothes felt unbearably heavy, and even her eyelids had weight. Her ears tuned in to sounds ordinarily out of human range, strange calls from animals, and the scurrying of unseen creatures around them. The air remained cold and humid, the smell of pine overpowering.

Something buzzed in her ear, making her Spirit leave her abruptly. Beside her, Lev stood silently, arms crossed, also looking down at the river.

'Aren't you cold?' she asked, taking in his light flannel shirt flapping over a T-shirt.

He laughed. 'You forget, I am from Siberia.'

'And how are things at…home?'

The smile left him. 'It's no longer home.' He continued to stare into the forest. 'I was going to tell you when I got the chance. I went back there. I…well, there were some things to take care of. I don't think my dad would've wanted me to run away like this.'

'You haven't run away,' said Maya. 'You have a life here. You're working really hard.'

Lev didn't say anything. He sat on the bench before them, and Maya got down next to him.

'So, you're not staying with your aunt then?'

He shook his head. 'As far as they know, I'm in a home.'

'Oh, Lev, don't tell me you're full-time in Lam! That's not good for you.'

He shook his head again. 'I go home with Chiyo every few days.'

'That's good, right? Isn't it?'

He hesitated. 'Yeah, it's good, I guess. Better than the alternatives.'

'If things were different, I'd take you home with me.'

Lev nodded. 'Sands, I missed you.' he said suddenly.

'Me too.'

Of course she had, but it was only since coming face to face with him that she'd understood exactly how much. Back in Roz, her schoolmates thought her weird, even her family were wary of her. And Noah had left.

Sudden tears stung her eyes and Maya turned away, embarrassed. She stood. 'Let's get something to eat,' she said.

4

IT ALL COMES DOWN TO MATHS

'It's all about mathematics,' Noah said.

Lev groaned. 'Of course it is.'

'Didn't we already know that?' Maya ventured.

'But now we know exactly what.'

'Which is?' Chiyo asked.

'Thandolwethusian theory and subjective mathematics.' He took in their blank stares and nodded to emphasize his point. It didn't help.

The four of them had congregated in Noah's living room in Roz. His flat was identical to the one Maya lived in, though far more austere. Walls lined with bookshelves, black and chrome sofas, and muted lighting—neat and sparse. It suited him, Maya decided.

'Thandolwethusian theory, as in, all the stuff behind how Roz and Lam are connected, how to figure out who can be a future Halvard and all that sort of thing?' Lev asked.

Maya turned to stare at Lev instead. Looked like she had a lot to catch up on.

'Exactly,' Noah said.

'Then what's subjective maths?' Lev went on. 'Isn't mathematics absolutely the opposite of subjective? It isn't based on anyone's assumption. Numbers don't change based on someone's opinion either. Right?'

'Well, yes and no. Measurements, numbers, formulas, axioms—they are all accepted truths. But where did they come from? Who defined them and decided they would be absolute truths? What if there are other such truths out there? Other ways to measure, deduce, analyze?'

'You mean, it's like how people say artificial intelligence is neutral, but it's not really?' Maya asked. 'Because somebody had to program it first, and they would have programmed it with the things they knew and believed to be true.'

'Something like that.'

Too busy feeling pleased with herself, she missed something Chiyo asked. When she tuned back in, Noah was speaking again.

'Like the advanced mathematics that model future generations of Halvard. In the same way, the outcomes keep shifting depending on an untold number of parameters.'

'Like the pandemic?' Lev said.

'Yes, but the pandemic could have been part of the model too.'

'Okay, I think I'm lost again,' said Maya. 'Could you *please* stop speaking in geek and explain in words that poor Preferred like me can understand?' She added hastily, 'I mean, er, respectfully speaking.'

'Sorry,' said Noah. 'Let's see if I can find an analogy. Imagine that you have to describe a turbulent sea using words. But in a language that is unknown by anyone except a select few. Every word that you write depends on the word that came before it, which comes from the one before that, and so on. If you or anyone else makes a change anywhere in the middle, it can throw the whole composition off. But it is imperative that the final result is still a description of a stormy sea.'

'Is the stormy sea meant to be the Prophecy?' Chiyo asked.

Noah nodded.

'Thandolwethusian theory is central to subjective mathematics,' he continued, 'and Halvard who work in this field mainly concern themselves with trying to model how the Sands works, or which humans have the potential to channel Spirit, and so on. And that is as far as I know. Which, as you can tell, is not much.

'Now, coming to the Prophecy—do you recall the Oparian birth chart that narrows the window for potential Halvard who might be the Shadow?'

Everyone nodded—till a few months back, they had believed that Maya was outside the birth window in the chart, and clearly they had been stupendously wrong.

'The Prophecy is full of other such bits, all of which come together to define what has to happen, when, in what sequence, how, and so on.'

Maya leaned forward. 'So now that you know this, you know what it's all about?'

Noah shook his head. 'I'm afraid it's a task that is beyond our combined abilities. And even if we had the theoretical knowledge, we'd need the original, hand-drawn version of the Prophecy to just be able to read the many layers of the Proto text. If at all we *could* read them.'

Lev and Maya exchanged a look. They had known that the Prophecy had been written in high-level, multi-layered Proto—so complex that most Halvard would have trouble reading it. Even when copied using special scanners that could capture the deep, Illusion-based notations of complex Proto, it was nearly impossible to make a faithful copy beyond a few levels.

'Is there *anything* new we know?' Chiyo asked, a hint of frustration in her voice.

'We know for certain that it wasn't written for a specific "chosen one"'—Noah made air quotes around the words. 'The Warriors were the ones who *chose* Yazid for the role. And Maya, by falling just outside the more obvious parameters of the Oparian window, somehow slipped under their radar. Lev, however, was considered a possibility.'

'Which is why the attack at the Tower happened,' Lev said, fingering his T-shirt's neck. 'They needed me gone.'

'But aren't there any number of potential Halvard in that birth window?' Maya asked. 'In a few years, they'll all start getting Summoned.'

'Which is where the subjective nature of the calculations comes in,' said Noah. 'Not every potential Halvard is a potential Shadow. But what specifically makes it work and what tears the calculations apart is something we don't know.'

They swallowed that in silence.

'Is that how the seal in the cave was triggered, then?' Lev asked. 'Because of all of this subjectivity…type of thing?'[11]

'Possibly.'

'So somehow, either I or Yazid managed to trigger it,' Maya added.

---

[11] The cave being the one where the Key had been hidden. It had been sealed shut until Maya and Yazid had somehow opened it.

'What I don't get is,' Lev went on, 'if both you and he are in the birth window, how come he couldn't take the Key but you could? Why did it burn him and not you?'

Everyone turned to Noah for an explanation, but he shrugged. 'I don't know. All I can tell you is that the Key is central to defeating the Sands of Time. But I have no idea how.'

'Defeat?' Maya asked. 'Not destroy? You're sure of that?'

'Reasonably sure.'

'That is interesting,' Chiyo put in. 'The Warrior ideology is to control the Sands, so it makes sense that they don't want to end it, just get it to do what they want.'

'Which is what?' pressed Maya.

Chiyo shrugged. 'I guess only a Warrior could tell you that, but one of the first lines of the Prophecy says, "The Sands of Time must not rule us."'

In the silence that followed, a pressure-cooker whistle went off in a neighbouring house, making them all jump.

'Perhaps the Warriors miscalculated,' said Lev finally. 'About Yazid, I mean. If you do so many complicated sums, you are bound to make a mistake some time, right? Maybe he just wasn't strong enough and you were, Maya.'

'I think,' said Chiyo, her words slow and careful, 'that this proves what we thought before is true—any of you three could have been the Shadow. Yazid was picked because Kilyana is a Warrior, and Noah and I aren't. As to why he couldn't claim the Key, I think we are just missing something.'

They sat silently thinking about this.

'What should we do now?' Chiyo asked finally. 'What does Nira say?'

'She doesn't really see what we can do,' said Noah. 'We go on as usual, just keep Maya and Lev as close to us as we can, which we do anyway. And keep a lookout for anything unusual.'

'But...' started Lev. He seemed to struggle to get this thoughts together. 'I mean, how can we do that? We can't pretend nothing happened?'

Noah spread his hands. 'What else can we do? Most people believe the Prophecy is just a myth. Anyone claiming otherwise risks outing themselves as Warriors. Moreover, as long as we have the Key, the Warriors can't do anything.'

'They can try to get the Key back.'

'They would need to get you too,' Lev pointed out.

Because you are their great hope, the Shadow.

Nobody said that, of course.

'What about Yazid?' Maya asked.

Which, of course, was a rhetorical question. Maya didn't want to think about it, follow the thread of logic leading from the fact that Yazid was no longer important to the Warriors to that he was still missing.

There was nothing much to say after that, and the meeting broke up. When Lev and Chiyo had gone, Maya remained where she was, on the rug, hugging her knees. 'For a moment,' she said quietly, 'I thought there was a possibility that there were other candidates for being the Shadow. That I might not be evil.'

'You're not evil,' said Noah. 'The Key gives you some power, but we don't know what yet. Whatever it is, it can't make you do anything unless you choose to.'

Maya nodded, running her fingers through the tassels at the edge of the rug. She really wanted to believe him.

~

Once back training at the Halvard Castle, Maya found that her reputation for having exceptional strength of Spirit—and of course, being only thirteen, the youngest Preferred in history—had preceded her. New Preferred whispered about her when she passed by, which was annoying.

'So rude,' she complained.

'In a couple of days, you'll be part of the scenery,' Noah said.

'Great.' She rubbed her hand along the underside of her thigh, trying to sooth her sore hamstrings. Noah's eyebrow twitched, like he'd been about to raise it but changed his mind.

'Not too late to get some Healing,' he said mildly.

'I'm fine,' said Maya through teeth gritted. There was pride at stake here, though why she couldn't say—Noah knew fully well how much her legs hurt.

'All right, then,' he said, pushing his tablet towards her. 'Let's talk about your schedule.'

She had thought being back at the Castle, restarting her training, being around Lev would ease the unsettled feeling inside her, but she had been wrong. There was so much still out of her control—the Warriors' plans, whether Yazid was okay, her family's unease. And not being able to do anything about all of that.

'Credit for your thoughts?' Noah's voice interrupted her descent into the rabbit hole.

'Huh, pardon? Sorry, I was…'

'Learning four Powers is not going to be easy, but we'll take it one step at a time.'

'No, that's not what—' Oops. 'I mean, yeah, sure.'

Noah's gimlet gaze pinned her, but he didn't push it.

'Can I come stay at the Castle?'

'You still have a week of school left.'

'I mean, after my vacations begin, of course,' Maya replied. She would have happily traded the last week of school for the Castle, to be honest.

'It's best not to stir things up too much at home. Let's give it a week or two for things to settle.'

It was rather unlike Noah to put things off, but when it came to dealing with her parents, he tended to be uncharacteristically nervous. Not that she could blame him—it was going to be an uphill job all the way.

'It's never going to settle, you know that, right?' Maya reminded him. 'And anyway, do I *really* need to go to school? I'm learning much more here.'

'Yes, you do really need to go to school.'

Maya rolled her eyes. She didn't agree, but it wasn't an argument she could win.

'By the way, you might be interested to hear,' Noah continued like she hadn't reacted, 'Chiyo has been taking on small groups of Preferred for self-defence and combat training. She's agreed to have you.'

Maya's flagging spirits did a quick about turn. 'That's awesome! When do we start?'

'Soon. We need to work on your fitness levels first.'

'Oh, right.' She had a sudden surge of appreciation for her Watcher. 'Thank you for everything, Noah.'

'You don't have to thank me, it's my job. Now look, here's someone to see you.'

Maya turned as the dark, lithe figure of Owen skidded to a halt next to her. 'Hey, the grapevine is right. You're back. Hi Noah.'

Noah nodded. Maya grinned at him. He was her favourite among the newer Preferred—but not new enough to look at her like she had a nose in the middle of her forehead.

'Yep, I'm back. How are you?'

'I'm great,' said Owen, smiling back at her. 'It's good to have you back. Will you be moving back into your old room?'

'Soon. Hopefully.' She squinted at him. 'You seem—I don't know. Something's different about you. Your voice…?'

Not just his voice, deeper and lower, there was a happy glow about him, his smile reaching his dancing brown eyes, and a spring in his step. Quite a change from the reticent Owen she remembered. He seemed wider around the shoulders too, and his smooth cheeks were covered in fuzzy hair.

'Hey, is that a beard?'

His grin got wider. 'Yes. Hormone therapy works great with a more efficient metabolism. Also.' He ran his fingers across his chest. 'I got top surgery.'

'Awesome!'

'Isn't it? Okay, I gotta run now. See you around. Bye, Noah.'

'Bye,' said Maya, watching him disappear into the Castle.

Noah cleared his throat.

Maya jumped.

'Somcthing bothering you?'

'No…I…just…thinking.'

'What about?'

'That I'm happy for Owen—happy that he can get the right, you know, the hormones and whatever that he wasn't getting in Roz. I'm glad that people here don't get all hyper about gender and all.'

'They don't, but there are other things they get "hyper" about, as you say.'

She nodded absently, and then said, 'Science is amazing, isn't it?'

Noah smiled. 'It is.'

5

MAYA MAKES A KEY DISCOVERY

Noah hadn't been exaggerating about stepping up her training. Just the physical part wiped her out, not to mention the constant use of Spirit. Then again, with more Spirit, she learnt very fast too.

Despite everything else, Maya's mood lifted at least a notch or two whenever she was at the Castle—an extra notch for Healing with Stephen. And with Owen in the same batch. Even though Stephen decreed that his Healing students had to compulsorily sign in class, even if they were speaking aloud, which meant extra Proto sign lessons for Maya.

'Over the next few weeks, we'll be working with shells,' the Healer announced one day, about a week after Maya was back. 'Anyone used shells before?'

'Seashells?' Diede, one of the Preferred inducted while Maya had been away, asked cheekily. 'I've listened to the sea in them.'

The others sniggered. Stephen narrowed his eyes at Diede.

'Artefacts that require Spirit channelled into them in order to function?' Mingmei called out.

'Close, but not quite there. Shells magnify Spirit for a specific function. A shell made to stop bleeding will let you Heal a wound with a fraction of the Spirit you'd normally need. Or a shell to create a certain Illusion will help you do that more easily than you otherwise could.'

'Isn't the use of shells outlawed?' asked Kari. 'I thought they're dangerous.'

'They are, except for Healing,' replied Stephen. He picked up his tablet and tapped around on it. 'And you're right about shells being dangerous. Some of you might have heard of the Nikau Auxilliary.'

'Something to do with Newton's third law of motion?' Owen frowned as he tried to remember. 'Every action has an equal and opposite reaction, but…relating to Spirit in some way.'

'Every artefact driven by Spirit causes a reaction proportionate to the value of its Nikau Auxilliary,' Stephen began. The lightboard in front of the room came to life, as he streamed data from his tablet.

'The reaction is determined by factors such as the amount of Spirit used, the shell's function, its duration of use, and so on. Sometimes these reactions can be severe, so every Healer must know how to analyze shells.'

'What kind of reactions are we talking about?' Maya asked. 'Like explosions and things catching fire?'

'There have been rumours of spontaneous combustion for sure,' said Stephen, but he was smiling. 'No, Maya, no explosions or fires. They're mostly relatively harmless, at least Healing shells—pain, dizziness, nausea, similar to Healing after-effects. I have used a shell that tickles and another that makes you run to the nearest restroom.'

A laugh went around the room, but Stephen quickly brought them back to the calculations on the whiteboard about how to quickly estimate a shell's reaction using Nikau's formula.

'If for some reason you are unable to estimate if a shell is safe, you shouldn't use it. Just so you know, they have caused deaths. And definitely do *not* use a shell whose function you don't know. There is no way to determine what an unknown shell is for without extensive testing, and without knowing that, you cannot calculate the risks.

'When used properly, though, shells are invaluable to Healers, especially in conditions where we need to perform Spirit-intensive tasks repeatedly. But don't think of them as simple magnifiers of Sprit—the skill still comes from the user.'

There was a silence as everyone digested all this.

'You mean,' said Maya, 'if someone *can* Heal, then shells can help, but if you can't, then a shell is of no use?'

Stephen nodded. 'Exactly. You can't take a ball and two nets and expect a game, right?' Some of the others looked perplexed, but it made perfect sense to Maya. 'You need players to go out there, have a plan and do the job. Similarly, you have to direct shells. You have to have the skill to perform the procedure in the first place. And you cannot use any shell for any purpose. They are, as I said, very specific in function.'

He leaned over the items on the table and picked out something that looked like two rings joined together. 'This is what a typical Healing shell looks like. You must have seen Healers wearing them. This is a very weak one, to stop bleeding. You couldn't take it and, say, try to mend a broken bone.

'Now, I won't go into the construction of shells or the different kinds—though I can give you a list of books to look up if any of you is interested. Right now, I'd like you all to take turns and try this shell out. Once you have experienced it, perhaps you will understand better. Who wants to go first? Diede?'

Diede shrugged and stepped up. He took the double ring from Stephen and slipped it on the first two fingers of his right hand. Meanwhile, Stephen erased the lightboard and wrote a Healing exercise on it.

It was a routine one, using a dummy simulating a simple cut, but Diede's eyes popped wide as he the simulated injury healed before their eyes.

'Wow,' he said, nodding at Stephen. 'Yeah, this is something else.'

'Now do you understand?'

'Heck, yeah,' said Diede, handing the shell back. 'What was that you said about having a reaction? Is it the slight buzzing in my head I feel?'

Stephen nodded. 'Yes, that's it. That's the most that routine Healing shells will trouble you.'

Maya watched with interest as Mingmei tried it next.

'Shells are made of a metal alloy, usually silvery grey to black in colour, but you can't identify one on sight,' Stephen went on. 'Some people can identify them by touch—for better or for worse, I happen to be one. I'd be interested to know if any of you can. I haven't come across too many people...your Watcher is one of them, Maya.'

'Really?' said Maya surprised.

'Come on, take a turn yourself and see if you are sensitive to shells as well. It is a super-normal ability, so there's a good chance.'

Stephen slipped the two rings on her fingers. At first, Maya was startled by how cold the metal was, considering so many people had handled it. Then the coolness shifted to a deep, almost unnatural, chill that seeped right into her core. She couldn't describe the feeling in words, but it was familiar. The shell felt heavy too, extraordinarily so for something so small.

Then she remembered why it felt so familiar. She gasped, disgusted. She wanted to rip it off and throw it as far as she could. But, of course, that wasn't an option. So she swallowed and clenched her other fist. Despite her dread, excitement stirred within her. She had solved a little mystery she hadn't known needed solving.

'Maya?'

Stephen's voice snapped her back to the present.

Maya flinched. 'Uh, sorry,' she said. 'Is…is it supposed to feel like this?' She raised her hand with the shell. 'Kind of like it's freezing, but like, from the inside, and it's so heavy, it feels like I'm wearing a brick.'

The Healer's eyes gleamed. 'Exactly. So you can feel shells, just like Noah.'

Maya didn't respond. Her mind was racing. 'Can a shell harm you?'

'Yes, they can be dangerous. I believe I said that just now.'

'How come?'

'The Nikau Auxilliary?' Diede called. 'You're losing your touch, *Wunderkind*.'

Stephen told him to button it, but Maya didn't care. 'Can a shell harm some people and not others?'

'Sure. If used under the Spirit threshold or used for something it's not intended for. Or if the user isn't skilled enough. If the reaction of a Healing shell seems to overwhelm you, you are probably not using enough Spirit with it. That's not a very scientific way of going about it, but with approved Healing shells, you're quite safe.'

~

'The Key is a shell.'

Noah's eyes widened by a fraction. 'How do you know?'

'We did shells in Healing today. I touched one. You know, the numbing, strange cold.'

He exhaled slowly. 'I see.'

'How come some people can feel shells but not others? Stephen said it's a super-normal ability. What's that?'

'Some traits that are common to a'fin. It is a strange sort of heredity, referred to as super-normality. Haven't you noticed a'fin pairs are often good at the same things? Take Chiyo and Lev's physical strength, for instance. Luu and Val's uncanny head for numbers. Wahid and Mingmei are both ambidextrous. Things like that.'

'I see,' said Maya. 'Does it help knowing the Key is a shell?'

'It does. We know now that it is intended for a specific function that needs the use of Spirit.'

'If only we could find out what that function is.'

'If only.' His brows were knitted together like he was deep in thought.

~

Maya's training with Chiyo began. It was, as expected, intense. Maya was in a small group with Owen and a new preferred called Mine. Her joy at being in yet another class with Owen was short-lived because he was useless at combat and kept getting yelled at. To be fair, they all got yelled at quite a bit, but within a fortnight or so, Maya could already tell that the incessant drills and exercises, and Chiyo's obsession with technique, were all paying off. Even Owen managed to land some blows.

Meanwhile, if she'd thought her double life would be easier now that her parents knew, she was mistaken. The tension at home was thick enough to cut with a knife. The only time she felt close to normal was when she was at the Castle.

But the illusion of normality at the Castle was just that, an illusion. Things *weren't* normal. They hadn't been since they had found out about the Prophecy and gone in search of the Key. Even Noah wasn't normal. He was outwardly the same, but he had become her shadow—no pun intended. When she wasn't in a class, she almost never found herself without him by her side. She wasn't allowed to leave the Castle premises without telling him, either.

'You've become a helicopter,' she grumbled. 'It's like how Kilyana used to be with Yazid.'

Of course, she was apologizing immediately, mortified that she'd compared him to Kilyana.

'I know, I know, it's all right,' Noah reassured her for the dozenth time. 'We are all under some stress, so let yourself off the hook. I'm not upset, am I?'

'You should be,' Maya muttered, going back to reading third level Proto, which was needlessly complicated and made worse by the fact that she had no idea what the text was trying to say.

'How about I stop following you around, but you make sure you stay somewhere public, like the courtyard or the library or the gymnasium?'

'Sure, thanks.'

It was unfair to go off on Noah, who did his best to accommodate her—except that he was procrastinating about her coming to stay at the Castle.

Maya held her head over the dancing text staring up at her. Sometimes these days it felt like the Key and the Prophecy and everything else had all happened to someone else. That there was no Shadow, and especially that she wasn't it.

And yet there was a pitch-black dagger—always chilled despite being wrapped in a torn piece of blanket, at the bottom of a cardboard carton piled with old toys from her childhood, and the whole thing pushed under her bed, as far as it could go—to remind her that everything was wrong and she was the reason for it.

6

NOAH IS EMBARRASSING AS USUAL

Maya, Lev and their Watchers met for a quick confab on the Portal Road at the end of a long and busy day of training. Noah had already told Chiyo about the Key being a shell, but no one knew what to do with that information.

'What does Nira say?' Chiyo asked.

'I haven't been able to speak with her,' Noah replied. 'She's been travelling a lot lately. Any word from Rafa?'

Rafa—or Halvard Rafael—was Chiyo's former Watcher. He was also a minor Elite Guard, and always off on some mission or another.

Chiyo sighed. 'I did actually manage to meet him, but there's very little he knows about shells. Says there's a lab in Kirnara that tests them, but obviously we can't send it there.'

'Are we certain there's nothing in the Prophecy?' Lev chimed in.

'Oh, I'm certain there *is*, but I'm less sure how to find it and how to read it,' Noah replied. To Chiyo he said: 'Maybe you should have a go. Your Proto is far better than mine.'

'I can if you like, but I'm not sure I'll get very far. Now that we know it's super high-level Proto, there's no telling what crucial bit is missing and where.'

Maya gripped the railing with her hands, so hard that her hands hurt. They had two copies of the Prophecy, but even the one that was more detailed was still missing at least a dozen layers of the original text.

'I hate this. Just hanging around, doing *nothing*.'

Silence from the others—she wasn't the only one frustrated. She was glad, for once, that nobody reminded her again that as long as they had the Key safely in their possession, the Warriors were rendered helpless too. She didn't want platitudes. She wanted to know if Yazid was okay. No one else, not even Noah, had seen the way he had struggled against Kilyana's control, trying to warn her. Or heard his horrible cries when the Key had burnt his hands.

~

'Ugh, this is boring,' Maya groaned. 'Why do we have to mug up laws and stuff when we can just look them up. Ready? Next question: what's Directive 7C?'

'Okay, I actually know this one.' Lev held up one finger. 'The High Council's Directive 7C recommends that no two Halvard may formalize any relationship between themselves. Violation incurs a fine of seven years of security credits.'

Quizzing each other on Lam laws was better than trying to learn them on their own. These days they barely spent much time with each other. During the precious few hours Maya spent at the Castle, they were both mostly busy with classes. The only time they met was if something was cancelled or rescheduled, and even then, it was to practise this, revise that.

'Correct. But what does it even mean?' Maya turned to Noah for a reply.

'It means exactly what it says,' Noah said. 'Halvard are discouraged from having any formal relationship between them.'

'What's a *formal* relationship?' asked Lev.

'Anything that's conferred by law—marriages and adoptions, for instance.'

'Wait, Halvard can't get married?'

'But Chiyo's married,' protested Maya. 'Aren't you, Chiyo? And you were too. Wahid's married, and, and—'

'Marry each other,' Chiyo clarified.

'Why?' asked Lev.

'It is felt that it might interfere with their primary loyalties, which are to the Sands of Time and the High Council.'

'But,' Maya scratched her head, puzzled, 'aren't Stephen and Jan married?'

'So many Halvard are together,' Lev added. 'Like, you know, everyone knows about Zavia and Luu, and then—'

'There's nothing to stop people from getting together, formally or informally,' said Chiyo. 'Plus, 7C is a directive, not a law, even though it carries high penalties. No one can put you in prison for it. Halvard have even challenged it.'

'Wait, what do you mean "getting together"?' Maya asked.

Lev looked upwards to the sky. 'You know, *getting together*.'

Maya gazed at him quizzically, when it suddenly fell into place.

'Oh! That's what Owen and Mingmei were arguing about. In the zines. Now it makes sense!'

'Zines? The ones Diede is always going on about? Please don't tell me you've been reading them.'

'Why? What are they?'

'It's some ridiculous series about,' Lev darted a glance at Chiyo and lowered his voice, 'well, er, sort of romantic stories, about Halvard.'

'Ew,' said Maya. 'Have you read any?'

'No!' Lev sounded outraged. But under the table, he signed to Maya, 'One or two, but don't tell Chiyo.'

Noah cleared his throat. 'It's a comic series that comes out every fortnight,' he said.

'Filled with, as you rightly say, Lev, Halvard romances,' Chiyo added. 'I wish I could say they were fine literature, but they are not.'

Lev's eyes popped wide open. 'You've read them?'

Chiyo shrugged. 'Sure. I'll read anything when I'm desperate, even vulgar, third-rate comics.'

'Can I read them?' Maya asked Noah.

Noah's eyebrows jumped to the top of his forehead. 'I wouldn't advise it. They are quite—let's just say they take quite a few liberties with the truth.'

'They are pretty graphic,' said Lev. Then he hastily added, 'I mean, that's what I've heard.'

'What do you mean graphic?' Maya asked. 'Like, there are pictures and all?'

'Lev, do you mind accompanying me upstairs?' Chiyo said before Lev could reply. She sounded very serious suddenly.

Lev glanced at Maya sheepishly. He gathered up his books quickly and followed Chiyo inside.

'Should I not have said that?' Maya asked. 'Is Lev going to get into trouble?'

‘I don’t know,’ Noah replied. He asked, a little too casually, ‘Have you read any of them?’

‘No! So no need to lecture me.’

She was starting to get an idea what they might be, though. Even if she only had a very vague notion what that would actually comprise. There were serious gaps in her knowledge about certain things.

She gritted her teeth. Lev probably thought she was some baby, right? Asking *What do you mean graphic? Pictures?* like that!

~

It was late—or early, depending on which side you looked at it from—when Maya left the Castle. A full schedule of classes and some tough training had dulled the prospect of dwelling on exactly how much of a dunce Lev thought she was, but she was sorely mistaken to think that Noah hadn’t taken note. He accompanied her to the Portal Road. And true to form, he was horribly direct about it all.

‘About what happened with Lev earlier today,’ he began.

‘Oh god.’ She leaned on the railing and dropped her head on her arm. ‘Can’t we just let it go? I’m so tired today.’

‘Bear with me a moment. I only wanted to ask, have you had any sex education at school?’

Oh my god, he said the s word!

‘No-o!’

‘I see. Have your parents—’

She rolled her eyes so hard, she almost gave herself whiplash. ‘Riiiight!’

Noah’s brow crinkled. ‘No? Nothing?’ He actually seemed concerned.

Maya shrugged. 'A couple of years back, Amma got me this book that explained about…' she trailed off, and then added in a whisper, 'periods.'

'And then?' asked Noah, like they were having a chat about what they'd eaten for breakfast.

'It was full of complicated diagrams and didn't make any sense.'

Noah didn't respond, and Maya found herself going on. 'I thought of looking it up on the internet, but someone's always hanging around the PC, and I don't want to try anything on my phone in case, you know,' she gave Noah a glance, 'it shows up on the bill or something.'

He nodded, like that was a perfectly normal thing to be concerned about. 'And what about at school?'

Maya shrugged again. 'There was a chapter in Manan's science book last year. I read it, but again there were those diagrams of insides and stuff. But I'm not a complete idiot, you know. I know *some* stuff.' Like from movies, but she didn't add that.

'I never thought you were an idiot,' said Noah. 'Do you think you might try and ask your parents?'

'Not much point getting another book I don't understand.' She sighed. 'I might as well read the zines.'

'Maya, look, the zines are quite unsuitable for a thirteen-year-old. In fact, they're unsuitable for most adults, unless they enjoy factual inaccuracies. But you know I won't forbid you from reading a book—I don't believe in censorship. I just want you to be equipped with the right tools and information so that you can handle what comes your way safely and responsibly.'

'What are you saying? I don't understand.'

'Suppose I have a word with your parents?'

Maya scoffed. 'About this? Forget it. They already hate you. If you talk to them about this, they will contact the Swedish embassy and have you deported or something. Anyway, if you have to talk to them, just ask if I could come stay at the Castle.' She blinked away the tears pooling in her eyes. How ridiculous. 'I'll find a book at the library or something about this stuff. Can I go now?'

Noah caught her arm before she could go. 'Wait.'

She yanked her arm away, angry for no reason. 'What?'

Talking to him was easy because he didn't seem to get flustered like other grown-ups she knew. But what was the point?

'I'm sorry that no one thought to give you this information. And I'm sorry that I didn't know.'

'It's not your fault,' she mumbled.

'It's my job to make sure you know the things you need to know.'

'Really? And what are you going to do about it?'

'Make sure you have the information you need.'

'*Re*-ally?' she asked, curiosity overcoming awkwardness.

'Yes.'

'And no books and diagrams?'

'I can't promise no diagrams, but I can promise you all the answers you want. I don't want you getting incorrect information from questionable sources—that's my worst nightmare. I doubt your parents will want that either.' He smiled at her uncertain face. 'And I don't think having a Healer ignorant of the facts of life is advisable.'

Maya blushed, but nodded. 'Thank you.'

'You're welcome.'

7

NIRA LENDS A EAR

'It's time for some sparring,' said Chiyo one day.

Maya and Owen looked at each other. Maya's heart sank. Would she have to hit him? She really didn't want to.

Chiyo had some conditions. 'Only kicks and only above the waist. You may use hands to defend yourself but not to attack. Spirit allowed, but no Illusion.'

The two Preferred nodded.

Chiyo looked at her watch. 'Ready? On my whistle.'

When Chiyo gave the signal, Maya and Owen circled each other. Maya filled herself with Spirit immediately and was ready for Owen's tentative kick. Noticing that he wasn't transferring his weight correctly, she skipped out of the way, making him stumble.

'Balance!' bellowed Chiyo. 'Technique is not for making your moves look pretty.'

They got under way again, kicking and ducking, jumping and rolling. Owen pulled himself together, but it wasn't difficult for Maya to defend, until Chiyo barked at her to attack more. So Maya aimed a leaping kick slightly above Owen's head. He ducked and she quickly used the other foot to catch him under the chin.

Owen grunted and nearly lost his balance again, and Chiyo called a halt.

'I'm sorry,' said Maya. 'I didn't mean to hurt you.'

Owen raised a hand to indicate it was fine. Chiyo went up to him and said something in a low voice. He came at her much more strongly after that, and Maya had to concentrate harder on keeping him at bay, ducking and weaving around his kicks. He had definitely improved, but even so, he wasn't able to touch her at all.

Chiyo's whistle called another halt. 'Owen, that's all for today. Cool down and you can go.'

'Thanks, Chiyo,' he said, looking visibly relieved.

Chiyo called Maya over. 'Why are you wasting my time?'

The words felt like a slap. 'I…what do you mean?'

'I was expecting you to have him on the floor in under sixty seconds. He will never be a fighter, his heart is not in it. But you…' Chiyo shook her head.

Maya swallowed. She glanced at Noah for support, but it was like he couldn't even hear what was going on. 'I don't understand.'

Chiyo caught Maya's shoulder. 'You can touch more Spirit than any Preferred I have ever trained,' she said in a low voice. 'I cannot believe this is the best you can do.'

'He's bigger and stronger than me,' protested Maya.

'No, he's not. With Spirit you're much stronger than him. And size counts for little. Or have I not taught you anything?'

Maya's ears burnt.

'Think about that. You are not like the others. Ordinary parameters don't apply to you.'

~

'What's wrong?' asked Lev.

'Nothing,' said Maya, turning away. She sat down on the bench to put on her shoes.

'I came to tell you something,' said Lev.

'Done something else wonderful, have you?'

'What do you mean?' He sounded bewildered.

Maya still wouldn't look at him. 'Ever since I've been back, it's been Lev this and Lev that. I'm getting a bit sick of it.' Her mouth motored on on its own. 'If you're so wonderful at everything, go get raised and leave me to live my life in peace.'

'What's the matter with you?'

'I'm not perfect like you, that's what the matter is with me.'

His mouth fell open. 'Wha—? Have I done something?'

'Just...go away!'

She stood up and shoved roughly past him. He stepped back, surprised.

Why was she taking it out on him? She didn't even want to. She walked away quickly, out of the training area, towards the courtyard where Noah would be waiting for her.

She stopped in her tracks. The last thing she wanted was to face Noah. She turned and went in the opposite direction. She was already in trouble, what difference would a little more make?

She might have gone home, but she couldn't leave the Castle without telling Noah, and she knew better than to disobey outright. So she found herself a quiet corner of the garden instead. Not that it made a great deal of difference, because she sensed Noah approaching before long.

He appeared from the trees next to her.

'Go away,' she snapped.

He settled on the bench beside her instead. 'Is this because of what Chiyo said?'

'It's probably because my evil side is finally showing itself,' Maya replied scathingly.

'Are you angry with me for not saying anything?'

She hadn't planned on admitting it, but now that he had brought it up himself, she laid into him. 'Angry? It was totally humiliating. How would you feel if you had to get a dressing down in front of your Watcher? Especially if he didn't even care.'

'What makes you think I don't care?'

'If you cared, you'd have stood up for me.'

'You don't defend what is indefensible,' said Noah.

'Oh great!' She threw up her hands. 'So now you think I'm useless too.'

'No one thinks you're useless, Maya. Chiyo is of the opinion you have a lot more potential than you displayed today.'

'So you also think I'm not doing my best?'

'I wouldn't challenge Chiyo's judgement about something she is an expert in and I'm not. She has never worked with anyone with as much Spirit as you. I believe you can touch more than Lev.'

'But we all know there's a reason for that,' snapped Maya. Her mind went back once again to the cool, sandy cave, of the chilled, heavy black dagger nestling innocently in her hand, Yazid and Kilyana watching, of Noah's disbelieving voice. Of horrible understanding descending on her that she was the Warriors' Shadow, the person they were depending on for giving them control of the Sands.

'Nonetheless.' Noah's voice in the present jerked her back to reality. 'She sets her standards very high for you.'

'Well, she'll have to lower them, then,' said Maya. 'Obviously I'm not good enough.'

'If Chiyo says you are, then you are,' Noah replied firmly. 'Maya, listen to me. I would be a bad Watcher if I didn't push you to the limits of your abilities. I know that Chiyo can teach you what is beyond me, and you shouldn't be deprived of the opportunity. I won't force you to continue, but don't give up just because you're angry.'

A few seconds of silence ensued. He was right as usual. So annoying.

She rubbed her forehead 'Maybe I'm PMS-ing or something.'

'Maybe it's just hard to be a thirteen-year-old Preferred learning four Powers.'

Maya sighed. 'Shit. I was so mean to Lev just now.' She grimaced. 'I might have even pushed him a little.'

Noah shook his head. 'Honestly, I can't imagine why you are so upset with Chiyo when it all comes so naturally to you.'

She groaned. 'Don't joke, Noah. I guess I should go find him and apologize.'

'You need to get to Illusion now. You can talk to him after. Did you know he's been selected for the Raising Day duel this year?'

'What? Really?'

The Raising Day duel was an old tradition—an unarmed face-off between two of the most skilled Preferred. It was less of a competition and more of an exhibition of their abilities. To be chosen for it was a great honour.

Maya said a rude word and Noah looked at her reproachfully. 'What's the matter now?'

'So that's what he came to tell me. Shit. I don't know why I'm such a—'

'No more swearing,' said Noah firmly.

~

She caught Lev on his way to a Guiding lesson with some of the others. He seemed to be the centre of their discussion, with Ray aiming some mock punches to his head and saying something that made the others laugh.

'Lev, can I speak with you?' Maya called.

Lev stopped and turned around. Unfortunately, everyone else stopped as well.

'I'm busy,' he said shortly.

'It won't take a minute,' said Maya. 'It's important.'

'Oh. So it's important when you say so?'

Val and Ray exchanged looks. 'We'll go on ahead,' said Val.

'No need,' said Lev, turning back to them. 'I'm coming.'

'Lev,' called Maya. She sighed. He was making this difficult. But perhaps she deserved it. 'Look, I am trying to apologize.'

Everyone stopped again. Ray spoke this time. 'Uh, we'll see you later.'

Lev stared at some Illusion art just above Maya's head when they had left.

'I'm sorry. I was really rude then. I heard about you being in the duel. I think it's great.'

Lev looked down at the floor. 'I came to tell you first.'

'Who will you be duelling against?'

'Kari.'

'Wow! That's amazing. I am really sorry for how I acted.'

'No big deal.'

'It *is* a big deal.'

A short, uncomfortable silence followed. 'It's all right. Is, um, is Chiyo giving you a hard time?'

It was Maya's turn to study the floor. 'She thinks I'm not pulling my weight.'

'Sorry about that.'

Maya shook her head. 'Don't be. She's right, I guess.'

They stood around awkwardly for a little while, not looking at each other. Then, Lev said, 'I have to go.'

'Yeah, me, too.'

'Okay then, see you later.'

'Yeah. Bye.'

~

As head of Network Security, Nira had access to all sorts of classified information, and even she hadn't been able to find anything to help them figure out the function of the Key. The use of shells for anything other than Healing had been banned in the 1920s, which was about a hundred years ago, and searching the Network or the Extranet, the special network that only Logicians had access to, only produced detailed reports of shell-related accidents and lengthy treatises about Healing.

'I don't believe any information is useless, though,' Nira told Noah over their encrypted Signal call in Roz. 'This now gives us context—that they want the Shadow to do something with it. Something related to the Sands, most likely.'

'But like Maya, I feel frustrated at being so helpless,' Noah said. 'Have you found out anything about Yazid and Kilyana?'

'No,' Nira admitted. 'But I've been going over what little documentation we have about backwoods settlements.' She was referring to small villages and itinerant folk in the more remote areas of Lam.

'You're convinced that's where they are?'

'Well, they *could* be hiding in one of the smaller towns or more remote villages. But the backwoods would be easier. Most of them have no connection with the High Council, no allegiance to the Warriors as far as we know, a healthy disdain of anyone who can hold Spirit. So my best guess is they're either lying low somewhere in the backwoods, or...'

Or they are dead. She didn't have to say the words.

'Unless they're being harboured by the Warriors.'

'They aren't being harboured by the Warriors, Noah.'

'How can you be so sure?'

There was a pause. 'I have my sources.'

Another pause, a longer one, this time from Noah's end. Mostly because he appeared to have lost his ability to speak.

'You—have connections? With the Warriors?'

'Don't make it sound like a bloody conspiracy,' said Nira. 'Of course I have connections. Where else do you think I've been getting copies of the Prophecy from? I can't say for certain, but I'm reasonably sure the Warriors don't know where they are.'

Noah closed his eyes and tried to process this information. Yes, in Network Security you crossed paths with official secrets all the time, so why should this be a surprise? Even back when he'd worked with Nira, she had been required to hold information she wasn't even allowed to share with him, not just her assistant, but her a'fin.

'He won't survive long,' he said at last. 'Not with the prolonged...scraping.' That was a word no a'fin could ever be comfortable with, because it referred to the complete control of another human being by exploiting the Link.

'I'm not giving up looking for him, Noah. I'm not sure what's worse, the Warriors finding him, or the Elites.'

'The thing is, once they do find him, they'll know that Maya has the Key.'

'Don't think I didn't think of that, smarty-pants. They may already know—we have no idea if Kilyana's made contact. Do you have a plan?'

Noah took a deep breath. 'No, but I was thinking, if anything happens to me—'

'You'll be leaving Maya alone and unprotected, in possession of an artefact that makes her much sought after by certain people,' Nira finished for him.

Hearing the words said out loud was like a punch in the gut.

'I know you will be careful, but you can't always plan for everything. You know that, right?'

'I do,' said Noah. Nira never stopped startling him the same way he surprised Maya when he read her so easily. 'And I've been thinking about that.'

'I'm all ears.'

She listened as Noah spoke, and he couldn't recall the last time they had had a conversation without her using one of her favourite swear words.

8

YAZID NEEDS A PLAN

The nights in Saroye were bright, especially on a clear day. The sky shone like a black silk cloth with millions of tiny jewels clustered together, burning with their own brilliance. Light clouds like whisps of veil floated across them. Yazid couldn't remember the sky being like this at home.

Home. What did that even mean?

Since the fugue of the initial weeks had passed, his old life receded into the realm of the surreal with each passing day. He had given up hope of ever going back home or to the Castle, of ever even seeing anyone he knew. How long had he been away? Had people forgotten him?

Sometimes he stared at the sharp rocks along the drop into the ravine, wondering if that would be the best way out.

Saroye, this little village or whatever it was, comprised a few dozen houses and a couple of shops. He wasn't sure he knew how to spell the name in English but he could write it phonetically in basic Proto. The Saroyen dialect was slightly different from the spoken Proto he had learnt. They used more of hissing, sibilant sounds, almost like lisping. It wasn't that difficult to follow, but it was harder to speak it their way. Not that anyone would notice—they would think it was a result of his speech coming back.

The word Saroye meant 'shifting place'. That's what Anje said, and it referred to the fact that the village didn't have a permanent location—it moved every few years.

Anje was a wizened old creature who was Saroye's de facto teacher. Children gathered at their doorstep every morning, learning to read and write and do basic calculations. Fortunately, Yazid was too old—people his age all worked—or he was afraid Kilyana would have made him go.

She was doing a sterling job assimilating into the community. It worried him because it didn't make sense. Kilyana was ambitious, and there was no way she was living her days out in an unknown backwoods village.

She had to have another plan. Whatever it was, it would have to include him, and that was horrifying to think of. He had to figure out a way to get away before that.

'Babani!' someone called out.

It took Yazid a couple of seconds to remember he was supposed to answer to that name. Babani and Semeri—those were the names Kilyana had given them.

He waved as a tall, rugged girl, about his own age, bounded uphill towards him.

Novocha was possibly his only friend around here. She lived with her family in the dwelling closest to his and Kilyana's, and in the early days had helped them a lot. When Novocha was around, Kilyana left him alone, so she was the only person Yazid felt safe around. For some reason, maybe the spark in her eyes, she also reminded him of Maya—even though she was much taller, taller even than Kilyana.

'Did you draw anything new?' she asked, sitting down on the doorstep next to him.

Yazid showed her a sketch of the view from the rocks behind the house—the drop of the ravine, the forest across the valley, the sinking sun.

'It's good. Is it finished? Can I take it?'

'No, I have some last touches to do,' he replied. Not that someone like Novocha would be able to see any difference. Only someone who knew there was second- and third-level Proto there would be able to, that too, only if they knew what to look for. 'Maybe you can take it by tomorrow.'

She nodded, and Yazid braced for her to ask why he made her keep some of his drawings. But she didn't and he breathed. He couldn't risk Kilyana finding his 'special' drawings.

'Why won't you make one that's for me?' she asked.

'Because you want me to draw birds just so and they don't sit still long enough.'

'In that case, make me something else. Can you draw my house, but make it look beautiful? With colours?'

Yazid laughed. He didn't do that much these days. 'Of course. I'll draw your beautiful house tomorrow. But you'll have to get me colours.'

'I will, thank you. But, oh, I came to ask you something else. They are making up the roster for the season's foraging expedition. Will you come?'

Yazid's eyebrows rose. 'You mean hunting?'

'Hunting, gathering, finding wood, and so on. All the adults have to go, of course, but we can volunteer too.'

The cogs in his brain whirred, but he caught himself. That sickening tug inside him, just above his navel—the only thing that caused him physical pain—cautioned him that if he did this, he would have to be sure Kilyana didn't catch on.

'What are you thinking?' Novocha prompted. 'Will you come or not? You must come. Only children and elders stay behind.'

'I would like to, but I will have to ask Semeri,' he said, quite truthfully.

~

The four of them were back in Noah's flat again. Maya burrowed into the sofa, trying not to fall asleep. She was worn out once again after training, lessons, and continual holding of Spirit. Noah and Chiyo's voices floated around her in a gentle hum, but she wasn't paying attention. What was the point—it wasn't like they could do anything about the Key.

Things had been somewhat strained with Lev since the Chiyo incident and her fight with him, even though they tried to keep up appearances. What was worst was that Maya still felt such an ass. Why did she always end up hurting those she cared about?

Lev seemed withdrawn these days, preferring to be alone rather than seeking out company. Maya was sure it was because of what she had said to him.

A sudden gloom enveloped her. *I've lost my best friend.*

Did she do these things because she was the Shadow? Was this really her evil side coming out?

She jumped when she felt Noah's hand on her arm. 'All right?' he asked. 'You seemed worlds away.'

'Sorry,' said Maya, giving herself a little shake. 'I was… thinking of something.'

Lev too was studying his shoes with great interest. Chiyo and Noah exchanged a brief glance, though neither said anything. Ugh. Of course they'd figured out something was wrong.

Chiyo came to sit on the sofa next to Maya while Noah leaned against the window, looking out through the crack in the curtains. Dawn was close, and it was raining hard, the kind of rain that drowned out all other sound.

'So, then, have you thought of anyone?' Chiyo said at long last, probably continuing whatever they had been talking about. 'Sometimes this feels like too big a secret for just the four of us—six, if you count Nira and Rafa.'

'Yes, I have,' Noah started, when the lights went out. They all jumped, but within a couple of seconds the power back-up kicked in. 'It's Stephen. He works with shells all the time. I trust him. He's dependable. And I want him to look after Maya if anything should happen to me.'

'No!' cried Maya, but nobody heard her.

Chiyo whistled through her teeth. 'Noah, I know he is a good friend of yours…'

'He's the only other person I trust,' said Noah quietly.

'I understand, but it's still too big a risk.'

'Conceivably, we are in danger anyway.'

'True, and I know that you and Stephen go a long way back, but I am not prepared to trust anyone else just yet.'

'But I am,' said Noah flatly. 'I appreciate the fact that you don't see beyond Lev's safety, but then you should understand that Maya is paramount to me.'

'If that is the case, how can you so casually just trust someone? Even if it is Stephen?'

'I trust you,' Noah pointed out, 'even though if we were to take the Prophecy literally, you should be the last person I should. And vice versa.'

Chiyo pressed her lips together. 'Okay, you've made your point. In any case, you have decided, haven't you?'

Maya exchanged a terrified look with Lev. You didn't need a Link to sense the tension in the room.

'Do you honestly suppose I would do anything to put Maya in danger?'

'No, I know you wouldn't. But—'

'It's fine,' interrupted Noah. 'You don't have to explain. I do understand. But I don't see a way out. I don't want to put Stephen in danger either. At the same time, I would like him here with us. Like you said, it's becoming too heavy a burden to keep to ourselves.'

'There has to be another way.'

'There is none that I can come up with. But you're right. I have made up my mind. Now it's up to you to decide if you're still in this with us.'

Maya gasped, and Lev's eyes widened. They looked at each other again, scared this time.

'That was uncalled for,' Chiyo said in a tight voice.

Noah sank down on the couch opposite them. He rubbed his hand over his face. Maya had no idea what was going on with him. He had probably blocked her. 'I'm sorry,' he said to Chiyo when he resurfaced. 'You're right, that was below the belt. I apologize.'

Chiyo nodded her acknowledgement.

'Thing is, we have no idea what kind of move the Warriors will make—if they do—or when,' Noah said. 'We don't even know if they know what happened to the Key, or if they'll try to get it. If they do make a move, I'm not such a fool to believe that we will see it coming. We can either sit around and wait for something to happen or we can try and figure out what the Key does. And Stephen knows more about shells than all of us combined.'

9

NOAH KEEPS A PROMISE

As urgent as telling Stephen was, Noah remained very much on the ball with his Watcher duties. A few days later, when they were making the best of the good weather by working outdoors near the lake behind the Castle, he stopped Maya just as she was about to get up and go home.

'I believe I have a promise to keep.'

Maya gave him a sharp look, her heart sinking with a suspicion that she knew exactly what he was talking about. 'What promise?'

Even though she dearly wanted to know this big secret that everyone else seemed to be in on, another part of her had slightly hoped that Noah would never bring up the subject again. There *had* to be a book in the library that explained everything, right?

He slotted a nano-SIM-sized drive into the side of his computer, 'I could make this really easy for you, you know that, right?'

Maya shrugged. 'You still could,' she mumbled. It would be so much easier if he *did* make her debilitating embarrassment go away.

'But I won't.' He glanced at her. 'Because this is far too important. Difficult or embarrassing questions are those that need to be asked and answered the most. And getting the wrong answers can be dangerous.'

Maya gave a noncommittal nod.

'Do you know why they're called the facts of life?'

'Um, because they describe how life happens?' Maya replied, rolling her eyes.

'Partly. These are the fundamental physiological processes and behaviours involved in human development, including sex and reproduction.'

'O M G!' said Maya, holding her head. 'Why do you keep saying it?'

'Saying what?'

'Never mind.' She pointed to the computer. 'What's that?'

'No books and no diagrams, you had said. So what I have here is an instructional film. I think you'll find it very informative. Once you've watched it, we'll talk. All right?'

'Yeah, sure.'

'If you prefer, we could ask one of our Healers to talk to you. Eidora maybe?'

Maya gulped in alarm. 'No way! I hardly know her. At least I know that you're not laughing at me.'

'Why would I laugh?' asked Noah, taken aback.

Maya drew up her legs and put her chin on her knee. 'I...well, I don't want you to think...it's not like I'm a pervert or anything.'

'I don't think that,' he said. 'Now, you watch the film. Meanwhile, I'll take a stroll to the other side of the lake.'

~

'Oh. My. God.' Maya decided it warranted the full form this time.

'You'll have to be more specific,' Noah responded.

'That film…um, it was very…detailed.'

'That was the whole point of it. It's an educational film for schoolchildren.'

'They tell schoolchildren all this?'

'Mmhmm.'

They strolled along the walkway that spanned the lake, stopping in the middle by unspoken mutual consent.

'You have questions, I suppose,' Noah said.

'Ha!' said Maya, 'Understatement of the year.' She placed her forehead on the cool stone of the walkway, watching the gently flowing water from the edges of her vision. Some part of her would be happiest to wipe away the past twenty or thirty minutes of her life. 'So…I don't know, it just sounds so…disgusting that I don't understand why. I mean, why do people do it?'

'Partly to keep the human race going. But mostly because, I guess, it feels good.'

Maya almost fell into the lake. '*What?*' she said when she'd composed herself. 'Did you just…no, never mind! I just…' She just threw up her hands.

'What?' asked Noah, puzzled.

'I can't believe you said that!'

'About feeling good? Because you asked, and it's the truth.' He leaned down next to her. 'I should add, not all people are sexual. Not everyone finds sex pleasurable or wants to do it.'

'The movies seem to imply it's great. Now that I know what they were talking about, I know they're all liars.'

Noah smiled. 'Let's not get sidetracked about the veracity of movies.'

'The what of movies?'

'Veracity. Accuracy.'

'Oh. But still.' Colour flooded Maya's face. 'It's gross and I'm never going to...you know!'

'Maybe, maybe not. There isn't one single universal human experience of sex or sexuality. It all depends. Between consenting people, though, it isn't disgusting at all.'

Maya's groan was muffled by her arms over her head. She poked one eye out. 'Could you please verify that Hanne was adopted?'

Noah laughed, but he didn't answer. Phew.

What he'd said had made her think, though. 'You mean, there are lots of things that are normal when it comes to... you know?'

'Normal is a very dangerous word. It makes us assume that some things could be abnormal.'

'Aren't there?'

'That's why consent matters—explicit consent between people who are capable of consenting.'

'What do you mean capable?'

'Children, for example, can't consent. Or someone who is intoxicated, unconscious, drugged, or someone who is being coerced or is afraid.'

'I see.' She drummed her fingers absently. 'I found it a little weird,' she added, 'that the movie also talked about, you know, stuff between—I mean, between people who are not, er, opposite genders.'

'You mean different genders,' said Noah lightly.

'Hmm?'

'Opposite implies two contrasting states. Whereas there are more than two genders.'

'Oh, right.'

'Why was it weird?'

Maya shrugged. 'I don't know. It just felt weird.'

'Can you describe weird for me?'

She screwed up her nose. 'Umm, odd? It felt strange. Like, uncomfortable maybe?' She gave a laugh. 'Okay, sure, the whole thing was uncomfortable, but this—like two boys or two girls,' with a glance at Noah, 'or other people—it was, maybe extra-uncomfortable.'

'Why did you think that was?'

'I don't know. I thought you might know. I mean, I know Kari has a girlfriend, and Owen said he's dated both girls and boys, and… They seriously want to tell school kids all this?'

'Don't schoolchildren who are not straight or are gender-diverse need information about their bodies and about safe sex?'

Maya stared at him. 'That's what you meant, right?' she said after a while. 'About normal being a dangerous word?'

Noah nodded, accompanied by a small smile.

'I think,' Maya said slowly, 'that if I had just been living in Roz, I might not have understood that. Here, there are so many different kinds of people.'

'Oh, there are different kinds of people in Roz too. It's just not safe enough for them to be themselves openly. So they hide.'

'Wow. That's…*awful*.'

'Yes.'

'We all need to stop assuming things about people.'

'That, and be able to ask and get answers without being afraid.'

Maya nodded. 'Thank you…for…this.'

'You're very welcome. If you have any more questions, anytime, you can ask me. As I said before, if I don't know the answer, I will find it for you.'

'I do have a question actually. Why are boys so obnoxious? Except Lev. He's okay.'

Noah thought for a while. 'My theory is, it's because adolescence is a strange, scary phase, and all of us, we don't really understand or know about what's happening to each other.'

That kind of made sense. Maya stared some more at the lake and sighed. 'I know I wanted to know all this, but…' she made a face. 'Argh!'

Noah patted her arm soothingly. 'You'll get over it. Now let's get you home before your mother's internet yoga class.'

10

STEPHEN HAS A SHOCK

Stephen and Jan had a house in the outskirts of Andara, away from the bustle of the city and its lively student population. But before seeking Stephen out there, Noah decided to check his study and then his room at the Castle first.

A sleepy face, one cheek marked with a criss-cross pattern, appeared when Noah knocked on the door of the latter.

Noah glanced at his watch. It was twenty past noon, but that meant nothing if Stephen had had a late night at the Dispensary. 'So sorry I woke you. I can come back.'

'What's the time? Sands! No, no, come in. I should be up. Have to be at work soon.'

'Are you all right?' Noah said, following him inside. Stephen wasn't necessarily good at pacing himself.

'I'm fine. I got back from Kirnara a few hours ago—couldn't use the Portal Road because I ran out of security credits and had to endure the train. There are some repairs going on at home, so thought I'd crash here. What's up?'

Noah followed Stephen inside. 'Needed to pick your brains. But…'

Stephen waved at him to be quiet. 'It's about time I was up. Tea?'

'Yes, thank you.'

Stephen's room was bigger than Noah's. There was a small outer annexe that had a long table pushed up against the wall, just under an immense window. There were some chairs around it, books and magazines were scattered on it. There was also a more comfortable seating arrangement, but Noah chose the table, picking up a journal and flicking through it.

The inner area was the bedroom, with a tiny kitchenette. A single wooden door, part ajar, led to the bathroom. There was a comfortable mess about the place. Despite being very organized about work, he seemed hopeless at keeping things in place.

'So, what is it?' Stephen asked after he got them tea and filled his cat Anfield's food bowl.

'A hypothetical question. Suppose you had a shell in front of you, what would you be able to tell about it?'

Stephen frowned thoughtfully. 'Hmm, well, my expertise is a bit one-track. Is this a Healing shell?'

'Probably not.'

'What is its Nikau number?'

'Unknown.'

'Then that's a tough one. You could send it to be tested—there's a place in Kirnara.'

'Suppose you couldn't send it there.'

'It's virtually impossible to tell the function of a shell otherwise. Is your hypothetical shell powerful?'

'Extremely. Can a very powerful shell hurt you?'

'Of course, as I'm sure you already know.'

'How? Walk me through it?'

Stephen scratched his chin. 'Is this some kind of a wind-up?'

Noah grimaced. He supposed it was a basic, newbie question, certainly not one a qualified Healer such as himself would ask. 'No, no. I'm just trying to get my head around how a shell would hurt someone on just touching it?'

'It won't,' said Stephen. 'No shell will hurt you if you just touch it or hold it.'

'Are you sure?'

'Positive.'

'Why not? Humour me.'

'Because a shell without Spirit is just any other object. Of course, the stronger a shell is, the higher its Spirit threshold, so the only potential danger is in trying to use it without knowing how to.'

Noah digested that. 'I see.'

'People like you and me, who are sensitive to shells, should be able to tell if they are too dangerous to attempt using,' Stephen continued.

Noah frowned. 'Wait, what? I didn't know that.'

'When you're using a Healing shell, how do you know how much Spirit to use?'

'The way I was taught. I test the shell with a bit of Spirit. If it works fine, I go with it. If not, I give it more.'

Stephen nodded. 'Because Healing shells are safe enough. But maybe because I work with shells day in and day out, I can now tell exactly how much Spirit a shell needs just by touching it. When I started out, I used trial and error, the same way you mentioned, but in time I discovered I didn't have to. I think you could learn to do that as well. Probably Maya, too.'

Noah was silent for a while, thinking.

Stephen drained his tea and set his mug down carefully. 'Are these really hypothetical questions?'

'Would it make a difference?'

'Maya was grilling me at length about shells some time back. Now you. I know you two are up to something. I'm not that clueless.'

Noah hesitated. Stephen was the last person he wanted to tell an outright lie to, and he wanted to break the news about the Prophecy to him as gently as possible.

'I never assumed you're clueless. The reason I'm asking you is that it's only Healers who work with shells nowadays, and you are the best Healer around here.'

Stephen narrowed his eyes. 'All right, I won't ask. But I just hope, whatever this project of yours is, you're not putting yourselves in danger.' He stood. 'Hang on, let me get dressed, and then we can go to the Dispensary and play with some shells if that'll help.'

'Sure. Thanks.'

When Stephen returned in his Halvard uniform, Noah's mind was made up. This was never going to be easy, and he might as well get it over with.

'Sit down for a moment, will you?' he said. 'You're right, there's...something you ought to know. It is going to be a bit of a shock.'

It was.

~

'Impossible,' said Stephen, and not for the first time. 'How many times do I have to say this—merely touching a shell will not harm anyone.'

'But I know what I saw,' insisted Maya. 'His hands were perfectly fine when he was bashing me up.'

'Maybe it was his first time touching a shell and he got spooked,' said Lev.

'I said I know what I saw!'

Lev clamped his mouth shut and looked away.

'He screamed, and there was blood on the...thing...and that smell...'

'There is a perfectly simple explanation, then,' said Stephen. 'Yazid tried to direct Spirit into the shell, it wasn't enough, and the shell reacted. The reaction was a bad one.'

Everyone stared at Stephen, who was kneading his forehead like he had a headache. 'Sands help me, I don't believe you all are in the middle of all this. Where is this Key? May I see it?'

'I'll get it,' said Maya. She was back in a few minutes with a small package made out of a piece of pink fleece blanket. She set it down on the table and unwrapped it. In uneasy silence, the five of them stared at the small black dagger. It was about five inches long, plain and unadorned, crafted out of a single piece of metal, so dark that light seemed to end near it.

Stephen reached out towards it, and Maya caught his arm in alarm. 'Don't!'

'Trust me on this,' said Stephen, and picked the Key up.

He dropped it immediately.

Maya jumped up with a cry and grabbed his hand. Even Noah half rose from his seat.

But Stephen's hands were fine. He opened his mouth, shut it, opened it again. He seemed to have lost his power of speech.

'This…' he said finally. He cleared his throat. 'This is a very, *very* powerful shell. Feeding it a trickle of Spirit should destroy any living organism in contact with it.'

More silence. Then Noah spoke.

'Do you have any idea what it might be for?' he asked.

Stephen shook his head. 'Impossible to say.' He looked at his hand again. 'My instincts tell me that it is a vile instrument. We have to find a way to destroy it.'

'Shells can't be destroyed,' said Chiyo quietly.

Stephen held his head again. 'I have a very bad feeling about this. No good can come of this.' He stood and paced the floor as the others watched. 'Explain to me once again why we cannot go to the High Council,' he said, stopping in front of them.

Noah rattled off the reasons: 'One, the study of the Prophecy is banned and we'll get into trouble about that. Specifically, I will, and that leaves Maya unprotected. Two, you know the official line about the Warriors. It's our word against that of the powers-that-be. We have no proof that this is a true Warrior conspiracy. Who believes the Prophecy, even?'

'Three, Warriors are rumoured to have people in the High Council even,' Chiyo continued. 'Four…'

'All right, all right,' said Stephen, raising his hands in a gesture of surrender. He sat down again.

Maya had never seen him this disturbed.

~

Kilyana rarely bothered to tell him anything, but Yazid was beginning to piece things together from the snatched conversations with her High Council contact through the recalcitrant radio. He knew, for instance, that Maya having the Key had put them all in a flap, and that heads were going to roll because they had missed this possibility in their planning.

He also figured that Kilyana was negotiating for the two of them to safely return into the Warriors' fold. He suppressed a shiver, listening to her trying to convince whoever was on the other side of the line that he, Yazid, was still the rightful owner of the Key based on his advantageous position in the Oparian birth chart that shaved down the list of possible contenders to him, Maya and Lev.

Getting the Key had been a huge responsibility—the start of the culmination of a couple of thousand years of carefully laid plans—and he had failed. Why would they want him back? What could Kilyana possibly negotiate that they would agree to having them back.

And if she did manage to do so, he was definitely going to jump into the ravine. Anything would be better than being Kilyana's and the Warriors' plaything.

'And how do you propose to get it back?' she was saying into the pinhead-sized microphone.

She paused to listen. 'I see, and who is this, if I may ask?'

Another pause, followed by a sneer. '*Him*? With respect, Councillor, he's too old for it. He's going to fall down dead chasing a teenager around.' Pause. 'Yes, that makes sense.' Kilyana nodded when she heard the response. 'Oh. And in the eventuality she does end up using the Key?'

Yazid held his breath. He knew very well what would happen if Maya ever used the Key. On the other hand—

Kilyana gave a derisive laugh. 'Again, with *respect*, Councillor, your threats are empty.' The way she said 'respect' sounded exactly the opposite of what the word meant. 'We all know what happened when you tried to eliminate Lev? You need us.'

His head spun. *Eliminate* Lev? Like, kill him? When had that happened? *What* had happened? Was Lev alive? Okay?

Kilyana looked over her shoulder at him, and he fought to control himself, looking down at his book.

'What threats?' he asked Kilyana when she had finished her conversation.

'Not your concern.'

'Why are we still hiding if they know everything?'

'Not for long,' she said. 'Just as soon as they get the Key back from that girl, we'll go back. And you have to be ready.'

His gut twisted at the implication of being ready. Instead, he forced himself to ask: 'Will they harm her?'

Kilyana gave him another sharp look. 'Don't concern yourself with trivial issues.'

A knock on the door stopped further conversation. Yazid got up to answer it and found Yaroslaya, one of the villagers who was particularly friendly with Kilyana. Rather, someone she had *allowed* to get friendly with her.

Yaroslaya grinned cheerfully at Yazid. 'Looking better by the day.' He looked over his head at Kilyana and waved a handful of papers. 'The roster for the foraging expedition—I trust I can put you both down?'

It took Yazid all of his will to stay neutral as Kilyana and Yaroslaya discussed plans. Kilyana finally said, 'Yes, put me down, but I think Babani is not yet strong enough.'

He couldn't help his twinge of dismay, and a moment later, a sickening twist deep inside seared through him. He groaned, and clutched his stomach. Through a haze of pain, he heard Kilyana exclaim, and herd Yaroslaya out with excuses of 'I must tend to him'.

He collapsed on his bed, gasping as Kilyana came and stood over him. 'So weak,' she said, words dripping with disgust.

'Yes, yes, I am weak!' he cried. 'I don't want this!'

She bent down to him. 'You will want it,' she said in a low, calm voice. 'You will want it, for the love of all those who are dearest to you.'

The words sank into him as Kilyana retreated to her end of their tiny house. He went cold at the possibilities of what she had meant. Even his tears dried up. He lay in the darkness, thinking.

Moonlight streaked in through the gap in the curtains, falling on his almost-ruined hand. He stared at it—would it all be worth it some day?

He thought of his family often. He missed them, his kid brothers and sisters, especially the youngest one, Sara. She had eyes like his—one lighter than the other. She would tug at his legs and yell incomprehensibly till he picked her up and took her over the fields to watch birds. She loved watching birds, but she couldn't hear them. If he closed his eyes and thought hard, he could still feel those strong little arms around his neck. Maybe she'd forgotten him. Babies were like that, weren't they?

He felt his eyes stinging, and took a deep breath. He concentrated on the feeling of needing to see her again.

There was one thing he had learnt in these past few months: Kilyana could scrape him clean, inside-out, for all she wished, she could inflict all the pain she wanted. But as long as he concentrated on his *feelings*, she had no idea what he was actually *thinking* about.

And that was how Yazid was going to make his plans.

11

MAYA HAS SOME MIXED NEWS

Finally, *finally*, Noah gave her the nod to come stay at the Castle. When Maya returned to her room, the one she shared with Val and Mingmei, it felt like a homecoming. There had been some tense scenes with her parents—and there had definitely been some behind-the-scenes drama between Noah and her parents that he refused to talk of—so in some ways this didn't feel like a victory.

But then, for the next few weeks she could put her family's silent disapproval out of her mind.

Staying at the Castle meant you had to pay for your boarding and lodging, which Preferred did by working as volunteers. Maya applied at the Dispensary for the volunteer's post she had before. Things with Lev were still a bit stilted, so working in her free time suited her very well.

But it also meant getting used to a new routine, and some sort of jet-lag because of the difference in time zones and the way that time passed.

'Am I getting Homesick Syndrome all over again?' she asked Noah, holding her throbbing head.

'No, you only get it the once. Once you're acclimatized, you're done for life.' He pointed to a covered glass. 'Drink that. Sweetberry with coldwort.' Seeing Maya's disgusted expression, he went on to add, 'It will make you feel better. You are exhausted with touching too much Spirit.'

Maya peered at the drink with suspicion. 'Why can't you just Heal me?'

'You know very well that you can't Heal exhaustion.'

She sipped the drink carefully, even though she knew from past experience that coldwort was tasteless and it worked fast.

'Perhaps this will cheer you up,' Noah said as she put the glass down. 'I have put in a request to visit the Network headquarters at Kirnara. So you can see for yourself exactly how communications work here.'

Maya's mouth dropped open. 'Really? Can I really go and see it. Go inside and all, you mean?'

'Yes, inside and all.'

'Don't make fun of me. Or do, I don't care! When do we go? Will we use the Portal Road?'

'We'll go by train,' said Noah. 'Kirnara is the capital of the Union of Southern Provinces, in case you have forgotten—and does not have free Portal Road access.'

'Train sounds fun,' said Maya. 'I've never seen a Lam train.'

It was either the coldwort or the news, but she was feeling a hundred per cent better.

'Now, let's get back to work. Where were we?' He opened a thick volume called *Here, There, Everywhere: An Introduction to Quantum Mechanics*.

For a change, Maya found her thoughts drifting to how much she had advanced in her training rather than about how hard the work was. Her Logic studies with Noah were going great, and Stephen had recently announced that his beginners' batch would be ready to move up to intermediate Healing soon. Even her problems at home seemed trivial all of a sudden.

~

'I don't understand,' said Chiyo, throwing the flat, brown discs, the size of quarter plates, up in the air one after the other, 'why you and Maya seem to be avoiding each other. It's hard on both of you.'

As the discs flew up in the air, Lev kept up a series of spinning kicks at them. He jumped, kicked, twisted and landed back on his feet in his starting stance, and did it all over again. And again. The discs, specially made for this kind of training, split into two or three when hit correctly.

They stopped when Chiyo had released all twenty. Lev was sweating and just slightly out of breath. 'Sorry. Didn't catch a word,' he lied.

Chiyo narrowed her eyes at him, but didn't push it. She bent to collect the discs. 'You're wasting too much energy—it's not efficient. Perhaps you should try a double kick with each jump.'

'Oh, come on—'

'Ready?' She flung two discs at him.

Lev jumped, kicked one, twisted, kicked the other, and landed back on his feet, perfectly balanced. His face was flushed and indignant.

'That's not fair! I wasn't ready.'

'Perfect. Here's another.' Chiyo chucked another couple of discs at him, but they clattered to the ground as Lev didn't move. He stared at Chiyo.

'What did you say?' he asked.

'I said perfect.' She pointed to the floor. 'You got power and timing both right. Why are you so surprised? Are you not satisfied with your performance?'

'You really think that was perfect?'

Chiyo looked surprised. 'Yes, Lev. I wouldn't have said it otherwise, now, would I?'

'Thanks,' mumbled Lev, bending to pick up the discs. Chiyo was uncharacteristically relaxed today. Usually, she remained in total control while training. She never let him know what she was feeling—unless it was disapproval, of course.

'They don't pick names out of a hat for the Raising Day duel, you know,' she said.

'Will I ever be as good as you?'

'I've been learning since before I could even talk properly. You, however, have far more Spirit at your disposal than I do. Yes, if you work hard, you will be just as good, but at different things. Especially considering you're much bigger than I am.'

~

'The knowledge you have is more than adequate for first-aid Healing,' Stephen said to his class. He smiled at the expectant faces. 'It has been a pleasure teaching you all. Your Watchers have already informed me about your future plans and I wish you all the best.'

The Preferred who would not be continuing with Healing left, and Maya was left with Owen, Mingmei and Diede.

'My new intermediate batch begins next week,' the Healer informed them. 'Lev and Kari will be joining you lot.' He regarded them thoughtfully. 'Now, there's a little catch. I like to interview each one of my prospective intermediate students individually, if possible their Watchers, too, before I start teaching them. If I am satisfied with your commitment and ability to make a competent Healer, you may continue.'

'But that's not the way other instructors do it,' said Diede, frowning. 'Learning a Power is voluntary.'

'Who cares?' said Mingmei in a low voice to Maya. 'Any time he wants to interview me in private, he's welcome to.'

Maya bit her lip to keep herself from grinning. Owen, also sitting in the first row with them, heard and coughed politely.

Stephen glanced at the three of them. 'I'm glad that makes you happy,' he said.

Mingmei blushed.

'Well, Diede,' said Stephen, 'Healing is different from the other Powers because of its proximity to life and death. I like to be sure of the Healers I am turning out.'

They took a moment to digest that.

'You mean,' said Owen slowly, 'you want to—what—test us or something?'

'Let's say, I like to be sure that the Preferred I take in are up to this,' said Stephen. He tossed a sheet of paper on Maya's desk. 'This lists the times I am available the next few days. Please choose any slot that's convenient for you. One of you return it to me later.'

'So I guess we are not celebrating just yet,' said Diede, running his finger down Stephen's schedule sheet. 'Can I take this evening? I'm not free any other time.' He signed his name and handed the paper on.

'What do you think he wants from us?' Maya asked. 'Okay, I'm taking the noon slot tomorrow.'

'It's not like you have to worry about getting in,' said Diede slyly.

'What's that supposed to mean?' demanded Maya, stung by his tone.

He shrugged. 'Your being Noah's Preferred and all.'

'Diede,' said Owen warningly.

'It's pretty well known Noah and Stephen are like that.' Diede crossed his first two fingers, and looked challengingly at Maya.

Maya fumed, but before she could say any more, Owen grabbed her hand. 'Come on, let's get something to eat.'

Before she could protest, he pulled her out of the instruction hall and nearly drove her into Noah, who was walking towards the classroom. He stared at Owen's retreating back.

'What happened?'

'Nothing,' said Maya, too angry to have even noticed that Owen had been holding her hand.

'Are you sure?'

'I *said* nothing.'

'All right,' said Noah mildly.

Maya rubbed her eyes. 'Sorry.'

By the time they reached the courtyard, Maya's rage had simmered down to irritation. She found a table while Noah got her something to drink.

'You've done well,' he said when he came back with sweet-lime tea. 'I am proud of you.'

'Really?' said Maya, feeling better momentarily. 'Well, I'm not in yet. Stephen's having some sort of entrance test.'

They didn't have a chance to discuss it any further because an admin volunteer came up and handed Maya an envelope.

'What's this?' she asked, turning it over. It was a plain off-white envelope with her name on it. The flap was held down with a golden hourglass seal.

'Apparently, you're in demand with one of the High Council,' said the volunteer. 'Well, get a move on. I need a reply.'

Maya slid a finger under the seal and opened the envelope. A matching sheet of paper slid out. Maya read it and frowned before holding it out to Noah. He read it and looked up at the volunteer.

'She'll be there,' he told her.

He waited till the volunteer departed to address Maya's rising panic.

'It's nothing to get nervous about. Councillors often choose to talk with Preferred. Especially those who might be showing good progress.'

'Why does it feel like I'm in trouble, then?'

'If you were, I would have known before you did.' He nodded to the upper end of the courtyard. 'And look, it seems you're not the only one who's got a summons.'

Sure enough, some others in the courtyard had those white envelopes. But it didn't make her feel much better. 'Will you come with me?'

Noah shook his head. 'When a member of the High Council requests a meeting with you, the invitation is only for you. If I go with you, that would be bad etiquette.'

12

STEPHEN DOES A TEST

'I must congratulate you on your progress,' said Councillor Enol, leaning back on his chair and studying Maya.

'Thank you, Councillor,' said Maya politely.

Enol regarded her with a slight frown. 'You seem nervous,' he said. He pointed to a chair. 'Please sit. I assure you, you have not been called here for any transgression on your part. I just wanted to speak to you about how your training is coming along.'

Maya sat down stiffly on the edge of the chair, her back rigid, arms folded on her lap. She tried to keep her face impassive.

'You are one of our most promising Preferred,' went on Enol. 'Tell me, Maya, if you were not going to be a Halvard, what would you have wanted to be?'

'Um.' She racked her brains. 'I am not sure, Halvard, I mean, Councillor. It's a bit hard to remember what I thought back then. Things have changed so much this past year.'

Councillor Enol bared his teeth in a smile. It looked like a snarl. 'I dare say you would have done well anyway. I hope you know that you are free to pursue a career in Amrozan as well. Plenty of Halvard hold important positions there.'

Maya nodded.

'And what Power would you like to be raised as?'

'I think I'd like to be a Healer or a Logician,' she said. 'Maybe someday, if I am good enough, I'd like to try for the Elite Guards.'

Enol smiled. 'The Elite Guards, eh? That's rather high ambition for a thirteen-year-old. Do you know the youngest age at which a Defender has been recruited to the Elites?'

'Fifty-five,' said Maya. 'Halvard Rafael Canas.' In other words, Chiyo's mysterious Rafa.

Enol nodded. 'That's right. But then, you're used to breaking age barriers, aren't you?' He smiled at her again. She wished he wouldn't. 'Don't ever let anyone tell you you're too young to do something.'

'Yes, Councillor,' said Maya, blushing.

'So tell me, how is your family taking this?'

'Oh, they are freaking out,' said Maya, beginning to get a little confused about Enol. The Preferred all thought of him as a frightening, unapproachable dragon who only yelled at people. But he seemed almost nice right now. Normal, really. 'They just want me to give it up. They keep begging Noah.'

Enol smiled and shook his head. 'Never changes. They haven't a clue what's going on in your life, but still want to control it, right?'

Maya stared at him in surprise. 'Yeah.' She added quickly, 'But they're okay, my family.'

'They usually are,' said Enol. 'They just don't like the thought of their children facing something they themselves can't understand.'

'I guess,' said Maya.

'And I know.'

'Oh?'

'Oh yes,' said Enol. He screwed his eyes thoughtfully. 'Let me see, when my youngest daughter went off to start a musical band, I nearly had a stroke, and when my older son settled in a backwoods island, I wasn't sure whether to shoot him or myself.'

Maya almost laughed, but caught herself and smiled politely.

'I have a grandson your age,' continued Enol. 'His parents are in a state of shock because he came home one day with his, well,' he paused and scratched an eyelid delicately, 'navel pierced.'

'Ouch!' That came out before she could stop herself.

Enol laughed. 'Exactly what I said.'

'My brother had a phase when he wanted to get his ear pierced. My parents had a cow.'

'A what?'

'A cow. That means they hit the roof.'

'That's an interesting expression. What about you? Have you done anything to make them hit any roofs?'

Maya shrugged. 'Not unless you count this Preferred thing.'

'Oh, that's right up there, I'm sure,' said the Councillor.

There was a short silence.

'You know, Maya, deciding to Summon you was a rather extreme sort of experiment. Even Lev and Yazid. We worried that you were all too young to be Summoned, and the strain of learning the Powers would be too much. Indeed, when Yazid deserted, we feared we were right to have been worried.'

Maya froze. She thought of Noah and kept her face as blank as possible. Enol had said 'deserted'. Did that mean he thought he'd just run off because the work was too hard?

'Have you ever wondered why we didn't wait a few more years?' the Councillor continued.

Maya jerked herself back into animation. 'I have, Councillor.'

'Well, the thing is,' said Enol, 'you are so strong that you might have been able to reach for your Spirit soon, even without guidance. That might have been dangerous, as you can imagine.'

She supposed she could.

'But I am delighted to report,' he said, 'that the experiment was a success with you and Lev at least. You are so young and yet you have the power to effect change in the worlds that you could never have imagined. Don't you find that amazing?'

'I do, Councillor,' said Maya.

'Well,' he said, getting up. 'I think you should go back to your Watcher. It's been nice talking to you.'

'Same here,' said Maya. And she actually meant it. Well, a little.

'Come back again some time. I'd love to chat more.'

~

Noah was waiting for her in the courtyard. When she approached, he didn't need to ask. He just put his hand out and when she took it, transported them to the Portal Road.

'What happened?'

'You were thinking it, weren't you? That what if Enol is the Warrior in the High Council?'

'The thought crossed my mind,' Noah admitted.

'I don't think he is.'

'Why do you say that?'

'He's kind of nice. He talked, he joked, he asked me about my family, my work. He even thinks Yazid is just a runaway. He's so…ordinary! Everyone knows he has a temper, but he was quite cheerful.'

'Not all Warriors are ranting, evil people, spouting anti-Sands slogans,' Noah said. 'People are rarely all good or all bad. Some of them could be ordinary like you or I. It is what they believe in that makes them dangerous. It's not the same as being cruel or nasty.'

'What do you mean?'

'This isn't to do with Enol per se,' Noah said. 'But as individuals, Warriors are likely to be ordinary people. Some will be pleasant, cheerful, kind, funny—just like anyone else. They have certain ideas of how things should be, which is different from the way we see it.'

'But they are bad guys, Noah. Why are you trying to understand them? Make them seem rational and reasonable?'

'I'm a Logician, Maya. So are you. That's what we do. Good and bad are relative. Don't you see, for them, *we* are the bad guys.'

Maya stared at him, flabbergasted. Was he crazy?

'Don't worry, I haven't lost my mind. In any case, we don't have to agree with them. We just need to understand how they think, and perhaps it will help us figure out what they want and why.'

~

A few minutes past noon the following day, Maya found herself with her Watcher, in Stephen's office at the Dispensary.

'For years now, I have been talking to my students,' he said, 'asking them why they want to be Healers.' He took off his glasses and polished them with a cloth.

Maya wondered idly why he didn't wear lenses like everyone else.

'But I don't know what to tell you. You are stronger than anyone else I have come across, and I know that you have the potential to be a skilled Healer if you choose to be.'

He looked towards Maya again, and she stared at his table, unsure how to react. Should she say thank you?

Then she remembered Diede's words. Did she really have it easy because Noah and Stephen were friends?

Stephen gave a sudden laugh. 'You're getting more and more like Noah every day.'

Maya widened her eyes in indignation. Noah was amused, but remained silent.

'I mean, the way you keep a blank face and yet one can see your mind working away underneath.' He put his glasses back on. 'So, do you see yourself as a Healer?'

'Definitely,' said Maya. 'Though I might want to be raised as a Logician.'

Stephen nodded. 'I generally give my prospective intermediate students a Healing dummy test to see if they are capable of buffering, but,' he nodded towards Noah, 'Noah tells me you can do it.'

'I can?' Maya asked, surprised. 'I don't even know what buffering *is*.' She looked at Noah. That uneasiness about Diede's words resurfaced. 'Look, I want to do everything straight. I want to take the test like everyone else. I don't want you to let me into your class because—' She ground to a halt.

'Because what?' A frown appearing on Stephen. 'I've always been quite straight with you, Maya. If anything a bit harder on you because you have more potential.' He peered at her. 'What's going on?'

Maya was fiddling with the edge of Stephen's table. Noah was puzzled, too, but he kept his expression neutral. No one spoke.

'Is there a problem?' Stephen asked finally.

When Maya didn't reply, Noah got up. 'I'll wait outside,' he said.

Maya ran a finger along the base of Stephen's computer in the uncomfortable silence. 'I want to take the test like everyone else,' she repeated when Noah had left.

'All right.' Stephen got up and handed her a Healing dummy—a small cushion covered in something that looked like leather, but built to simulate various sicknesses and injuries.

'Buffering,' he said, 'is when you split your Spirit into two, and use one part to form a protective shield around yourself. You use the other part for the Healing. It's called buffering because if you can do it properly, you protect yourself against Healing side effects. It can also reduce shell reactions, and protect you from infection, as Healing requires skin-to-skin contact. But buffering isn't something everyone can master. It's a tricky skill. If you're a full-time Healer, it is impossible to survive without buffering.'

He explained to her how to do it. 'Do you remember when we were practising splinting techniques last week? I showed you how to immobilize the patient's limb temporarily? This is similar to a certain extent. Only, you do it to yourself.'

Maya frowned. 'But how's that possible? You can't Heal yourself.'

'It isn't Healing. Give me your hand.'

Maya extended her hand towards Stephen. In a few seconds, she couldn't feel her arm any more or move it. It was spooky!

'Now, this is what I would do to you if I were operating on your arm, setting a bone, and so on. Not only can you not feel your arm now, but in this state your arm is also protected from the outside world. And the rest of your body is protected from your arm, any infection that may be in it.'

'Okay, I think I get it,' said Maya, massaging her arm as the feeling came back into it. 'I have to do that to myself?'

'Yes. But you have to do it without feeling the numbness. It wouldn't do if you fell down in a helpless heap in the middle of a major procedure.'

'How do I do that?' Maya asked, perplexed.

'That,' said Stephen, his eyebrows raised, 'is the tricky part. It's almost as if you separate your physical body from your Spirit and protect it. It's nothing to do with strength of Spirit. It depends on your skill and concentration. I don't like to test publicly because it embarrasses people if they can't get it right. Shall we try it now?'

'Okay,' said Maya indecisively.

'Right. Take this Healing dummy. It simulates a simple blade wound. I want you to try to buffer while Healing it.' He reached across and put a finger lightly on her hand. She felt a slight tingling sensation and understood that Stephen was putting a mild Probe on her to see if she would be able to do it. 'You can start now.'

Maya shut her eyes and reached for her Spirit. She could do it without thinking now. She tried to imagine the outer edges of her body, and then to imagine that she was floating outside it so she could do what Stephen wanted her to. It was tricky. It reminded her of an Illusion exercise Alfiya made them do every other week, where they had to direct a flame through two closely placed barriers without touching either one. She said it was an exercise in control.

Maya concentrated. She felt sensation fading from her extremities—

The next thing she knew, she was lying on the floor.

Her face hot with embarrassment, she let Stephen help her up. He gave her some water.

'Don't worry,' he said kindly. 'It takes a bit of time to get the hang of it.'

'Maybe I can't do it,' Maya conceded, with a sinking heart.

But the Healer was shaking his head, smiling. 'You can. You have done it before. The reason I wasn't going to test you is that Noah told me how you saved his life. What you did was a far more complicated form of buffering.'

'Really?' Maya asked, surprised.

'Yes. Otherwise you'd have both died.' He stared at her for a moment. 'You not only buffered, you simultaneously gave him some of your Spirit. That is considered… impossible. Anyway, are you ready for another try?'

Maya nodded. This time she had a better idea what to do, and after a few false starts found it a fairly simple process. It was strange not feeling that sharp pain she usually got in her head just after Healing. It was a neat trick, but needed a good bit of skill.

Stephen nodded. 'There you are. Well done. Welcome to intermediate Healing.' He smiled at her.

Maya smiled back uncertainly. 'Thanks. Can I go?' She stood up.

'In a minute. Sit down. I want to talk to you.'

She sat back down.

'Are people giving you a hard time because I am friends with Noah?'

'I never said that!' cried Maya.

'No. But I can put two and two together.'

Maya studied her hands in her lap.

'If that's the case,' said Stephen, 'I am really sorry. But you're my best Healing student. That wouldn't change even if Noah and I were sworn enemies.'

'I guess I know that.'

'Then there is something else you should know,' said Stephen. 'Noah is a very close friend. I respect him far too much to keep you in my class if I thought you weren't up to it.' A pause. 'Do you understand that?'

That she understood perfectly. She flashed a smile at the Healer. 'Yes, I do. Thank you.'

13

MAYA GOES ON A FIELD TRIP

Whenever they were all in the Castle together, Noah and Chiyo and their Preferred met for dinner every night as a rule. These days, both Preferred pretended that everything was okay, while the Watchers pretended not to notice the awkwardness.

'All packed for Kirnara?' Lev asked, cutting his food into tiny pieces and arranging them on the plate.

'Yeah,' said Maya, staring at her plate fiercely, like if she didn't look, it would vanish into thin air before she had a chance to eat it.

From the corner of her eye, she noticed Noah look at Chiyo, who shook her head slightly. *Argh!*

'Well,' Chiyo said brightly. 'You've never seen Lam city except Andara, have you, Maya?'

Maya shook her head. Noah nudged her with his toe, and she swallowed her mouthful and said, 'No, I haven't. Not that I've seen much of Andara either.'

'Kirnara is a big city by Lam standards.' Chiyo smiled, 'Though probably not as big as Bangalore.'

Maya smiled politely. At least Chiyo was trying to be normal.

'How long will you be away?' Lev asked, still not looking at her.

'Couple of days.'

'Cool. Have a good trip.'

'Thanks.'

More silence except the sound of cutlery against plates. Finally, Noah cleared his throat.

'So, Lev, how is your training for the duel coming along?'

He looked up from his food finally. 'Pretty good. They told us all the rules and stuff today.'

'We met with an Inshain Master as well,' said Chiyo. 'He says he'll spend some time with Lev.'

Maya looked up at that. 'You're working with a Master?'

Inshain Masters were experts in combat. They were reputed to be a bit snooty when it came to sharing their knowledge unless their pupils were extraordinary. Chiyo was technically an Inshain Master herself, as in, she'd passed all the tests, but she didn't acknowledge the title as she was not Inshain herself.

Lev looked embarrassed. 'No big deal,' he said to his food.

'It's a big enough deal,' said Noah. 'Congratulations.'

'Thanks,' mumbled Lev.

Maya wished she could at least punch his shoulder to congratulate him.

~

Maya had been uncertain about self-driving trains, which had led to the burning of midnight oil poring over everything she could find on the subject. It didn't take her long to discover they were safer than taking a flight in Roz, with an operator always on duty to oversee the computers. They were environmentally friendly, with the outer body of the train being covered in solar panels that powered batteries and sent the excess into the electricity grid. And they were rather snazzy to look at as well, which meant she was looking forward to being in one.

She wasn't disappointed when they boarded their train late in the evening. The seats were wide and deep, and inclined almost horizontally, with enough leg room even for Noah. They stowed their bags under their seats, and Maya looked around. Not just roomy and comfortable, she had never seen a train like this one.

'It's like a glass cage,' she exclaimed. Except for the floor and a strip along the ceiling, the entire coach was transparent. 'But we couldn't see inside from the platform. Is it like that magic window thing, where you can only see out, but not in?'

'One-way glass, yes,' Noah replied. 'They have a way to control the transparency, so it doesn't get hot on a sunny day.'

'But wait, I read there were supposed to be solar panels on the outside. Where are they?'

'The exterior surface.'

'Coo-ool!'

The other seats filled up quickly. There were two other Halvard, the librarian Quin and another old man whose name Maya couldn't recall. They all exchanged greetings with each other.

'How old *is* Quin?' Maya whispered to Noah.

'Coming up to his centenary, I think.'

'Shouldn't he have retired or something? Is that ageist?'

'Probably.'

In a few minutes, a door-closing warning sounded on the intercom, and Maya and Noah pulled on their seatbelts. The doors shut with a loud hiss. The train gave a little lurch, and suddenly they were on their way.

Noah reached under his seat and pulled out two sandwiches, a couple of small bottles of sweetberry juice, and a large bar of chocolate. They ate in silence, and when he was sharing out the chocolate, Maya gave a gasp.

'What is it? Have you forgotten to bring something?'

'No, I…uh…I just remembered. Nira! She's going to be there, right? She works at the Network Headquarters.'

'You're in luck,' said Noah. 'She's out of town.'

Maya heaved a sigh of relief. Then she spent the next quarter hour apologizing to Noah, though he insisted there was no need and that he understood.

'Um, there's one other thing…'

'Yes?'

'Uh, well.' Maya shifted in her seat. She bit into some chocolate, then crossed and uncrossed her legs. 'I mean, I know it's none of my business and all.' She adjusted the seat a bit more, peered out of the window into pitch blackness, scratched her leg, and rotated her ankles.

'Are you working up to ask about Lian?' asked Noah finally.

'She has your old job, doesn't she? As Nira's assistant?'

'She does. Is that really all you were asking?'

Maya considered lying and saying yes; considered that Noah would realize she was regretting bringing this up and stop pushing the conversation any further.

It was all moot, of course.

'If you're worried that I am going to have a dalliance with her given the first chance, I can put your mind at rest right now,' he said.

Maya held her head and groaned. *This is your fault for starting this.*

'It's, er, not that. I mean, she's…nice.' *Stop lying! He knows you're lying!* 'And if you like her…'

'Of course I like her. She's one of my oldest friends. Don't you think a couple of decades from now you'll still like Lev?'

'You know that's not what I meant.'

The thing was, she had worked out why she was so hostile towards Lian. She wished she had a better word for it, but she was jealous. That was the simple truth. The idea of sharing Noah with someone was unthinkable. She'd never admit that to him, of course, and hopefully he hadn't figured that out.

'Then tell me what you meant.' He said it with kindness and curiosity. He actually wanted to know.

Maya hesitated. Of course he'd want to know—that was his job, to know everything and fix everything. She cast him a glance. He was leaning towards her, watching her.

Maya returned his stare. Having shared a Link for the better part of a year, she had learnt a lot about trust, faith, loyalty and respect. And most of it was impossible to put into words.

'All right,' he said when Maya remained silent. 'I'm doing some guesswork here, but do you want me to spell it out, about Lian and me?'

Yes, she did want that. Being Linked meant sharing some things you didn't want to. And whatever benefits that brought to her training, it also meant Noah knew far more about her than she would want another living soul to know. She also knew that she would be aware of many things that he wouldn't want to willingly share either.

He'd admitted last year that he and Lian had been together back when they were Preferred, but he also said he had no inclination of getting back with her. He had just reiterated that. That should be enough.

'No, you don't have to spell it out,' she said finally. There was only a very thin line of mutual respect that kept the Link from being intrusive.

He pressed his eyes closed in acknowledgement. 'Thank you.' As he settled back into his seat, he added: 'You've learnt more than I could have taught you.'

~

Halvard Jan—Stephen's husband and also (unfortunately) Lian's Watcher—had offered to put them up in Kirnara. They found him waiting at the arrival platform the next morning.

Jan looked like he had been carved carelessly out of a block of brown granite, with his broad frame, glistening, hairless head, randomly uneven features, and surprisingly tiny ears. And yet there was something innately pleasant about him—an air of a teddy bear.

When he spotted them, his face broke into a wide smile that crinkled the edges of his shining brown eyes.

'Good morning,' he called out to them. 'Welcome to Kirnara.'

Jan ruffled her hair and gave Noah a hug like they were old friends. 'It's good to see you.'

'You too, and thank you for letting us stay,' Noah replied. 'But you didn't have to pick us up—I know this city like the back of my hand.'

'It's no bother. I just got off work fifteen minutes ago.'

'You work here?' asked Maya, puzzled.

They had come out into the parking area. Jan pointed to a large building across the street. 'Right there.'

Kirnara Central Dispensary—okay, that made more sense.

Jan took them to his car, a tiny four-seater that she couldn't imagine both him and Noah fitting into. He unlocked it, got in and folded down the front passenger seat to turn it into a neat luggage hold for their bags.

Noah and Maya piled into the back. The car was small, but high, and Noah could raise his seat so he wouldn't have to tuck his knees under his chin.

Maya stared at the controls in fascination. 'It looks like a gaming console more than a car,' she said. There was no steering wheel, only a touchpad, a small screen above it, a joystick-like handle, some buttons and dials. A couple of pedals on the floor were the only normal-looking parts. 'Is this self-driving?'

'No such luck,' Jan replied. He pressed a button and everything lit up with a low whirr and the doors locked.

Maya was dying to ask more questions, but Noah preempted them. 'It's electric—all transport is electrified in Lam. The touchpad is used to steer, the rest are other controls, brake and accelerator on the floor, and the screen is customizable into a street map or a rearview camera, and various other things, I believe.'

'It's awesome!'

'Thank you,' Jan said, as they waited to turn into the main road.

'Did you have a car when you were in Kirnara?' Maya asked Noah.

'No. Kirnara has a perfectly good public transport network.'

'I'm so going to get one when I'm old enough.'

Kirnara seemed to belong to a different age from Andara. Unlike the laidback university culture of Andara—it was home to three major universities in Lam—this was more business-like and impersonal. The buildings were dizzying multi-storey structures, a peculiar mix of Andarean curves and odd angles, and something distinctive that Maya couldn't put a finger on.

Jan drove fast through the sparse traffic—a bit faster than Maya would have liked. Not just because she wanted to take in the views, but because her heart jumped up into her mouth each time he braked or changed lanes or turned a corner. Perhaps this was what being in a car actually felt like in a normal place, unlike in Bangalore, where one was perpetually stuck in traffic.

Noah remained oddly tense throughout the ride. He didn't speak, except when Maya asked something. A couple of times she glanced at him to find that he was keeping his eyes fixed on their bags in front of him rather than looking outside.

'Are you okay?' Maya whispered to him.

He gave her a tight smile and nodded. 'Don't like cars.'

Jan glanced at them through the rearview mirror. 'Nearly there.'

Noah nodded. 'Thanks.'

What a bizarre exchange. Maya filed it away for later, when Noah wasn't so tense.

14

MAYA FINDS HIDDEN DEPTHS

Jan was on the nineteenth floor of his building, the top floor. Maya had always been curious to see the inside of a Lam house, but when she got her wish, she was slightly disappointed. It was quite ordinary. Smaller than her home too.

His flat was tidy and comfortable, the floor covered in tiles that felt cool to Maya's bare feet. He had a lot of books, and many of them were about cooking. There was a big flat screen attached to one of the walls of his living room. Maya's eyes widened.

'Is that an RC?' The Castle had a rec console in its entertainment area, but there was always an old person watching the news, so she'd never really had a chance to use it.

Jan picked up a small tablet, about the size of a mobile phone, and passed it to Maya. 'Here, you can try it out.'

'Ooh, thank you.'

'I'll make us all some breakfast, shall I?' Jan said, rubbing his hands.

Noah started to protest, saying they'd eat out, but Jan stopped him. 'I'd have made some for me anyway. Also, I have some pancake batter I'd love your opinion on.'

'But you've been at work all night,' said Maya. 'Don't you want to sleep?'

'Not just yet. I want to wind down first, and cooking is how I do that. Meanwhile, you'll want to freshen up, I suppose. There's a bathroom through the hall, and another in my bedroom. Noah, you take that one as it's much more your size.'

Maya found no wonders in the shower and toilet either—except for the electronic bidet, that is. It was fancier than the ones at the Castle, but she desisted from experimenting. It would be most embarrassing if she got scalded.

Back in the dining area, Jan, in a big, red apron, was dishing out pancakes. He had changed into a dark T-shirt and Kirnaran-style trousers. His arms were rather hairy, which was funny, considering his head was absolutely bald.

Noah poured out orange juice and they sat down to eat. The pancakes, with date jaggery poured over them, were delicious.

'So, you like to cook?' Maya hazarded.

'Love it,' Jan replied. 'It's a bit limiting, though, when you have no one to feed. Even Stephen is mostly in Andara.'

They had about an hour to kill before leaving for the Network headquarters, so Maya explored Jan's living room. She found some photographs on the shelves that caught her attention. There was one of Lian's Raising Day, and a few with Stephen. She picked up a small frame containing a photograph of a baby with wispy brown hair, sitting on a wooden floor, wearing a nappy.

'Who's this?'

'That's my son,' said Jan. 'Erik. Though, he looks a lot different now and is a little bit bigger.'

'Oh,' said Maya. 'How big?'

'Here's a more recent photo—of Erik and his wife. I just got it last week.' He handed her another frame.

Maya studied it. Erik was fairer than Jan, with a pleasant, cheerful face. He had his arm around a very pregnant woman with dark, frizzy hair.

'Are you going to be a granddad?'

Jan smiled. 'Very soon.'

'Congratulations,' said Noah, while Maya studied Erik with interest.

'He looks nothing like you,' she pointed out.

'Fortunately, he takes after his mother,' Jan replied.

His words made something click in Maya's head. 'Er... his mother...?'

'Really, Maya,' said Noah softly behind her.

But Jan was vastly amused. 'From before I knew Stephen, if that's what you mean.'

Maya put the photo back, ears burning. Really, she needed to keep her mouth from running away from her brain sometimes.

~

They caught a bus to the Network headquarters, officially Network of the World, abbreviated to NEWorld (pronounced *new world*), a big grey-and-white building with sprawling lawns in the centre of town. It was the most crowded place Maya had visited so far—full of locals, and a few Halvard. No one spared Noah a glance, but Maya, in her Preferred grey, earned some curious stares.

The NEWorld building was hollow right in the middle, with the central rhombus-shaped hall stretching all the way up, the sky visible through the transparent ceiling.

Maya craned her neck up. 'So this is where you worked before you had me to babysit?'

'I wish you wouldn't put it like that.'

Black and white marble paved the floor. One side of the hall housed service counters. There were four lifts, one at each corner of the rhombus. The lifts were transparent, so you could see them going up and down with people inside.

'So, it's not just Halvard who work here?' Maya asked.

'It's mostly locals,' said Noah. 'With just a few Halvard.'

The tour took them most of the morning, but Maya barely noticed how much time passed. A couple of times they ran into people who recognized Noah and they had to stop and chat. At other places, people wanted to show them what they were doing. At the R&D department, for example, a Halvard demonstrated how they were trying to adapt Proto better for the Network, and was quite surprised when Maya had some probing questions. As they were leaving, the Halvard muttered something to Noah about how they got younger and younger with each passing day.

At the Hardware section, a spiky-haired individual with bright orange eyes showed off prototypes of the new comms models. 'These handheld models have a mini-RC built into them,' they explained excitedly to Maya. 'We've modelled them on smartphones from Roz.'

'But at the cost of the portability you have with these wrist models,' Noah pointed out.

'Smartphones are big in Roz right now,' they said. 'I believe you can do *any*thing on them.'

'He knows,' said Maya, hiding her grin.

Finally, they were on their way to Network Security, Noah's old workplace. Maya had been looking forward to it the whole time, but after spending a few minutes with a couple of Halvard at 'Decryption and Analysis', her head was already reeling.

'Aren't Network communications end-to-end encrypted?' She asked, puzzled. 'How do you decrypt them?'

'We have some tools that allow us to break encryption,' a Halvard called Sumiko, one of Noah's former colleagues, explained. 'It's not easy.'

'But then, what's the point of the encryption?'

'We only look into them when a particular transmission or communication is deemed suspicious,' she replied. 'We decrypt it, analyze it and trace it. It's rare for it to happen.'

'If it's so rare, why are there four of you? I mean, er, Halvard?'

Sumiko gave Noah a desperate look.

'You recall the Sadir uprising?' he said from behind them.

'Yeah, it happened a few years ago.'

Sumiko flashed him a smile. 'Thanks. Good example. They were using the data network and broadcast channels to spread their messages around Lam. We hunted them down by tracking the signals, and then decrypting any messages to and from them. That's how the Elites caught them.'

Maya leaned closer to Sumiko's screen, filled with ever-changing letters and numbers, a small box in the corner where something that looked like gears spun very fast, and a bigger one with lots of code. Whatever it was, it was beyond her, but she knew enough to understand that a very powerful decryption software was at work.

'What is happening here?'

'All I am allowed to tell you is that we're looking for a location, and it's somewhere in Roz.'

Maya's eyes widened. 'You can do that? I thought there are no communications possible between the worlds?'

'Oh, it's possible all right. Just complicated and needs some very expensive toys.'

'Remember I told you how the internet in Roz is monitored from here?' Noah said.

'Yeah,' said Maya. 'Silly of me, I never questioned that.'

'Come on, Lian can tell you more.'

'Pity you weren't here yesterday,' Sumiko said. 'You missed Nira.'

Yes, a pity.

Lian's office was at the far end of the corridor, with her name printed on the door. Noah knocked and they went in.

She was just as Maya remembered her. Tall and slender, dark hair coming down to her shoulders in a silky sheet, dark brown eyes. She smiled and stood as they entered.

'I've been expecting you.' She rose and came towards them. Maya tried to tone her disapproval down when Lian and Noah shared a brief hug. After all, she would be offended if Lev *didn't* hug her twenty years from now, wouldn't she?

Lian shook Maya's hand. 'Nice to meet again, Maya.'

'Same here,' mumbled Maya, stretching her lips in what she hoped would suffice for a smile.

The office was small and crowded with books. Lian had a computer terminal, and on her table were open books, an ordinary stylus, and a special one with some wires running from it to a box that looked like it belonged in the twentieth century.

'Would you like something to drink? Spiced tea, real tea, coffee.' She turned to Maya, 'Or milkshake,' then to Noah, smiling, 'or even cocoa?'

'Spiced tea will be nice,' said Noah at the same time as Maya said, 'Spiced tea, please.'

'My goodness. In a few years the only way to tell you two apart will be your slight difference in height.'

Maya pretended to smile again. *I'm going to pull a muscle in my lips at this rate. Do lips have muscles?*

Noah gave his Preferred a warning look as Lian pushed a button and said, 'Three spiced teas. Thanks.'

'How has Nira been treating you?' Noah asked.

Lian sighed. 'My vocabulary has improved!'

Noah gave a perfunctory smile and didn't take the subject further. Instead, he said: 'Maya would like you to tell her a little bit about how communications between Lam and Roz work.'

'Certainly,' said Lian. The door opened, and their spiced teas were brought in.

Lian launched into a detailed explanation as they drank. Maya forgot her grievances and found herself drawn into the explanation.

She was a good teacher, Maya had to admit—patient, with a knack for making complex things sound simple. She drew her diagrams, showed her some books, and even some documentation from her computer. The tech bit was fine, but Maya wasn't satisfied.

'But isn't that spying? Or hacking?' she asked.

'We call it ethical surveillance.'

Maya frowned. 'What if the person you suspect is innocent? They could just be going about their lives and you could be finding out about their personal stuff. Isn't that totally *un*ethical? Doesn't it violate the principles of—what's that thing, Noah, of the assumption of privacy or something? You were telling me about it last week.'

'The principles of privacy-first design.'

Lian narrowed her eyes at Noah. 'I see you've got to her, then.'

Noah raised his hands in denial. 'No, I haven't, I promise.'

She turned back to Maya, and gazed at her thoughtfully. 'These are good questions, very good questions, but no easy answers. You remember contact tracing during the pandemic?'

Maya nodded.

'That was a level of surveillance considered appropriate in the interests of public health in Roz. Similarly, we weighed the pros and cons, and decided that in the greater interests of the worlds, we needed to use this technology. You see, a right to privacy isn't absolute, not when it overlaps with other rights of other people.' She pointed to a thick volume on the shelf behind her desk. 'That is our ethical surveillance manual, with all the rules and regulations and conditions we have to follow. So, you can imagine, it's not done without a great deal of thought.'

It kind of made sense, though. When Maya had no further questions, they thanked Lian and declined her invitation to join her for lunch at the NEWorld canteen.

'I wanted to show Maya a bit of the city, and try some local food,' Noah told Lian. 'You're welcome to join us.'

'Afraid I can't,' Lian said. 'We are monitoring a situation, so can't leave the building till the relief shift arrives.'

Aw, what a pity. Not!

But Maya's heart was not in it. She was beginning to have some grudging respect for Lian after their conversation. At least Noah's former job was in good hands. Probably.

As they waited for the lift to arrive, she saw a figure disappearing down the corridor and round the corner. 'Look, Noah, isn't that Quin?'

When Noah looked, the corridor was empty.

'Funny he's here too, just like he was on the train. Is he following us or something?'

Noah ushered her into the lift. 'All this talk of security has gone to your head.'

~

'All right, all right, I was being judge-y about Lian,' said Maya as they waited for their food at a pretty little restaurant set in the middle of a park. 'So you can stop being so smug.'

Noah's eyebrows rose. 'Smug? What do you mean?'

'Why else are you feeling pleased with yourself.'

'Oh, that.' He looked down at his hands around a glass of cool water, a faint smile touching his face for a second. 'I am pleased, but not with myself, as it happens. But never mind. About Lian—Nira picked her out from half a dozen extremely qualified people. That should tell you something.'

'What did she mean when she said you had got to me?'

'She was referring to the argument about ethical surveillance.'

'Aha! So there *is* something.'

'Elaborate, please.'

'Noah, this is not a class,' Maya moaned, but he wouldn't budge. 'Okay, fine, but I don't know what to elaborate about.'

Their food arrived. A salad with bean sprouts and nuts, sticky rice, grilled fish in a red sauce, and a vegetable broth on the side. Noah didn't speak till they had served themselves and started eating.

'What bit of the conversation made you feel there were still unanswered questions?'

Maya gave it some thought. The food was *really* good, even though they had dialled down the spices quite a lot—apparently there was a term for that in restaurants, 'Halvard special'.

'The argument about contact tracing,' she said at last. 'Something doesn't add up.'

'Because the comparison wasn't a fair one,' Noah conceded. 'Can you think why?'

Maya chewed on her salad. 'Mm, no. I can't figure it out.'

'It's about consent. In Roz, we knew what was going on with contact tracing. With this surveillance, the people being surveilled don't know of it.'

'Is that ethical?'

'Not in my book, no. But,' he raised an index finger to emphasize this point, 'she was right about one thing, that this is a complex and layered matter. That's why there's a twelve-hundred-page manual to read.'

'But you still did the same job she is doing.'

'I know. So perhaps it's hypocritical of me, but I questioned it, and Lian doesn't. I feel that makes a difference.'

'What does Nira think?'

'You'll have to ask her yourself.'

Maya made a face and went back to her food. 'I get the feeling Lian doesn't like working with Nira.'

'Honestly, I don't think they've taken to each other.'

'I guess Lian's okay, really,' said Maya, sighing. She tried to mean it very hard.

Noah gave her a small smile. 'You don't have to like her for me.'

'Are you sure?'

'Absolutely.'

15

LEV MAKES AN OVERTURE

Lev checked he had all his books before leaving his room. A quick breakfast with Chiyo at the courtyard, and then he had a full day.

He glanced towards the neighbouring room, the one Maya shared with Val and Mingmei. He did that every day, even though it had been a while since he and Maya had gone down for breakfast together.

He could refuse to talk to Chiyo about it all he wanted, but he couldn't deny it to himself—he and Maya were going through a rough patch. They were avoiding each other, in fact. Funny thing was, now that he thought about it, he couldn't say why, or what started it.

He considered knocking and finding out if she was in and was coming down any time soon. She would have been back late last evening, and maybe they could just pretend all these weeks of awkwardness hadn't happened. There was so much to say. He wanted to tell her all about his duel training and he wanted to find out all about Kirnara.

He was also dying to know about her meeting with Enol. He had a bad feeling about that. All he knew was what Noah had shared with Chiyo—that they'd had a pretty routine conversation about training and her goals and so on. But surely Maya had more to add? What had *she* thought about the interaction? What had she noticed? Were there any signs that Enol was sizing her up to join the Warriors?

Were there even any signs that Enol himself might be a Warrior?

It was a crazy thought, but Maya wouldn't think it crazy. She'd have something to say about it, and she'd want to know what he thought.

Then there was the other thing. Back when he himself had been going through stuff and was being horrible to everyone, including Maya, she had been there for him. She had held his hand through his worst times. Sometimes literally.

What if Maya was having a bad time too? What if her parents were angry? That always upset her so much.

To be dreadfully honest, avoiding Maya was rather hard on him too. His roommates Sebastien and Owen were okay, but they had their own stuff. Plus, they were years older than him. Ray was fun to be around, but he and Val were virtually joined at the hip. Kari was a great listener, but she preferred to be on her own.

The simple truth was, Lev didn't have any close friends apart from Maya, and he had more troubles than most people his age.

And he missed her.

The door opened and Val came out. She looked him up and down. 'What are you staring at our door like that for? Gone all Superman with X-ray vision?'

'If I had, what makes you think I'd choose your room?' shot back Lev.

'Ha, so witty. One of these days you'll bite your tongue off.'

Lev grinned. 'Is Maya in?'

'Very much.'

Maya was alone, brushing her hair, and surprised to see him. 'Oh,' she said. 'Hi.'

'Hi. So, you're back.' He trailed off and they stood staring awkwardly at each other.

'Yeah, um, yesterday. It was late.'

They studied the floor for a while and then:

'Look—' began Lev.

At the same time Maya said, 'I—'

They looked at each other again, and suddenly Maya laughed. Lev couldn't help smiling back.

'Are we fighting or what?' she asked.

'I don't know. I don't even remember what started it.'

'I don't either. And I don't care. Let's forget it, shall we?'

'Deal.' Lev stuck out a hand. 'Let's start all over. Good morning, Maya.'

Maya shook his hand solemnly. 'Good morning, Lev. How are you today?'

'Very well, thank you. And you?'

That set them off again. 'Maybe we should write a book about good manners,' Maya said.

'Sure. Overnight bestseller.'

They left the room and wandered towards the ramp going down.

'So, how was Kirnara?'

'It was great, I have *so* much to tell you.'

‘I have so much to ask you. Your meeting with Enol is at the top of my list.’

‘Forget Enol, guess who travelled with us to Kinara and back in the same trains, and was also at NEWorld?’

‘Who?’

Maya lowered her voice. ‘Quin!’

Lev’s mouth fell open. ‘The librarian? The one who caught us looking up you-know-what and got you in trouble for it?’[12]

‘Exactly! Doesn’t it seem suspicious to you?’

‘How do you mean?’

‘I don’t know. It just bothers me. Do you think he’s a—?’ She raised her eyebrow significantly. ‘And he knows about my having the…thing? And so he was following us?’

‘Why to Kinara, though?’

‘Who knows? To keep an eye on us?’

Lev considered that. ‘What does Noah say?’

Maya grimaced. ‘That my imagination is running wild.’

‘Do you think he’s right?’

Maya sighed. ‘He usually is.’ As they approached the courtyard, she added, ‘I wish we could do more stuff together. I hardly ever get to see you these days. Apart from Illusion, we don’t even have any classes together.’

‘We’ll have Healing together soon,’ Lev reminded her. ‘Oh, I know—train with me in the morning. I really need a sparring partner.’

‘I go swimming in the morning.’

---

[12] Last year, Quin had caught them looking up information on the Prophecy at the library. This was long before Maya and Lev had any inkling of what it was all about.

'Come swimming in the evening, silly. That's when I go. Or I could swim in the morning and we could train in the evening. Whatever.'

'You wouldn't mind that?'

'Of course not. Will Noah agree?'

'I think so. Will Chiyo?'

'Let's ask them right away.'

~

Halvard Alfiya walked up and down the front of the room, addressing her intermediate Illusion batch: 'In the old days, when the world was yet to be united under the High Council's command, and skirmishes among factions were frequent, Halvard were mainly warriors.'

She had to stop as a collective gasp went around the class. She shook her head impatiently. 'As in, people who fight, defending lands and their people. I'm sure you are all aware of the history of Lam, so I won't go into details. Back then, every Halvard had to be equipped with the Power of Illusion. Can you tell me why?'

Maya, Lev, Owen, Mingmei and Za-Ab, all shook their heads.

Alfiya threw up her hands like she was giving up. 'Because defensive Illusion was one of their main protections. Any guesses why that would be so?'

'Because Healing was too time-consuming?' Mingmei ventured.

'Yes, good. What else?'

'Body armour was crap,' Owen contributed doubtfully.

'Yes, another good point. Anything else?'

'Healing isn't preventive?' Za-Ab was also unsure, signing slower than he usually would.

'Also correct, and a very important point. Healing takes place after the fact, is relatively slow, and Spirit-intensive.'

'Maybe they didn't have good equipment for Healing?' Maya ventured.

'Yes, you're right. If we go back in time when body armour was bulky and unreliable, and there were no modern medicines and equipment, injured Halvard only had touch Healing against injuries—or first-aid healing, as we say these days. And a wonderful Power though Healing is, it isn't always the best solution. A bone that is instantly Healed, for instance, will never be as good as one that is allowed to Heal by itself. Knitting a gash without first cleaning it could cause an infection that could prove fatal.

'Moreover, every Halvard had to be able to protect not just themselves, but also those they led, often troops of non-Halvard soldiers. Illusion could be used for camouflage, for physical defence, for strategy, and more. Thus, it was imparted as essential training to each and every Halvard.

'Nowadays the situation is very different. Illusion is not a very difficult Power to master, so most Halvard are trained Illusionists, but fewer and fewer practising ones. Neither are Preferred always taught the more intricate nuances of the Power any more. The only working Illusionists are those like me, who teach, those who practise Illusion art, or the Elite Guards, who use other advanced techniques in their line of work.'

'Well, if it's so useless, why is she boring us to death about it?' Maya whispered to Lev.

Lev opened his mouth to answer, but Alfiya's dark, beady eyes came to rest on him, and he coughed innocently instead.

'The main reason Halvard do choose to qualify in Illusion,' she continued, an eye still on Maya and Lev, 'is not just because it is a relatively easy Power to learn, but also because small tricks of Illusion have their uses in everyday life, as I am sure you have found out for yourselves. Who has ever bound a falling item in an Illusion to keep it from shattering on the floor?'

Maya raised her hand sheepishly. She had dropped her mother's precious crystal vase once and had only just managed to keep it from breaking with an air cushion. And there was that one time her brother had caught her too. She found a grinning Owen raising his hand, and even Mingmei did. 'I'm learning wheelchair combat with Illusion,' she added.

'So you see,' said Alfiya, 'it has everyday uses. It was how we secured civilian victims in the Kendark war too.'

'You were in the Kendark Civil War, Halvard?' Lev asked.

'I was,' Alfiya replied. 'You'll find very few Halvard over a certain age who weren't there. Anyway, I want you to leave your books here, get your anti-impacts and meet me in practice arena three in,' she glanced at her watch, 'ten minutes. I want you to meet someone who will take you through a basic defensive Illusion course for the rest of the week. I trust you will find it entertaining at the very least.'

~

Any way that Yazid examined Kilyana's words from, he always ended up at the same conclusion: that unless he did what she asked—what the Warriors asked—people would suffer, people he loved, people who were innocent.

'Do you think they'll just let us—let you—walk away without consequences?' she had asked him.

'What about the consequences of all those broken promises?' he argued. 'Everything you promised, everything *they* promised, has been a lie. The Key is gone. We are fugitives, hiding, scared.'

He braced for the twist of pain that always came when he defied her. But this time, she didn't bother. She just laughed. 'But we have you.'

'I am weak and pathetic, remember?'

She laughed again. 'You are not. Do you know how I know you are ready again? It's because you push me, you argue, you fight me. Even though you know what will come.'

She paused, as Yazid clenched his fists against the pain, and squeezed his eyes till tears fell. But he did not cry out.

'See? You are fighting back.'

He gasped as she released him, breathing fast, unable to speak for several seconds. It didn't matter, for Kilyana wasn't done talking.

'And here's something I know about you. That you will do anything, undergo any suffering, if it keeps those you love from feeling pain.'

The worst part was, she was right. The best part, though, was that she had no idea of the extent of his desperation, of what he was willing to sacrifice.

16

RAISING DAY ROLLS AROUND

The five of them from Maya's Illusion batch were joined by Kari, Ray and Sebastien as they arrived at the practice arena with an air of excitement that would have put to shame any kindergarten group off for a picnic. Waiting with Alfiya was Halvard Ariba, overseer of Preferred, and with them a swarthy-complexioned Halvard.

His neatly cropped greying hair, and trim salt-and-pepper beard could have been unremarkable, but the silver stripe in his lapel made the Preferred gape at him with undisguised awe.

He was an Elite Guard.

'Good afternoon,' Ariba said as they took places along the circular bench that ran the perimeter of the arena.

'Good afternoon,' the Preferred greeted her back in chorus, which made Maya want to giggle.

'This is Halvard James,' she said, gesturing at the man, who bowed his head slightly. 'He is my Watcher,' Ariba added, much to the surprise of the Preferred. It was strange to think of the dignified Ariba as ever having had a

Watcher to run after her, and even stranger that they were still Linked. 'He works in the Elite Guards' Training Unit in Scale End, Ing, instructing newly inducted Elites in advanced defensive techniques.'

By now the Preferred had stopped zipping up their anti-impacts to listen, trying to surreptitiously sum up James. It was hard to imagine this man—who was at least four inches shorter than Ariba—with his bow legs and his uniform stretched slightly over his middle, as a dashing Elite.

'Good day,' Halvard James spoke in Proto, and signed so fast that Maya would never have been able to keep up. 'I am very pleased to meet you all. Ariba and I will teach you some defensive Illusion techniques. Nothing very complex—for that you'll have to come and visit me in Scale End.'

He had a deep voice and a pronounced accent that made Maya quite certain he was from her part of the world.

After a quick round of introductions, James asked, 'Has any of you ever seen an inverted Illusion? No? Oh dear, how sad.'

And then he vanished.

The Preferred gasped.

'It's an Illusion!' cried out Ray, when he spotted Ariba smiling.

'Yes, but how did he do it?' she asked.

Everyone looked around the room. There was no sign of him. Maya reached for her Spirit wondering if she would spot the telltale shimmer of an Illusion, but of course, he was far too skilled for that. If there hadn't been so many people in the room, she could have tried to listen for his breathing.

But wait—Illusions could be shattered by brute force. Back when she, Lev and their Watchers had been on the hunt for the Key, Noah had shattered a trio of syncing assassins' Illusion with his and Maya's combined Spirit. Surely that was worth a try.

Filling herself with as much Spirit as she could take in, she battered hard in the direction James had been standing.

The way Maya directed her Spirit caused no harm to anything or anyone apart from any air-based Illusion in the vicinity. With no warning, James suddenly appeared, standing exactly where he had been. Everyone jumped.

'Who did that?' he asked the Preferred. 'That was foolish. You can get hurt.'

Most of the Preferred looked bewildered. Only Lev glanced at Maya. She flushed.

'Um, I did,' she said after a few seconds, raising her hand. The thought of keeping quiet had crossed her mind, but Noah's face floated up unbidden in her mind's eye. 'I'm sorry.'

But James wasn't angry, just concerned. He came over and Maya felt the mild tingle of a Probe go through her. He looked at her curiously.

'That was effective, but not the most efficient way to break an inverted Illusion.' He turned to the others. 'Let's establish some ground rules here. No Illusions or shields unless either Ariba or I instruct you, okay? We will show you the correct shields for every Illusion.' He turned back to Maya. 'I don't know how you managed it—I've seen full Halvard rendered unconscious when they've tried that.'

Maya's ears went hot. She couldn't believe she had been so foolish. Noah had hammered into her how important it was that she didn't call undue attention to herself by showing off her strength. She almost forgot to listen to James who was now drawing diagrams in the air about angles of vision and how to make a spectator's line of sight slide across you so that you wouldn't be visible to them.

Two days later most of the Preferred were still struggling with the inverted Illusion. Lev and Maya were the only ones strong enough to master it, but even then it took far too much skill for them to do it successfully all the time. James laughed it off and said it didn't matter, as technically using inverted Illusions in public places, including the Halvard Castle premises, was illegal unless under the supervision of a trained Illusionist. They moved on to other defensive and shielding techniques.

By the time the week was over, Halvard James went back to Ing the undisputed hero of his Illusion students, and the Castle rang with proclamations of 'James this' and 'James that' (he had asked them to dispense with the Halvard on the first day). It was only the excitement of Raising Day that finally relegated him to the background.

~

These were arguably the best summer holidays of Maya's life. Being at the Castle meant getting out of being forced to visit two sets of grandparents, and having to field their comments about her body (not thin enough), her hair (not neat enough), her interests (not feminine enough), and so on.

She did go home for breaks now and again, but Manan had inadvertently been deflecting attention from her for a while. First, his board exams results had been less than satisfactory, and second, he had been insisting that he did not want to study science. Since Amma and Appa had only so much outrage to spare, and as Manan was about to bring shame on the family by wanting to be a penniless artist or some such, it left Maya more or less free to do as she pleased.

Residing at the Castle meant a full day of training, working, classes, reading, revising and more. Noah and Chiyo put their heads together to merge her and Lev's schedules as much as possible. They were in the same intermediate Healing and Illusion classes, they worked together with Noah on Logic though they were doing different things, and they also teamed up for as much physical training as possible.

Meanwhile, excitement ramped up at the Castle for Raising Day—the annual ceremony to induct new Halvard. It took place during what they called the 'turn of the season', when the cold winter turned into a marginally less cold spring. Raising Day was celebrated on the first Friday of June, and this time, among the Preferred being raised were some of Lev and Maya's friends: Ray, Val and Za-Ab.

But more than that, it was Lev's preparation for the duel that occupied the two of them. Maya helped him, drilling through forms and strategies together until they were coming out of her ears. Sometimes they also sparred, though that meant Maya getting flattened sooner or later. Still, it was actually really good practice for her too. While she didn't have Lev's skill, she did have more Spirit, and this helped her experiment in ways she wouldn't have been able to otherwise.

~

The Castle took on a festive air as visitors for Raising Day began to pour in. The residential wing was packed to the rafters, and the guest quarters were full. Some Halvard were even rooming with their friends and colleagues. The families of Preferred being raised were invited to stay as well, though most Roz natives tended to be too spooked by Lam to stay overnight.

On Friday morning, when Maya and Noah were having breakfast with Chiyo and a restless Lev, for this was the day of the duel, Noah casually remarked: 'By the way, Nira is here. She wants to know if you'll drop in to see her after breakfast.'

Maya choked on her cereal; Noah thumped her on the back.

'She's very keen to meet you,' he added mildly, though Maya was very well aware of how amused and entertained he was by all this.

'You're lucky,' said Lev. 'I've never even come close to meeting Rafa. Sometimes I doubt he even exists.'

He gave Chiyo a cheeky side-eye, but she only shrugged. 'Sometimes I doubt his existence myself,' she responded. 'Are you done, Lev? Let's go—we have plenty to do. Noah, say hello to any old friends you run into.'

Noah nodded.

'Good luck, Lev,' Maya called after them. 'Will I see you before the duel?'

'Thanks, and sure. I'll be in the—' But Chiyo had dragged him inside before he could complete the sentence.

'She's not going to eat you,' Noah told her when they were alone.

Maya made a face. 'I just don't want to make an ass of myself.'

'You won't. Have some faith in yourself.'

'But she's *famous* and all.'

'So are you,' Noah reminded her.

But being famous as the youngest Preferred of all time was hardly the same thing as being famous for creating the Extranet, drawing up the Kendark Peace Treaty, and half a dozen other things.

17

NIRA PROMISES TO WATCH HER LANGUAGE

Maya's first impression of Nira was: *This can't be her.* She remembered her face from a video chat they had had months ago, but the rest of her seemed like a cut–paste job from a whole other person.

Beneath a big head of curly black hair sprinkled with grey, Nira looked much younger than the late fifties or so she should have been, especially her eyes, bright and sparkling. Back when they'd last spoken, she had given Noah a dressing down that had been so bad that Maya had accidentally intervened. Therefore, reconciling that commanding, assertive, angry person with this tiny one in front of her was completely nuts.

Despite being the smallest person in the room, she had a presence that pushed even Noah into the background. In the same black and silver uniform as her former a'fin, Nira somehow looked like someone in charge, while Noah seemed like he was about to melt into the curtains.

She had a Guide's badge pinned to her jacket under the silver hourglass insignia of Halvard. Another surprise for Maya, as she'd always assumed she had been raised as a Logician.

And even though she was shorter than Maya, when Maya touched her fist to her heart—as a mark of respect to her Watcher's Watcher—she had a funny feeling she was looking up higher than Noah to see her.

The formalities dispensed, Nira held out a hand, beaming. 'Such a pleasure to meet you at last.'

Maya shook her hand and smiled back uncertainly. 'Nice to meet you too.'

'All those nasty things Noah has told you—all lies.'

She smiled at Maya and pointed to the sofa. 'Please sit down. I was just making tea. Would you like some? I have my own—genuine Sri Lankan tea, not the crap you get here.'

Noah cleared his throat delicately.

Maya grinned at him before saying, 'I'd love some. Thank you.'

'I hear you are keen on Healing,' Nira said when they were drinking their tea—definitely a much finer beverage than the Castle had ever produced. 'And Noah tells me you are a good Logician as well. Plus, you're being trained in unarmed combat by Chiyo.'

'Um, yes, ma'am, I mean, Halvard,' said Maya, squirming with embarrassment.

'Impressive. Chiyo doesn't give her time unless she is sure her students are exceptional.'

That was news to Maya. Chiyo thought she was good? 'Lev is in the duel today,' she said, to deflect attention from herself.

'Yes, I know. I've seen Kari in action at the Watchers' Tower, and I am keen to see how Lev handles her.'

They talked about training, and the Castle, and the Watchers' Tower, which Maya had not yet visited. Nira told them of the time she and Noah had spent there when he had been training to be a Watcher. His training, of course, had been cut short as he had been asked to Summon Maya years before he should have had to.

'Do you regret it?' Noah asked her. 'That I never completed my training?' He was being playful, though you wouldn't know to look at him.

'You could train your entire life and never feel ready to Summon your a'fin. I certainly didn't feel ready when I had to get you.'

Noah's eyebrow twitched, surprised. 'Really? I didn't know that.'

'What was Noah like as a Preferred?' Maya asked, setting her cup down and sitting up straighter. This should be interesting.

Nira studied Noah for a second or two. 'Hmm, let's see. He was different from what he is now, very different. When I met him at the Portal Road for the first time, he was this extremely thin, extremely tall, bespectacled teenager, all pimply and rebellious. Very gobby too.'

That made Noah laugh, and Maya's mouth fell open. 'He *was*?'

'I assure you, she's exaggerating,' said Noah. 'I was shy and retiring. And had great skin.'

Nira was smiling too, so Maya assumed the truth was somewhere in the middle.

'If gobby means talkative, I can't imagine Noah being that,' Maya mused.

'Well, he wasn't really a chatterbox,' Nira conceded, 'but every time he opened his mouth, it was to argue. So rude and argumentative.' She made a face. 'I think he was a bit like me.'

That made everyone laugh.

Noah steered the topic away from his wild young days to Nira's work, about which Maya had dozens of questions, of course. She didn't even know how much time had passed, when Nira slapped a hand to her forehead. 'I am supposed to meet the High Council and their guests before lunch. What's the time? Oh f—'

Noah cleared his throat loudly, drowning out the second syllable of that word.

Maya tried not to grin.

'Fine, fine,' grumbled Nira. 'I will try to set a good example and watch my language. Happy?'

'Thank you.'

~

Maya spent the rest of her morning helping Lev run through some drills, and by the time Noah came to get her for lunch, the courtyard was emptying.

'Where's everyone off to?' Maya asked, as they settled down with their food.

'The raising ceremony will begin soon, I guess.'

'Don't you want to see it?' Preferred, of course, were not invited.

Noah shook his head. 'Watchers are not allowed to. The next time I witness it, it will be when you are raised.'

The thought of being raised was alarming. 'Wow. I feel like I'll *never* be ready.'

Noah didn't reply. Maya sensed a variety of emotions roiling through him, and for a moment, that scared her. 'You think so too, right? That I'll never be ready? I'm too young?'

He shook his head. 'Oh, I'm certain you'll be more than ready next year. It's just that I don't feel like I'll be ready.'

She stared at his impassive face. 'Will you…I mean, you won't…are you going to stop being my Watcher after I'm raised?'

'I'll be your Watcher for a long, long time to come, Maya. Until you don't want me to be anymore.'

Funny that the thought of being Watcher-less was so alarming. They resumed eating in silence.

'What'll happen after the raising?' Maya asked.

'After the ceremony and presentation of badges, is the duel. Then we take a break to calm our frazzled nerves and change for the evening banquet, where the new Halvard will be presented. After that, we will proceed to let our hair down for the rest of the night.'

'I've never been to a banquet before.'

'Even if you had, I doubt it would have been anything like this one.'

'How?'

But Noah wouldn't say anything except, 'You'll see soon enough.'

Just as they finished eating, a voice hailed her. It was Owen, along with a bunch of other Preferred. He jogged up to their table.

'Hey, Maya. Busy?'

'Nope,' said Maya. 'Where are you off to?'

'Last minute touches to the arena for the duel. Want to come?'

'Sure. Can I go, Noah?'

He nodded, and Maya skipped off with Owen. The others had gone on ahead, and Maya hugged herself in delight. She might have a tiny crush on Owen, she had to admit.

'Some of us have a little pool going about the duel,' he said. 'Fancy a shot?' Then he grimaced. 'Oops, sorry. I shouldn't be corrupting you.'

'A pool?' asked Maya, perplexed.

'You know, a kind of bet.'

'Like, gambling?' Maya's eyes widened.

'Apparently it's a tradition as old as the duel itself. Not that anyone admits that.'

'Yes, I want to bet,' said Maya immediately. 'I bet on Lev. Oh, but wait, I don't have any Lam money.'

'It can be anything, not just money. So far, we have seven different currencies, one cactus shaped like a…well, something rude, three books, an iPad—which of course, doesn't work in Lam—and an Andarean flute.'

'Ooh, can I bet my brother's mobile phone?'

Owen laughed, and Maya hugged herself in glee.

'Do you think next time it'll be our turn?' he asked.

'Noah thinks so, but I don't think I'd ever know enough to be a Halvard.'

'Yeah, same.' He glanced at her. 'But you shouldn't worry, you're really clever.'

Maya laughed. 'Who told you that?'

Owen didn't laugh back. 'You're seriously strong, aren't you? You're doing all that advanced Logic with Noah, and you're really far more talented than any of us in Illusion. You were the first to get that inverted Illusion when James was here.'

'Oh that,' said Maya. Damn it—she had just been paid a compliment and this was the perfect chance to say something clever and funny, but she was tongue-tied. Which was rather inconvenient, because she always wanted to say clever and funny things when Owen was around.

This time Owen did laugh. 'It's not just "oh that",' he said. 'I think it's cool that you're so young and yet so accomplished.'

Maya almost tripped and fell flat on her face. Had he just said she was cool?

And he thinks I'm accomplished!

18

LEV MAKES HIS MARK

The arena was milling with people. Newly raised Halvard, all important in their new uniforms and shining silver badges, were filing in, taking up most of the front row along with their Watchers, who in turn all looked like proud parents on prize-giving day.

Chiyo, as Watcher to one of the duellists, had a place reserved right in front, next to the aisle where the competitors would be entering from. She had managed to save seats in the next row for Noah and Maya.

To Maya's delight, Jan joined them, and there was no sign of Lian.

The High Council had seats on the opposite side from theirs, near the ground-level stage. In all, the main arena, a large indoor auditorium, held about five hundred people. Shining black seats were arranged neatly in ascending concentric rows all around the stage. Black and silver ribbons decorated the walls.

Maya shifted impatiently from one foot to the other as the arena filled. Lev must be chewing his nails off—she herself was so nervous, she felt like she would pass out if things didn't happen soon.

Nine Preferred had been raised that day, which made eighteen including their Watchers. At least fifty others were visiting, and the Castle itself had about a dozen more Preferred and their Watchers, plus many Halvard and non-Halvard working there. Plus, the invitees of the newly raised and the High Council's guests. Maya couldn't concentrate enough to count how many in all that would be, but the arena was full, which was a good indicator.

'Where's Chiyo disappeared?' she asked when she'd given up counting.

'To be with Lev,' Noah replied patiently. Maya had just trod on his toe, though his uniform boots were quite resilient and it hadn't hurt him.

'When will it start?'

'It would be rude to start before time and before the High Council get here, don't you think?'

'Oh.' Then, 'Sorry, am I asking too many questions?'

'Not at all.'

'Did you just *lie*? Sorry, I'll try to be quiet. What's the time?'

'Don't you have a watch?'

'Yeah. I meant, how much longer?'

'Not long. Here come the High Council.'

A cheer accompanied them.

'Oh good.' A few seconds later: 'How long do you think it will last?'

'Till one of them overcomes the other,' Noah replied.

'Do you think Lev will win?'

'It's not about winning.'

'I know, I know. But still?'

'I think they are well matched.'

'Will they be using bare hands or are they allowed weapons?'

'You and Lev have been talking of nothing else these past weeks. I'm sure you know the rules better than me.'

'So-*rry*. Just making conversation. Where *are* they?'

'Patience is a virtue.'

'What's that got to do with—Jan, why are you laughing?'

'You're a real riot,' said Jan.

'Did I say anything funny?'

'I wish I'd had Li when she was a little bit younger,' said Jan to Noah. 'Might have been fun.'

'Oh, it's fun all right. I am being punished for the sins of my past,' said Noah drily.

Maya opened her mouth to protest before she noticed he was pulling her leg.

'What about me?' she said, after a few moments of thought. 'I am too young to have a past, but I'm still being punished.'

That made Jan laugh more.

Another big cheer went up around the arena as two figures emerged, wearing protective anti-impact suits that covered them from neck down. The flushed, slightly nervous faces of Lev and Kari looked around in bewilderment at such a big and noisy crowd.

They walked down the aisle and entered the transparent enclosure in the centre. It was much like a squash court but without a roof. With them were their Watchers, a Halvard who would be refereeing the duel, and a Healer.

Lev had his neck craned towards the crowd. Maya jumped up and down—only once on Noah's foot—waving, till he saw her.

'Good luck!' she yelled at him.

He smiled back in a watery way. Chiyo gave him his mouth guard and helmet. He pulled them on as everyone else left the enclosure. Kari was ready too.

Chiyo came to her seat, smiling. She seemed much calmer than Maya thought she ought to be.

'Is Kari good?' Maya asked.

Chiyo looked surprised at the question. 'Lev is slightly outclassed here, if I were to be absolutely honest.'

'So have you bet on them or what?' Maya asked Chiyo.

'Maya!' said Noah. It was the closest she had ever known him to be mortified. Jan wiped his eyes.

The referee secured the door of the enclosure. They made a sign and the two contestants bowed to each other.

A hush fell over the arena.

~

Only minutes later, the arena was roaring. But Maya wasn't among those cheering.

The duel was very much in progress, most of the audience thoroughly enjoying it, calling out instructions and chanting, but Maya was on her feet, nails between teeth, muttering to herself.

Strict rules applied to the duel, mainly that the two duellists could only use approved moves and forms. They were allowed Spirit and Illusion, but it was almost impossible for the audience to see either. Illusion was also really hard when they were both moving about so much.

So far it had been quite tame, more like a dance than a fight. Both Kari and Lev were very good, flowing in and out of movements so fast that sometimes they were just two blurs. These early few minutes were about sizing each other up.

Covered from head to foot as they were, the easiest way to tell Lev and Kari apart was that Lev was slightly taller. He seemed to depend more on keeping out of the way and trying to get his opponent unbalanced. Kari, on the other hand, was very quick. She liked to dictate terms and Lev seemed content to let her. Maya knew, having sparred with Lev, that he liked to bide his time.

Neither of them made much contact during the early part of the duel. Kari landed a crunching blow to Lev's shoulder early on, and he took her legs out from under her with a sweeping kick. And just as Maya was wondering why the transparent box enclosed the two duellists, Lev tried his sweeping kick again. Kari let herself fall to her left, but her legs kicked out, and she did a little two-step, gravity-defying run on the vertical wall, hand on the floor for support, gaining momentum to swing out and catch Lev low on his back.

A renewed roar went up as Lev fell to his knees, rolled, and was up even before Maya could register any alarm.

'Oh, brilliant move,' Chiyo muttered.

Maya glared at the back of her head. Whose side was she on?

Lev feinted a good old-fashioned punch to the side of her head and Kari ducked easily. But that was just what he wanted her to do. He brought up his knee up to make contact with the side of her head. Kari's Watcher shouted out to her.

'Yeah, Lev!' yelled Maya.

But Chiyo tsked. 'He's beginning to get frustrated.'

'It looks to me like they both are,' said Noah, who looked like he was watching the news.

'It's still early, though.'

Lev was advancing on Kari now, attacking more, making use of his longer reach. He would strike and retreat. He caught her on the side once soon after the knee to the head, but she reached out in a flash of movement, caught his leg and twisted.

With a cry of frustration, Lev's entire body flipped over and he fell face down. He put his hands flat on the floor to break his fall, using the momentum to turn, and kicking out and up to catch Kari under the chin. She deflected with her arm, but it forced her to step back.

And on and on they went, faster and harder. The crowd was loving it, the chants and rhythmic claps reverberating around the arena until the floor itself vibrated.

Kari backed into a wall, using it to brace herself as she launched forward. She flew through the air, at an angle to Lev, nearly parallel to the ground, one leg drawn up, the other outstretched. Her foot hooked Lev at the waist; her other leg straightened, catching him on the other side, almost spinning him around.

Lev turned with the momentum, pivoting around on his foot until he faced Kari yet again, but she was already moving.

Maya was out in the aisle by now, standing next to Chiyo, fists clenched, one in her mouth.

Kari's furious volley of kicks and blows, blurred even with Maya's Spirit-enhanced vision, pushed Lev back and back, until he suddenly went down. Kari dropped a second later, her legs tangled with Lev's.

Nikos, Kari's Watcher, bit back a cry of frustration before Maya understood what had happened. Lev had taken her legs taken out from under her, pulling them forward so she ended up on her back. Her few seconds of surprise were all it took for Lev to bind her with an Illusion.

But only for a second. She broke out of it, and raised herself just enough to use the same sweeping kick Lev had used on her earlier. He jumped to get out of the way, and Maya remembered the rest of it like a slow motion replay.

He had jumped, but he didn't land back down, at least not in the regular sense.

One of Chiyo's greatest skills was her ability to change positions in midair. It was all about timing and prioritizing, she always used to say. Maya understood the theory of it, but she had never managed to execute it.

As he jumped, Lev let his upper body drop, at the same time, kicking out behind him. He broke his fall with his hands, but used his arms like springs to push himself back up. At the same time, his feet made contact with the wall of the enclosure. And just like one pushed off from the side of a swimming pool, Lev launched himself forward just as he lifted off the floor.

It happened so quickly that Kari was in the middle of following through with her kick, still low on the ground. Lev flew over her, landing on his hands. He rolled over and came to his feet. By the time Kari turned to face him, Lev was already in position.

The first of his double kicks caught her on the shoulder, the other on the side of her face. She fell back against the wall, while Lev landed square on the ground, knees bent, shoulders back, head still. He raised his arms, almost as if he was going to hug her.

Kari grunted with effort, but she couldn't move. The Illusion that bound her shimmered for all to see.

As the seconds ticked by, the arena quietened. There was pin-drop silence as the referee raised their right hand, index finger up—like a cricket umpire indicating out. Their left hand pointed at Lev.

Then, there was some real cheering. Maya screamed with joy, and before she could stop herself, threw her arms around Chiyo.

Lev and Kari took off their helmets and mouth guards and clasped hands. Sweat poured down their flushed faces. Lev grinned at Kari, and the older Preferred put an arm around him and said something as they left the enclosure. Even the newly raised Halvard were jumping up and down.

Eidora, the Healer on duty for the duel, checked them over and gave them any Healing they might need. Then they were free to return to the Watchers.

Chiyo patted Lev's cheek and said, 'I thought she had got you with the Airborne Birl.' She hugged him and then let him go.

Maya could hardly believe how calm Chiyo was, but a second later, when Noah put an arm around her, she hugged him back rather tightly.

'So?' asked Lev, coming to stand before Maya.

'You were awesome!' said Maya, grabbing his arm. 'It was the best thing I've *ever* seen.'

She threw her arms around his neck, and he squeezed back fiercely. 'Thanks.'

19

NOAH CLEANS UP WELL

Noah had been right—they did need a couple of hours to calm down after that adrenaline-thumping performance. And of course, to get ready for the banquet.

Folks were said to get out their fanciest and shiniest stuff for the Raising Day banquet, but Maya had never really been into clothes and dressing up. Mostly because she had never liked the way she looked. Which put her in a bit of a bind because the only fancy clothes she had was something Amma had forced her into for an aunt's wedding. That had been back in pre-pandemic times, and Maya was at least six inches taller now.

Amma would have probably happily taken her shopping if she had asked, but Maya didn't want to get into the inevitable tussle over what she liked and what her mother did. Noah had also offered, but she didn't think it was any use buying Andarean finery that she would grow out of in months.

Ultimately, it was Mingmei, her roommate, who came to her aid. She had a sister of a similar height and build to Maya, from whom she sourced an ink-blue dress with little silver flowers all over. It was made of a soft, velvety material, buttoned down the front with a belt around the waist. It was slightly loose on Maya, but Mingmei adjusted it by pinning some gathers in the back, under the belt, so it looked just fine. She also offered shoes, but Maya wasn't sure if Mingmei's adaptive footwear was actually adapted for walking and dancing. So she borrowed Amma's cool zip-up boots.

She wished she could do something about her hair, but Mingmei told her that people in Andara were actually *paying* to get their hair frizzed, so she was right with the times.

Finally, when Maya was absolutely sure there was nothing more she could do to get any fancier, there was a knock on the door.

~

Maya gasped. That was all she was capable of.

Noah was wearing a formal Kirnaran suit—like she'd seen on mannequins in shop windows during her trip. Trousers in a rich cream that tapered at the ankles—any longer, and they would have gathered like a churidar—and a top of the same colour, with long, straight sleeves and a short, square collar that buttoned at his neck. Over that, he had a deep maroon sleeveless overrobe that fell in a single piece till his hips and then split into panels that swirled when he walked. The edges of the panels were embroidered in gold thread in a fine geometric pattern. The pattern was also on the edges of his sleeves and along the collar, these in same maroon of the overrobe. Even his shoes were embroidered along the sides.

'Thank you,' he said, dipping his head to one side, in response to her unspoken words. 'You look great yourself.'

'I…uh…thank…I mean…' Maya battled to get her tongue around the words she meant to say as she continued to survey Noah, even walking around him once.

It wasn't just his clothes—his face was different too. He wasn't so pale. His usual planes and angles had softened somehow, his eyebrows were more, well, visible, and his entire face was…

Maya gasped again. 'Oh my god, are you wearing *make-up*?'

One darkened eyebrow rose in a very familiar fashion. 'Do I take that as disapproval?'

Maya considered the question.

Manan had this cream he used to hide his pimples with, which she'd always laughed at. Appa dyed his hair, and hit the roof if anyone touched his moisturizer.

But those weren't the same. Or were they?

Plus, if she did decide to disapprove, what did it mean about who was allowed to use make-up? Only women? Was Luu, Val's Watcher, who was non-binary, allowed? Was Owen not allowed because he was a trans man? Or Arian who was agender?

Maya's already overtaxed brain was beginning to hurt. She studied Noah closely again. What he had done to his face was a work of art, and if anyone had to be 'allowed', it should definitely be him.

'You look great,' she said at last, 'so I thoroughly approve.' She waved a hand in the direction of his face. 'Can you do that for me too? I mean not today, but some day?'

'Certainly.' He offered her his arm. 'Shall we?'

~

In the few hours they'd been occupied with the duel and getting ready, the courtyard had been completely transformed. Fairy lights glittered from trees and bushes, and extra tables, chairs and benches were packed between the usual tables, all the way up to the lawns. The food counter stretched many times longer than usual.

Along the front of the training wing where the Castle abutted the courtyard, the platform had been converted into a makeshift stage. There, an Ing band in matching red, black and white costumes, tuned up and tested their systems. The area in front of it had been cleared for dancing, covered with temporary flooring.

Guests had started to trickle in, and already a variety of Lam and Roz finery was on display. Saris, sherwanis, kilts, ponchos, flax skirts and wooden jewellery; intricately embroidered Ing robes; beaded tops and flowy trousers of Kendarkis; the split robes of Kirnarans; the plain gowns and coloured sashes of the Inshai warriors.

'Incredible,' Maya breathed. 'You guys really know how to party.'

'Just once a year, we certainly do,' Noah replied. 'Come on, I think I see Chiyo there.'

But Maya was distracted once again, this time by the band. 'Why can't we hear them? I can see them playing. Wait…there's an Illusion around them. Why, Noah?'

'I nearly forgot,' Noah said. He backtracked to a small basket hanging from a lamppost—and there were others around the courtyard—and picked something out. He came back and handed Maya a tiny black disc smaller than a fingernail. 'Hearbuds.' Peeling off a sticky backing, he pasted it somewhere behind his ear. 'Here, let me.'

He stuck one behind Maya's ear, over the hard bone of the skull. Immediately, soft tunes from the band filled Maya's hearing.

'Whoa! Did you say *hear*buds?'

'Mmhm, because they aren't *ear*buds.'

'Clever. I guess not everyone likes the loud music.'

'You can adjust the volume by moving it away from the bony part of your head.'

Chiyo waved to them from her table. She was wearing trousers with a jacket patterned with a profusion of colourful flowers, and had piled her hair on one side of her head. She looked very much…not like herself. In a good way.

'Wow, look at you two,' she said, giving them the once-over.

'Not so bad yourself,' Noah said, sitting down across from her.

Maya wriggled in embarrassment. 'Um, where's Lev?'

'Went to check out the food,' Chiyo nodded over Maya's shoulder. 'Actually, will you go and rescue him? I get the feeling he's not really enjoying the attention.'

20

LEV AND MAYA ATTEND A BANQUET

Lev definitely wasn't.

For all the talk of the Raising Day duel being just a tradition, having won it had sent his popularity through the roof. Arian and Mine, both newish Preferred, had accosted him at the drinks counter, telling him how wonderful he had been.

Arian had just asked if he had any *plans* after the banquet—in a way that made him wonder if the word had any hidden meaning—when he spotted Maya.

'Lev,' she called to him. 'Come on!'

'Got to go!' he said hurriedly to the two Preferred, and escaped.

'What's going on?' Maya asked.

'I don't know,' Lev said, pulling his silky wraparound shirt straight. He'd rather fancied himself in it at first, plus Owen had mentioned the sea-green brought out the colour of his eyes. But now he had developed an irrational notion that the tie at his hip would come undone, and the shirt would fall open. 'I think they were, maybe, flirting with me.'

Maya coughed a very fake cough. 'Oh, er, and did you flirt back?'

'First of all, I know you were laughing just now. Second, they're technically adults, so ew. And third, Chiyo will flay me.'

'I think maybe she'll flay them first,' Maya said. Sure enough, his Watcher was frowning at the retreating backs of Mine and Arian weaving through the trees.

Safe from his wannabe fan club, he and Maya loaded themselves with snacks and went back to their table. In a few minutes, the music stopped, and everyone turned towards the stage, where the lights had dimmed. It was time for the official proceedings to commence.

One by one, the newly raised Halvard, in their ceremonial uniforms—slightly different from their everyday ones, with long, knee-length overrobes, golden sashes, and all their badges instead of the single ones they wore daily—were presented.

Once the cheers died down, the band struck up again, playing the Halvard anthem, 'The ground beneath our feet'. The new Halvard's Watchers stepped forward, and they paired off for the Andarean five-step, a complex dance-march type of thing that made Lev's eyes water.

'Phew, I hundred per cent won't be ready for that next year.'

'What?' Maya looked startled.

'You know, if we're raised next year, which Chiyo says is very likely, we'll have to do that too.'

'No way! I'll look like a cartoon with Noah. Plus, can you imagine Noah in a *dance*?'

Lev stole a glance at Noah. 'To be honest, after today, I don't think he can ever surprise me. Sorry, I don't mean—'

But Maya laughed. 'Yeah, I know, he looks great. Even I can see that!'

Whoops and cheers rose again, as the Andarean five-step disintegrated into a free-for-all. The Watchers retreated, which was a sign for others to join the new Halvard.

Someone pulled on his arm. 'Come on!'

It was Mingmei, clutching his wrist and powering forward in her wheelchair, almost pulling him down. He grabbed Maya in turn, and they surged forward, along with Owen, Sebastien and Kari, and into the fray.

Ray, Val and Za-Ab—the newly raised—and their still-Preferred friends formed a ring, and jumped and swayed and laughed and screamed till Lev's throat and feet threatened to give up. He spotted Maya with Owen in one corner, away from the main crowd of dancers, playing some bizarre game where they were trying to jump on each other's shoes. He debated whether to join them or to go get a drink, when he noticed a movement behind them.

In the shadows behind Owen and Maya, stood someone whose outline felt familiar. They were still, facing the two Preferred and their crazy dance. Lev probably wouldn't have noticed them had it not been for something glinting near their face, catching some light from the courtyard. He drew in some Spirit to sharpen his senses, and the shadows coalesced into the features of Lian, one of the Halvard who had saved his life when he had been attacked at the Tower. She wasn't just standing there idly, she was watching Owen and Maya.

Why though? And why did she have that intent expression, like she was afraid or worried?

'Le-ev? What's the matter, can't you hear me?' Someone was shaking him.

Lev jumped. 'Uh, sorry, I…' He looked down at Maya and then back to the shadows, but Lian had disappeared.

~

Finally, tired from the dancing, Maya and Lev returned to their Watchers. At least she'd got to dance with Owen! If that could be called dancing.

I have to remember to clean Amma's shoes really well before I return them.

Lev went off to source some sweetberry to drink, as Maya plopped down next to Noah. 'That was fun. Hey, are those fish fingers?'

The courtyard was teeming by now. Noah and Chiyo kept disappearing to catch up with someone or the other, and many people came to meet them too. Nira came by their table briefly, very dapper in a sari, with Jan in tow, who looked like his tie was strangling him. Lian stopped by for a bit, and a couple of Halvard they'd met at NEWorld.

The crowd thinned in the second hour. The older Halvard retired for the night, and others who'd had their fill left. The band took a break, and as Maya, Lev and their Watchers sat around a plate of snacks, all made out of flower parts, a new voice said, 'I hope I'm not interrupting.'

Maya almost choked on her mouthful of deep-fried spicy sweet pea flower petals. For there was Ariba, in a striking beaded jacket and flowing trousers that draped her shoes, looking nothing like the Overseer of Preferred tasked with keeping them all in line.

She smiled at Maya. 'I was wondering if I might borrow Noah for a dance or two.' To Noah, she added, 'I have it on good authority that the band will resume soon with a fusion waltz medley.'

Maya stared at Ariba, then turned to Noah. 'Those words did not make sense to me.'

'I'll take that as a yes then,' said Noah. He stood and took the arm Ariba offered as they headed towards where the musicians were taking up their places again.

'Seriously?' said Maya to Chiyo. 'I mean…' She spread her hands.

'Watch,' Chiyo replied.

So Maya watched. Noah had surprised her many times in the year or so she'd known him—heck he'd surprised the life out of her just two hours ago—but this, this was something else.

He moved to the music like…like he was air, weightless and flowing. Like his bones were made of jelly. His strides devoured the dance floor like he owned the space. Ariba was pretty good herself—she kept up with him, or he kept up with her, whatever—but Maya couldn't take her eyes off her Watcher.

One by one, other dancers moved away leaving the floor to Noah and Ariba, and a few others who seemed to know what they were doing. Even among those other dancers, Noah remained untouched.

And then, there was the other thing, invisible to everyone else—an unbridled joy that burst from within him. He wasn't just good at this, he was *loving* it.

Someone tapped her on the shoulder—it was Za-Ab, calling her and Lev over for photographs. Maya tore her eyes away and followed. Ray and Val had got all their friends together, and Luu stood by patiently with a camera as they arranged themselves.

Maya and Val sat on the bench, pulling Mingmei next to them. Lev, Sebastien and Kari sprawled on the ground.

Finally, Owen, Diede and Za-Ab jumped up on the table and knelt so they could be in the frame. This, of course, took a lot of adjustment and arguing and a good quarter of an hour, but Owen was right behind Maya, holding on to her shoulders for support, so she didn't really mind at all.

All too soon, though, it was over. Owen jumped down from the table and disappeared with the others. An inexplicable melancholy descended on Maya.

She sat on the steps bordering the courtyard, in a spot of relative darkness and rested her head against the column next to her. A yawn almost cracked her jaw. It was nearly midnight, and she considered going to look for Noah or Lev, and see if they were thinking of calling it a night.

Before she could decide, someone stepped up next to her and sat down with a groan.

'Hello, you,' said Stephen. 'Why so glum?'

'Hi.' Maya smiled back at him. 'I guess I'm banqueted out. Where have you been? Don't you want to dance or something?'

'Ha, no. I've got two left feet. Probably start a stampede if I went up there.'

'You might start a stampede for different reasons,' said Maya without thinking, and slapped herself mentally. She really needed to learn to think before opening her mouth. To change the subject, she said, 'Noah really surprised me with his moves.'

Stephen's eyes widened. 'Did he now? I'm delighted to hear that. It's been a while.'

'A while?'

'The dancing. There was a time you had to peel him off the dance floor on Raising Day.'

Maya laughed. 'I can't imagine that. But then, I couldn't imagine him dancing either. He really enjoyed it.'

Stephen turned his head towards her. He nodded, but his expression remained serious.

'Why are you looking at me like that?' Maya asked.

'I was thinking about Noah. We'd all been a little worried when he had to Summon you early. But you've been really good for him.' He smiled then.

'He's been good for me too,' said Maya.

'I can see that. You complement each other well. This is the first time he's been at a Raising Day banquet since… for years.'

Maya noticed the hesitation. 'Were you going to say, "since Hanne"?'

He grimaced. 'I wasn't sure if you knew about her.'

'Did you know her?'

Stephen nodded slowly. 'I did. A delightful, noisy, tiny version of Noah…' He tapered off like he couldn't bear to continue. He rubbed his face and sighed. 'I'm sorry, I don't think any of us ever got over it.'

'It's okay. I don't want to rake up painful memories.' She studied Stephen. 'Hey, why are you in your uniform?'

'I just got off work,' he said.

'You look tired, you need some time on the bench.'

'And you should watch yourself with the football talk. Jan says I'm corrupting you.'

Maya laughed and jumped up. 'He was around somewhere. Shall I go find him for you?'

Stephen took the hand she held out and pulled himself to his feet. 'No need, he's gone home and I'm going to go join him.'

'And I'll go find Noah.'

21

YAZID DELIVERS A MESSAGE

'Did you have a good time, then?' Noah asked as they trudged back to their rooms.

'Yeah.'

'Why so despondent?'

Maya shrugged.

'Want to share?' he asked.

She was about to shrug again, but changed her mind. 'Do you think anyone would ever like me?'

The question ignited a spark of surprise in Noah. 'Plenty of people already like you, and I'm certain many others will in the future.'

'No-o, I don't mean that kind of like.'

Noah paused for a second. 'Do you mean in the romantic sense?'

Argh. Of course he was going to be all direct and literal about it. 'You know what, forget it.'

Instead of replying, Noah paused at the door to his room and nodded at it. 'Come inside for a bit, will you?'

'I'm going to regret this, right?' Maya grumbled, but followed him in nonetheless. She was dying to take her shoes off.

Noah undid his overrobe and slipped out of it, throwing it on the back of a chair. He went to get them water, while Maya wrestled with her footwear.

'Did you mean someone specifically, or were you asking in general?' said Noah finally. He'd perched himself at the edge of his desk, looking down at Maya, sprawled on his rug.

She considered how to answer that. Lying to him was pointless, and she didn't want to tell the truth and have to listen to some lecture on how she was too young to be thinking of stuff like that. Not that Noah had ever used that line on her, but at the end of the day, all grown-ups were the same—they liked to tell you what they thought was best for you.

She decided to ask him a question back: 'When you and Lian were, like, boyfriend–girlfriend.' *Ew!* 'Did Nira know? And Jan?'

'Of course. Everyone knew. It wasn't a secret.'

'No, I don't mean that. I mean, did your Watchers figure out that you *liked* each other or, you know, if you…like… ohmygodforgetit!' She jumped up and grabbed her shoes. 'Just forget this conversation, okay. I'm just…just random, stupid thoughts in my head, and I—'

'It's all right,' Noah said, interrupting her. 'Let's see if I can answer that unasked question to your satisfaction. Watchers can't know *every*thing, but,' he smiled faintly, 'it does cramp your style sometimes.'

Maya smiled back uncertainly. 'Sorry, I don't mean to be nosey.'

'You're a logician in the making, being nosey goes with the territory.'

Maya was looking forward to bed. She had the room to herself that night. From the way Mingmei had been stuck to Sebastien the last time Maya had spotted her, she doubted her roommate would be back any time soon. Val had already moved into her upgraded Halvard's quarters, though she was probably going to party all night.

She put her mother's boots carefully by the door—as a reminder to give them a clean in the morning (perhaps some Illusion would be required)—and walked towards her cubicle. She thought about checking next door if Lev and Owen wanted a midnight feast, but another gigantic yawn changed her mind.

Maya raised her hand to her cubicle door, frowning. Why was it shut? She didn't usually shut it. Shaking her head, she pushed it open and stepped inside, yawning again. But a movement caught her eye and she froze.

Something stirred inside her cubicle, something dark and shapeless. Something that had been crouching on the other side of the bed, shrouded in the part darkness.

Maya would have screamed if her tongue hadn't been stuck to the roof of her mouth. Across her, the thing unfurled into the shape of a person. Someone about as tall as she, but thinner, covered in a thick, dark garment pulled over their head.

They pushed the hood back to reveal a hollow, bony face, with straggly, shoulder-length hair. They looked familiar, but Maya couldn't place them. Their face was clammy and eyes rimmed with dark shadows.

Without thinking, she reached for her Spirit and assumed a fighting stance. All her tiredness melted away; she was fully alert.

She could scream, but only to startle the unwelcome visitor, because the thick stone walls around her would muffle any sound beyond the walls of the room. Her heart thudded so hard that she was sure it was audible all over the Castle anyway.

Plus, she only had to stall till Noah got here, which should be any second now.

But the person before her made no attempt to attack. Instead, their shoulders drooped and hands raised in surrender.

'Please.' Their voice was hoarse, like they hadn't spoken for a long time and wasn't used to it. 'Don't hurt me.'

The hands—one normal, the other scarred and disfigured.

'You have to listen to me. Please.'

The eyes. Maya's legs almost gave away from underneath her.

The eyes—two different shades of brown.

~

Jan and Anfield the cat were stretched out on the sofa, fast asleep, when Stephen reached home. He nudged the human awake, decided to leave the feline alone.

'Why aren't you in bed?' he asked.

Jan sat up and stretched. 'There's something I wanted to talk to you about.'

'Can't it wait till morning?'

'Best not.'

Stephen groaned. He pointed to the kitchen. 'First I need a drink.'

He came back minutes later, with a tea for himself and some revolting herbal drink that Jan swore helped him sleep better. When he sat, his back twinged in protest. Maya was right, he did need some time on the bench. They were two Healers short at the Dispensary, and covering for them, as well as keeping up with his teaching load was sometimes just too much. He wasn't a spring chicken, after all.

He yawned and rubbed his eyes wearily. 'Sorry. Sure it can't wait till morning?'

Jan blew out his cheeks. 'Tomorrow morning, Li and I are voluntarily releasing our Link.'

Tea sloshed to the floor. For a moment, Stephen truly feared that he had lost his mind as well as his sense of hearing. 'What?' he asked finally.

'You heard me. We decided that it was time.'

Stephen stared at him, but waiting did nothing to dispel his disbelief. It made no sense. 'But why? She's still in training to be a Watcher herself. It's not the best timing.'

'Li wants her freedom. I want to give it to her. I don't think I have anything else left to give her.'

So it was real. It was happening. 'Are you sure?'

'I feel she's drifting away from me, like I don't know what she wants any more. This is the one thing I can give her.'

'So it's not a mutual decision?'

'It is and it is not. It's complicated. I want to do this for her.'

Stephen could think of a dozen different ways to counter that, but he didn't argue. His own experience of having a Linked Watcher had been tragically short—she had died in the Kendark War, before he had even been raised—so he was in no position to offer any insight.

'How long have you been thinking this way?'

'We just decided a few days ago. I'm sorry I didn't tell you sooner.'

'Doesn't matter. But this is crazy, JC. You're not ready for this. Give it some time. Think about it, all right? Talk to Li.'

Jan shook his head. A tear dropped to his cheek and on to his sleeve. 'We've talked and talked. It's decided.'

No words that Stephen could offer could fix this. Despair smashed his heart in a million pieces. 'I'm so sorry.'

~

'Everything I know, everything I remember, it's all in there,' Yazid continued, pointing to the haphazard roll of papers he had pushed into Maya's hands.

Maya stood, speechless, motionless, as he spoke. Words tumbled out of him. He panted like he had been running for miles.

'They want to get the…get it back. From you. You have it, right, the thing from the cave?'

'The Key?'

He nodded.

'Yes, I…it's…safe. It's not here.'

'Good. Hide it… Whatever you do, Maya, don't use it.' He stopped, gasping for breath. 'It is bad.'

Maya reeled. 'But what…I mean, how…how did you get here? Where have you been? '

'I can't stay,' he rasped, clutching his stomach and grimacing like it hurt. 'I came to warn you. They may harm you to get the…ah…remember that. Oh…and Lev…I know they tried to…is he all right?

Maya nodded. 'He's fine.'

'They are…everywhere…even in the Council… in the Elites… She…she lied to me. About the…the… everything…the thing from the cave…rest of it… You understand?' He stared at Maya.

'I…yes. You mean about the Prophecy and the Warriors and all?'

'Yes… There are words…things…I can't say…' His speech had become more and more laboured.

Horrible understanding fell into place. 'You're being compelled?'

He gave a mirthless laugh. 'A lot more…than compelled. We are staying in a…place…outside High Council… Ki-K-she is afraid that we…not welcome…until the…item is returned… You understand?'

'Yes. But—'

'Look,' gasped Yazid. It was getting harder to make his words out. 'I don't have time…came to warn you… She's gone…for a few days…food gathering…that's why…I could come… But I have to go now…'

Where the hell is Noah? Why is he taking so long?

'Wait!' Maya cried. 'Don't go. The Elites—they will protect you.'

'Can't trust… No time…too long here…I have to return.'

'But you're not—are you safe? You look…not good.'

'Not good…but…too late… Just…don't use…it… I have to go… This pain…too much.'

He slipped past her, but Maya grabbed his arm. 'Wait!' She thrust something at him. 'Take this. Yes, I know it doesn't work, but just keep it. Turn it on. Hide it from Kilyana.'

He nodded, but he was shaking so hard that Maya didn't even know if he heard her. And then he was gone.

Maya's legs finally gave out from under her.

22

MAYA READS BETWEEN THE LINES

'*Yazid* was in your room?' Lev sniggered. 'Are you sure it wasn't Owen?'

Maya glared at him. 'You don't believe me?'

'Sure, I believe you. How much angel wine did you have tonight?'

Maya clenched her fists.

'Lev,' warned Chiyo. She turned to Maya. 'What exactly happened?'

So Maya recounted the bizarre conversation again, with Noah filling in with what he remembered from Maya's first report.

'Sands!' breathed Chiyo when Maya finished. She walked to the window and back, a deep frown cleaving her brow.

No one spoke. When Maya caught Lev's eye, he mouthed 'sorry' at her.

'So, how exactly did he manage to get away?' Maya asked finally. Amid all the questions she wanted answers to, this one was the easiest to ask. Though it made her sick just thinking about it. 'He said it was worse than being compelled.'

'Not without putting his own health at risk,' said Noah quietly.

'Proximity matters,' Chiyo added. 'The further Kilyana is from him, the easier it will be to resist. But "easy" is a euphemism. He must have been in agony.'

'He risked his life to warn us,' said Lev. 'Can I see those drawings again?'

Maya handed him the drawings Yazid had given her and turned back to the Watchers. 'So this is proof that he's being forced by Kilyana to do bad things, isn't it? He said we can't trust the Elites, but surely there's some way?'

Lev snorted. 'We all know what the Elites think. That the Warriors are history.'

'I'm sure the Elites know more than they let on,' said Noah, 'but it all comes down to who he could trust. And after his Watcher's betrayal, that must be difficult.'

'He trusts us because we stopped him from getting the Key?' asked Maya.

'I guess.'

They fell into a huddle of silence again, with rustling from Lev as he pored over Yazid's drawings.

'He said, there are Warriors everywhere, even among Elites and the High Council,' Maya said. 'So that's confirmation.'

'Did he have any names?' Chiyo leaned forward.

'No, but he also said he put all the information he has in the drawings.'

Lev waved a sheet of paper at them. 'These drawings are excellent, but they're just drawings. Of buildings and trees and mountains.'

'Oh no, they are not.' Maya snatched one from him. 'It's a kind of Illusion art he was experimenting with—Illusion with Proto. It's second-level Proto, but the first layer isn't text, it's drawings. Like this one…oh, it's actually third-level Proto, wow, okay, let me see.'

She started to read, turning the drawing this way and that: '"K used the radio again. Charger didn't work so she used Spirit. She called the Councillor again and told them about M. K wants the Key back before she returns." And so it goes on.'

Maya picked up another drawing, this one of a landscape at night, heavily shaded to depict a dark sky with stars. 'This one is actually a map. A place called Zaa-row-ee. Zaroey? There's a river, some cliffs, forest, houses. Have you heard of this place, Noah?'

When she looked up, everyone was staring at her. Lev's mouth was in the shape of an O, Chiyo's eyes wide open, and while Noah remained deadpan, Maya was all too aware of his surprise.

'Well, I'll be damned,' said Chiyo slowly. She picked up the drawings one by one and studied them. Noah reached for some others.

Lev bent over the one in his hand. 'What the hell.' He didn't actually say 'hell', but nobody bothered to reprimand him.

'This is a journal,' said Noah finally, 'of the last few months. This is amazing work. How did you know?'

Maya shrugged. 'We used to do this little game last year when we were bored in history—turning drawings into words or words into drawings. He always drew really well, but I think Kilyana didn't approve, so he hid it from her.'

'Wow, so you two developed your own secret language?' Lev looked almost jealous.

'It was more his thing, because whatever I try to draw looks like mashed potatoes.'

'Whatever it is, it's brilliant.' Chiyo said.

'So now we know where Kilyana is hiding,' said Lev. 'We can find them, right? At this Zaroey place?'

'Saroye,' Chiyo said, reading it slowly. 'He mentions here it's a backwoods village—Nira was right about that.'

'Uh, sorry, there's one more thing,' said Maya, raising her hand like she was in class.

Noah's eyebrows went up. 'Go on.'

'I gave him my mobile phone. I told him to turn it on. We can track it, right?'

~

'Ow, Noah, let go!' Maya wriggled out of his grasp, mortified.

'I would hug you too if I didn't think I'd be punched in the face,' said Chiyo.

'I don't care,' declared Lev, lurching over and managing to get one arm around Maya before she pushed him away.

'Stop it, all of you! He risked his life to warn us. We have to save him, get him away from Kilyana.'

Noah cleared his throat and sat back down on the rug, quite composed now. 'Sorry about that spontaneous display of admiration,' he said drily. 'Yes, we can track it, but it isn't a straightforward process.'

'Won't Nira know how?'

'She will.' He looked at his watch.

Lev chewed his lower lip. 'Thing is, if Kilyana figures out what he's been up to tonight, it will be bad for him, won't it?'

'What I don't get is, how can Kilyana hurt him without hurting herself?' Maya mused. 'Is it all part of this scraping business?'

'Let's just say you wouldn't want to know,' Chiyo said grimly. 'We trained at the Tower together. She has a super-normal ability to bear pain. She can do…terrible things.'

'Meanwhile,' said Noah, 'we also know that there is a Warrior spy among us who wants the Key and might not hesitate to hurt Maya to get it.'

Maya glanced at Lev. 'I think I know who it is,' she said.

'Quin?' Lev asked.

'The librarian?' Chiyo said incredulously.

'He did follow us to Kirnara and to NEWorld,' said Maya. 'And he came back with us too. And I seem to keep running into him all the time.'

'Come to think of it,' said Lev, 'so do I.'

'That's because both of you are spending a good bit of your time in the library,' said Chiyo. 'And Lev, he does take your advanced Guiding classes.'

'Yeah, but I met him in the gym yesterday!'

'Really?' Maya said. 'Funny, but he always seems to be there in the courtyard whenever I go for a meal.'

'Honestly,' said Noah, 'the man might be close to a hundred, but he does have a right to keep himself in shape and eat. I am sorry to disappoint you, but a Warrior spy is likely to be more difficult to spot.'

'Why would they want to spy on us?' Lev asked. 'I mean, it's not as if we're hiding.'

'Yazid said they want the Key, even though he couldn't say the word,' said Maya frowning. 'He got rather excited about it. It doesn't make much sense to me. What could they do with just the Key and not the person who can use it?'

'Perhaps the answers lie in the drawings,' said Noah, picking up all the sheets of paper. 'First, we have these journals entries to transcribe. Then, I'll talk to Nira.'

23

STEPHEN DOES SOME REASSURING

Sleep was suddenly the last thing on the agenda. After the quickest change of clothes Maya and Lev had ever done, they all met back in Noah's room, and divided the papers out between themselves.

Yazid had given her about a dozen drawings, each one intricate and detailed, with text below the visible layer, and sometimes another layer beneath that. He had kept careful logs, rich with detail, and it filled them in on what had happened to him after the fiasco in the cave where he and Maya had found the Key.

But while there was a lot of text, there wasn't necessarily much useful information. Yazid had recorded everything he could think of or remember, including his thoughts, names of his neighbours, their daily schedule and more. It was impossible to tell what might be relevant and what not without reading it all.

The reading itself was the easiest part of the operation. The problem was figuring out what went where, which bit came after which. And if all that wasn't complicated enough, because the text was hidden under the drawings, it didn't necessarily go in the same direction all the time, but twisted and turned with the lines and curves of the mountains or the shape of a leaf or a detail of architecture.

About an hour into the transcribing, Lev held his head. 'When I'm a Halvard, I'm going to invent a machine that reads multi-level Proto.'

'If this was an episode of *Doctor Who*, we would connect an Illusion scanner to a 3D printer and a car battery, install some self-driving solar train software, and somehow create a Proto reader,' mused Maya. She flexed her fingers and picked her stylus back up.

They were all transcribing the text by hand into their e-notebooks, which automatically saved and converted everything into a computer readable format. Once that was all done, Noah was going to try to put them in order and see if anything became clearer.

The sky was lightening by the time they neared the end of their work.

Since their failed attempt to retrieve the Key, Kilyana had indeed 'gone dark', as Chiyo put it, hiding with Yazid in a backwoods village, waiting for him to recover. Apart from his hand injury, he had temporarily lost his ability to reach his Spirit and to talk, probably from shock. Plus, if he hadn't been able to return to Roz in at least four months now, there would be other long-term physiological changes he was dealing with. He had looked shockingly emaciated anyway.

Having managed to fix up the radio, Kilyana had also been in regular touch with the Warriors. She had been negotiating for her and Yazid to return safely into their fold, and for the Key to be retrieved from Maya.

The Warriors had known for a couple of months that the Key was with Maya, and they had deputed someone to keep an eye on her. Yazid said it was a 'he', someone Kilyana wasn't happy about. Later he also mentioned that there might be someone else, who Kilyana did approve of.

'This bit is interesting,' said Chiyo, breaking an almost hour-long silence. 'He says here that according to Kilyana, among all three of you, something in his position in the Oparian birth chart gives Yazid an advantage.'

'Maybe that's why the Warriors chose him to be their Shadow?' Lev suggested.

'Possible. But I still think it was more to do with her already being a Warrior.'

They went back to work, and it was just minutes later when Noah broke the silence again with a single word.

'He,' he said.

Everyone looked up.

'What?' asked Chiyo.

'The Councillor who's the Warrior—Kilyana referred to him as "he".'

That was a bizarre statement, but no one cared about grammar.

'So that's either Enol or Ryder,' said Maya. She glanced at Lev. 'I find it hard to believe it could be Enol. He was so *normal* and *nice*. It must be Ryder.'

'What if it's both?' Lev asked.

'If you had to guess?' Noah asked Chiyo.

Chiyo blew out her cheeks. 'Enol makes sense—to groom the Watcher who would then train the Shadow. But I don't want to speculate.'

'Sorry to wake you so early, but I really need to talk to you,' said Noah by way of a greeting.

But Stephen didn't look like he had been woken. He looked like he was ready to head back to work without having been to sleep at all.

'My least favourite words these days,' he replied. He moved aside. 'Come in.'

Noah hesitated. 'Are you all right? You look terrible.'

'Ha, thank you. I'm fine, just didn't sleep well.'

Noah followed him through the house to the porch outside the dining room, where he seemed to have been having breakfast. 'Is, er, Jan around?'

Stephen indicated somewhere inside. 'Probably in the bathroom.'

'Okay, then, very quickly.' Speaking quietly, he proceeded to fill Stephen in on the happenings of the early hours of the morning.

The first question he asked was: 'Is Maya in any immediate danger?'

Trust him to draw out the one detail that was making Noah's insides coil with anxiety.

'I suppose not any more than she has been these past two months.'

There, it was out now. The absolute terror that came with the knowledge that she had been watched, followed, monitored, Sands knew what else, all without him knowing. Even though he hadn't said it in so many words, Stephen had known him long enough and well enough to figure that out.

'That possibility had always been there,' Stephen reminded him. 'We knew that. All that's happened is that it's been confirmed.'

'I know, but—' Noah sighed, letting his shoulders droop. 'Just knowing that anything could have happened, any time. Anywhere. At home, at school, at all the thousand places where I'm not around.'

'But it didn't,' Stephen reminded him.

'I wish she could have had a more experienced Watcher. At least not a half-trained one.'

'There's no such thing as a fully trained Watcher,' said Stephen firmly. As Nira had said less than twenty-four hours ago. 'And in these past few months that we've all been hoping and praying that she was not in the Warriors' radar, you have brought her that much closer to being a powerful Halvard who will be a force to reckon with very soon.'

Noah didn't comment. He didn't think he deserved such credit—or the kindness.

'Tell me, does Maya know of her potential?' asked Stephen.

'She has an idea, but I doubt she really understands yet.'

'What about the Key, where is it?'

Noah pressed a hand to his forehead. 'She refuses to part with it. She won't even let me keep it.'

Stephen said a bad word that he kept for special occasions. 'I have a secure vault at the Dispensary…' he began, trailing off as Noah shook his head.

'You're welcome to try and convince her.'

He sat back and waited as Stephen turned this new information over in his head.

'Yazid is the one in more immediate danger right now,' Stephen said finally. 'Can you track the movable phone?'

'Mobile phone. Theoretically, but I'm less certain how one can do that, well, unofficially.'

'I suppose that could be an argument to make this whole thing official.'

That thought had crossed Noah's mind more than once. 'Chiyo and I have discussed it at length. Problem is, it's a rather fantastic story, that too from a thirteen-year-old, with no proof to back it up. The Elites wouldn't be inclined to believe us, and it would be out of the jurisdiction of any civil defence set-up.'

'You have the drawings as proof.'

'Of what exactly? That someone drew them? It's a diplomacy nightmare—there's no way the High Council would sign off on a mission to swoop in on a backwoods village based on a handful of drawings whose provenance can't be ascertained.'

'Hmm.'

'But more important than that,' Noah reminded him, 'now we know for certain that either Enol or Ryder is in with the Warriors…' Instead of completing the sentence, he just raised his hands. The Elites reported to the High Council—the conclusions were clear as spring water.

'You're not thinking of launching your own rescue mission, are you?' Stephen's voice rose with incredulity. 'That's insane.'

'I think,' said Noah, speaking slowly, because this was another torment he would live with for a long time, 'we owe it to him. We stood by twisting our hands as he was being tortured by his Watcher. We knew he was being scraped, and we did *nothing*!' Noah leaned forward to emphasize his words. 'Yet he risked his life to warn us.'

'You did it protect your own a'fin,' Stephen said. Ineffectual words.

'The point is, the system is broken—a law that criminalizes even a whiff of the Warriors.' He threw up his hands again. 'How can you trust a system that will arrest you on suspicion of collusion even if you bring them information?'

If Stephen had an answer to that question—rhetorical though it had been—Noah never got to know. A small noise alerted him from behind.

Jan stood there, dressed in his Halvard uniform, holding the doorframe like he needed it to keep him upright. 'What in the name of the flaming Sands!' he said, his voice unsteady. 'Warriors, Councillors, *scraping*?'

24

NOAH HAS TO GO AWAY

The Castle was unusually quiet for a weekend, though, possibly, people wanted to have a lie-in after the biggest party of the Halvard calendar. Either way, Maya was glad. Her eyes were still gritty from the scant sleep she had managed, and not even a hot shower at the Castle's excellent facilities did anything to rejuvenate her.

As Chiyo had had to return to Roz and had taken Lev with her, and as Noah had a number of things to do—like update Nira and Stephen—Maya spent her morning quietly in his room. She had loads of reading to finish for Healing, some mind-scrambling advanced Logic problems to solve, and a long list of Illusion exercises to practise. The mundanity of 'homework', as she and Lev called it, somehow soothed her frazzled nerves.

Nevertheless, she jumped when Noah opened the door and came in. He was blocking her—or no, to be precise, he was masking himself. Whatever it was, Maya was less able to pick up on his proximity or state of mind. That itself was telling, because it meant he was trying to avoid letting her know how rattled he himself was.

The closer he was, though, the less he was able to mask himself with efficiency, so Maya knew immediately that something was wrong.

'What happened?' she asked. Noah didn't reply immediately, so Maya added threateningly: 'Don't you dare lie to me and tell me it's nothing!'

'I wouldn't dream of it,' said Noah. He went and sat on his bed—in the midst of the madness, he'd actually made his bed; Maya's cubicle was a tip at this point—and took a deep breath. 'When I went to update Stephen, Jan accidentally overheard some of the conversation.'

'Shit.'

'Indeed.'

'Does this mean Lian will know too?'

Noah hesitated, weighed something up, and said: 'No. He assured me that and I believe him.'

'So what happens now?'

'He insisted we tell him, and he now knows about Yazid and Kilyana—'

'The Key?' Maya interrupted, too impatient for him to get to the point.

'No, he doesn't know anything about the Key. Or you.'

Maya breathed.

'On the bright side,' Noah continued, 'I suppose we have more numbers now.'

'And on the not-so-bright side?'

'I haven't thought that far yet.'

'What else? What did Nira say?'

'Nira has already gone back to Kirnara, so I have to go there to see her and find out about tracking the phone.'

'Great. When do we leave?'

Noah hesitated. 'It's just me, I'm afraid. I can use the Portal Road if I go alone—I have plenty of security credits, but I can't share them with you.'

'Please don't make me go home.'

'I don't want you to be alone in the Castle. Will you think about staying with Stephen and Jan for a couple of days? Their house is pretty secluded—you'll be safe there.'

Maya didn't have to think about it. Anything was better than being alone at the Castle or going home. 'Could I go there by the Portal Road? Then whoever is trailing me will think I've gone home.'

Noah nodded. 'That is the idea.'

There was something else bothering him, but Maya couldn't put a finger on it. 'How long will you be in Kirnara?'

There it was again, a twinge of disquiet. 'I am not sure—maybe a day or two.'

'There's something you're not telling me, Noah,' she said warningly.

The walls slammed down. 'Maya—'

'Oh no, you don't get to do that. Tell the whole truth or take me with you. And don't say no, because I will go to the station and catch a train. Which means you'll have to compel me to stay. And if you do that, it just proves that you don't trust me!'

'Maya,' said Noah again, leaning forward and grasping her arms. 'If I didn't trust you, I wouldn't be leaving you alone. It's not that. I can't take you because I need to see Nira alone.'

'Why?'

His arms fell back down. 'Nira left the banquet early last night because she felt unwell. She is in the Kirnara Central right now.'

Maya gasped. 'What happened?'

'She won't tell me. She doesn't want anyone to know. Insists it's nothing, probably ate something she's allergic to.'

'She had the world's best Healers here, and she went off to Kirnara?'

Noah smiled faintly. 'She hates a fuss. That's what she would have got here. Anyway, I'm sure she's right and it's nothing.'

Maya shook her head. 'No, you're not. You're afraid it *is* something.'

Noah dipped his head in acknowledgement at having been caught out. 'Sorry. Yes, I am afraid. She might look fragile, but Nira has always been extremely hale and hearty. Voluntarily admitting herself means she must have had some kind of…a scare.'

'Why are you being so *weird*? Why didn't you tell me this straight off?'

Noah took a deep breath. 'I suppose,' he said slowly, like he didn't really want to say any more, 'I suppose, I was afraid that articulating my fears would only magnify them.'

'That's the most illogical thing I've ever heard,' Maya declared.

Noah smiled wryly, 'There's a bit of mature, grown-up logic for you.'

Maya rolled her eyes. 'Have your fears magnified now?'

'Actually, I feel slightly less scared.'

He needed a hug, Maya decided.

~

Before he left for Kirnara, Noah went to have a 'little chat' with Maya's parents to let them know that there was a change of plans and that she wouldn't be coming home after all, not in the next couple of days at least. He didn't let her come, and so she had no idea how he wangled it. All she could tell was, it hadn't been easy.

'Being a Watcher is not all fun and games,' was all he would say when Maya asked.

Jan and Stephen's house was definitely secluded, in an odd sort of residential neighbourhood that blended quietly into the forest. Theirs was the last house, with nothing but trees on one side. On the other side, their closest neighbours were older people and their grown-up daughter, who were private folks themselves.

A porch ran all around the house, widening in the back to make a sit-out that led straight into the dining room. The sit-out had a beautiful wooden swing, and Maya instantly fell in love with it. She made herself comfortable on the swing's soft cushions with her books.

Maybe work would distract her again like it had in the morning. Noah had also left his laptop with her, so they could keep in touch through his secure communication app, the other end of which resided in Nira's computer.

But not even the challenge of unravelling Noah's impossible Logic problems could keep her mind from whirring with questions and possibilities. Finally, she gave up working, and booted up Noah's computer. She pulled up the transcribed text from Yazid's drawings. Maybe some small detail, something they'd missed or overlooked last night, would strike her and somehow help them locate him. She hoped her phone had enough charge to stay on long enough for it to be tracked.

The rhythmic motion of the swing, rustle of trees from the forest, chirps of the birds, and small sounds from inside the house must have calmed her, for the next thing Maya knew, she was waking up to gentle late afternoon sunrays on her face, something soft pressing into her middle, and the murmur of voices.

She stirred, waking Anfield, who looked annoyed at the sudden movement and jumped off. Jan was back from wherever he'd been all morning, and he and Stephen sat on chairs, talking in low voices.

'Hello, sleepyhead,' Jan called as she sat up. 'Were we too loud?'

Maya squinted at the sun. 'No, you weren't.' She grabbed at a book too close to the edge, and tucked it back with the computer. 'Sorry if I'm crashing your weekend plans.'

'You aren't. Delighted to have you here.'

But Jan himself looked a bit off. His eyes were sunken and without their usual sparkle, his face filled with extra lines. Why was *every*one falling ill?

'Are you sick?' she asked.

'Never!' said Jan in mock outrage. He started to rise. 'Excuse me, there are some cinnamon buns that aren't going to put themselves in the oven.'

But as he stood, Maya's Healer-in-training eyes noted the way he grasped the wooden supports of the porch to steady himself. She turned to Stephen as Jan retreated inside, a question in her expression.

'He's not ill as such,' Stephen said. 'Just a bit, well, stretched beyond his usual capacity. It actually helps, your being here.' He glanced towards the house. 'I hope you like sweet things—he bakes to make himself feel better, and nothing cheers him up more than having someone to feed.'

'He can keep the cinnamon buns coming,' Maya declared. 'Has Noah been in touch?'

Stephen nodded. 'Only to say that Nira's back home and he's with her.'

'What's wrong with Nira, do you know?'

'Nope. When Nira doesn't want you to know, there's no getting around it.'

Maya couldn't shake off the surreal experience of having coffee and cinnamon buns—which were the best she had ever had—while Noah was away, something was wrong with Nira, there was no Lev to talk to, and most of all, Yazid was in danger from things she couldn't even imagine.

Later that evening, they listened to the news on the RC. The High Councillor's Raising Day speech and the list of new Defenders were still among the headlines. A storm had caused a minor landslide somewhere, but no loss of life or property had been reported. A twelve-year-old somewhere had passed university examinations. Environmentalists were protesting a proposed road—

'Does the news go everywhere in Lam?' An idea was taking shape in Maya's head.

'Sure. Anywhere there's Network access,' Jan replied. 'Why do you ask?'

'I was thinking…by Network access, do you mean,' she tapped her watch, which was just an ordinary time-telling device unlike those belonging to Halvard, which were full comms devices, 'like this?'

She knew the answer, of course, but thc idea was revealing itself bit by bit.

'I'm not sure.' Stephen frowned, turning to Jan for conformation. 'There's something about trains I remember Noah explaining.'

'Trains?' Jan's question echoed Maya's bewilderment.

Then she laughed. 'Do you mean platforms?'

'Possible,' Stephen conceded.

'Ah, I get it now,' Jan said, shaking his head at Stephen. To Maya, he clarified: 'No. The comms signals are different. With news, anyone with a receiver tuned to the right waves can pick up the news, but it's harder, maybe even impossible, to do that with communications because they're encrypted.'

Maya nodded. She'd already known that. 'And does stuff happening in the Castle make it to the news usually? Not just Raising Day, but things like Halvard going missing with their Preferred?'

'Oh yes. Any scandal related to the Halvard Castle is much sought after. When you, Lev and Yazid were Summoned, for instance.'

Maya's eyes nearly popped out of her head. 'Really?'

'They couldn't disclose your names or photographs, but it was on the news.'

'They did post photographs and detailed descriptions when Yazid and Kilyana were declared missing, though,' Stephen added.

'So…' said Maya, weighing each word carefully, 'this would mean that any backwoods community that had their own RC-type receivers would have had access to that news, would know what they look like, and so on.'

'Correct.' Stephen leaned forward. Jan mirrored him. 'Go on.'

'Would they give sanctuary to someone who'd been involved with the High Council?'

The two Halvard considered that.

'They might,' Stephen said, 'if they were convinced that Yazid and Kilyana were in danger from the High Council.'

'Although,' Jan added, 'backwoods folks are not keen to associate with anyone who can hold Spirit. At least, that's the prevailing belief. And they might not want to get involved in the High Council's problems.'

'Which means, they wouldn't be likely to harbour Warriors either,' Stephen put in.

'Though there's no way to say for sure.'

Maya listened to the two of them throw ideas back and forth.

'How many such villages are there?' she asked.

'Hard to say,' Jan said. 'Some of them maintain the illusion of a relationship with the High Council—which is to say, they don't pretend it doesn't exist—but there may be dozens of others who are completely cut off.'

'What are you thinking?' Stephen asked.

'That Kilyana has probably taken Yazid to one of these remote, cut-off places. Maybe too remote for Network access, somewhere people have no idea who they might be. Because any risk of contact, even if it's with the High Council, would mean a risk of the Warriors finding them.'

It was a stretch, but still, it was something. She shared her idea with Noah when they spoke later in the night.

'That's a good point,' he said.

'You've already thought of this, haven't you?' Maya huffed.

'I have, but it's still good thinking.'

'Fine. So when will you do this tracking thing?'

'Tomorrow. Nira's feeling miraculously better after hearing our story. We had a couple of ideas on how to proceed without rattling any official alarm bells, and what you just said might make it a little easier.'

'We've already lost so much time. I hope Yazid is okay. And my phone, what if the battery runs out? It can last a couple of days if I'm not using it, but I don't know.'

'We'll do our best,' Noah assured her.

'I know, I know. Is Nira really okay to work?'

'She'd throw me out if I tried to keep her from solving this puzzle.'

25

NIRA DROPS A PIN

Noah hadn't been exaggerating about Nira's magical recovery. When he'd arrived at Kirnara, she had been grumpy and listless. By the time she'd been discharged from hospital, back home, and made Noah tell the story three times, the gleam in her eyes had returned, her back was straighter, and her speech was peppered with swear words. She retired early that night, claiming not tiredness, but that they'd have to be up at an unholy hour to get to her office.

They were installed at her desk even before the sun was fully up. The Network Security floor was deserted. Noah was uncomfortably aware that there should be skeletal staff on duty, probably two junior Halvard, but their paths didn't cross, and he heaved a sigh of relief when the door of Nira's office closed behind them.

'You never saw me do this,' said Nira.

'Do what?' Noah replied innocently.

'Good.'

She hunched over her computer—similar to his own laptop, the one he'd left with Maya, but with an assortment of peripherals attached to it, and some others connected wirelessly that you couldn't see.

Two of the monitors connected to her system flickered to life. She pointed to one of them. 'I want you to run all the standard tests for unusual or non-standard signals, with a particular focus on mapped backwoods settlements. I'm not expecting a hit, but at least we can rule that out. By the time you're done, I hope to have tweaked the tracking software to search for a more specific signal.'

Noah was already at work before she finished speaking.

~

They took a break for breakfast after a couple of hours. Noah had brought sandwiches, and Nira brewed them tea.

'There were twenty-seven pings from various High Council-administered regions and none from the known backwoods areas,' Noah reported as they ate. 'Of these, fifteen were at the Castle—probably Halvard or Raising Day visitors with mobiles and iPads. The rest are divided between Kirnara, Ekim, Fell, Himsa, and Snowce, all towns with working Halvard, and definitely not remote enough. So, this just leaves those villages and settlements and itinerant tribes that we don't know of. So far, all as expected.'

'It's like looking for a needle in a haystack, when you don't know where the haystack is,' Nira mused.

'Might even be an invisible haystack.'

'Hmm.'

She lapsed into silence, but Noah could see the cogs of her mind turning. He sat there trying to chew and breathe quietly so he wouldn't interrupt her thinking.

'Saroye. Something that moves or shifts,' she said suddenly. 'A town or a tribe's name?'

‘It could be both.’

‘Could be. But—hmm, forget I asked, there’s nothing on available records, so it’s irrelevant.’ She placed her half-eaten sandwich down and jumped up. ‘Did you prepare the hardware signature I asked for?’

‘Yes.’ Noah reached across and rifled through some papers. ‘We know the model of the phone and it’s less than a year old, so this is the closest I could get without an IMEI number.’

‘More than good enough once the signal scan gives us a result.’ She settled at her laptop again. ‘Ah, yes, the code has finished compiling.’

Noah stood behind her. ‘Are you launching the scan?’

‘Yes, as soon as you’ve stopped looming behind me, for f—’

‘All right, I’m getting a chair, keep your hair on.’ He smiled to himself as he pulled his chair over. If Nira was being irritable, that meant she was feeling optimistic.

The next few hours were an exercise in patience. The earlier scan that Noah had run was a broader one, picking up anything that fell outside Network comms range. The scanner was generally the first piece of tech called into play when the Network Security folks wanted to track dodgy signals. It responded based on the parameters fed in, and Noah had queried it with a simple command to report if it picked up anything non-standard, which could potentially include any Roz device, not just phones.

Now, they had fanned out and increased the scan area beyond High Council-marked territories. This was hard because comms towers were sparse in remote areas, so there was very little to bounce signals off. Nira had made some tweaks to make it easier, including reconfiguring the scanner's engine to zero in on specific frequencies emanating from Roz mobiles. Thankfully, they were of a completely different kind and range to Lam comms, so—unless Kilyana had managed to find a location that was truly in a blind spot—it was only a matter of time before something revealed itself.

'There!' cried Nira, making Noah jump.

They'd been staring at the screen for nearly an hour and Noah's eyes had started to glaze over. Nira—more used to doing this—seemed as alert as when they'd started out. She snatched the small printout that coughed out from a slit on the side of her computer and handed it to Noah.

Noah grabbed it and rolled over to his monitor to compare the readings with the signature he had built. This would usually have been done by the computer too, but it was simpler to do the comparison by hand than rewrite the code for yet another complex program.

He wasn't even halfway through when he could tell that this wasn't a match. 'No luck.'

'Try this one.' Nira handed him another piece of paper.

Forty-nine minutes and four comparisons later, Noah's pulse quickened. 'I think we have it.'

In seconds, Nira was looking over his shoulder, reconfirming his calculations, her eyes bright as diamonds. 'Sands, I think we do. Like the old days, isn't it?'

Noah was struck by a pang of nostalgia. 'Remember how we cracked the Sadir case? It was right here. We worked all night.'

'I bet you don't miss it.'

'Actually, I do. Sometimes.'

'I miss working with you, too,' Nira admitted. She clapped her hands. 'Anyway, no time to stand around and reminisce.'

She plucked the piece of paper from Noah's hand, darted back to her computer, and pulled up a different application. She tapped and scrolled, made some small changes here and there. 'There's a new terrain-mapping tool—classified, don't ask me—but anyway, aha, here it is, accounting for an error of point eighteen per cent, you're looking at Saroye.'

She ripped out another piece of paper and handed it to Noah. 'The coordinates. Now go and rescue that boy before the Warriors get him. Tell me, does Maya like chocolate?'

'Er, pardon? Yes, I mean, yes, she does.' Noah split his gaze between his former Watcher and the piece of paper she'd just handed him.

'Then after all this is done, buy her the biggest bar of chocolate you can find, and tell her I said she's an absolute f—'

'Yes, all right, I'll tell her she's brilliant, buy her a giant bar of chocolate from you, and keep all the four-letter words out of it.'

'Fantastic. Now what's the plan for the rescue mission?'

'That's Chiyo's territory. I suppose she and I will do a recon and then work out the details.'

'You're forgetting Maya and Lev,' reminded Nira.

'Really, Nira,' began Noah, 'we can't possibly put them into more dang—'

'Listen, stop thinking of Maya as a child all the time,' Nira snapped. 'She is a very powerful Halvard-to-be and you have to acknowledge that. You are a team. Can you Sync yet?'

'Yes.'

'And? What's it like?'

Noah sighed. He had already lost this argument. 'Like we could extinguish the sun if we wanted.'

'You see! You and Maya, plus Chiyo and Lev. Noah, the four of you together could take on the entire village if needed.'

She was right, of course, but Noah didn't say so. He didn't like the idea, but he wasn't going to be able to protect Maya forever. His job, after all, was not to shield her from danger, but teach her to face it.

'There isn't much time. Every hour could be crucial for him. You need a fast and strong team. Jan trained in search-and-rescue back in Kendark, and he knows a good deal about strategic approach in that north-eastern area. I would offer to come, but I'm useless out of doors and would probably fall off the mountain.'

'I'll keep you posted,' said Noah. Of course he wouldn't ask Jan, considering he was recently released, but that wasn't something he could share with Nira yet.

'You do that.' She stood. 'Go back now and make your plans. And stop worrying about me. I'm fine. I'm used to not being able to lie to you, and some old habits are hard to break.'

'Good. Promise me you'll let me know the next time you're out of sorts.'

Nira laughed. 'I will promise no such thing. I do *not* want you dropping everything to come running to me whenever I have a sniffle.'

'What about—' Noah swept a hand across the array of electronics on the table. 'There will be logs. How will you explain these searches?'

'You leave that to me.'

26

CHIYO PLANS A RECON MISSION

'Did you say you were short of Healers at the Dispensary?' Jan asked the next morning as he walked in and out of the kitchen, tending to his Andarean rice porridge on the stove and savoury buns in the oven, while making sure the fruit preserve was at exactly the right temperature on the dining table.

Stephen watched him with a mixture of amusement and irritation. He had known Jan would jump at the opportunity to cook for someone—and it did actually keep him from feeling low after his and Lian's release procedure—but Stephen worried that he would wear himself out. He was supposed to rest, after all.

The release, a rather harsh name for something so deeply personal and emotionally complex, was a short procedure, but it was precise and tricky, needing a Healer and Logician of high skill to work together. Neither Jan nor Lian would be showing any major physical symptoms, except feeling wobbly for a day or two. Wobbly in more ways than one.

'We are,' Stephen confirmed. 'Ever since Precious moved and Dagan retired. Roh-Ahn has been filling in now and again, but we all know it's not permanent. Why do you ask?'

'I was thinking,' said Jan, walking back into the dining room with a stack of plates in his arms, 'of applying for a transfer here.'

'Ryder would probably kiss you with gratitude.' Councillor Ryder was the Healers' representative on the High Council, responsible for all Healer appointments.

Jan grasped the back of a chair and stared down at the table. 'Good. I'll talk to him. There's no point hanging around in Kirnara, and it would be good to be home.'

The real reason, Stephen guessed, was probably that he still wanted to be close to Lian, who was transferring to the Castle with a new job.

'Good,' he repeated, trying to be playful because Jan hated sentimentality just as much as Nira. 'I hope he says yes, because travelling back and forth from Kirnara is draining my security credits at an alarming rate.'

Jan raised his hands from the chair back, changed his mind, and put them down again. 'Another thing.' He glanced out towards the hall, but it was silent and empty. His voice dropped. 'Tell me, is Maya all right?'

Stephen's eyes widened in surprise. 'She's—it's—well, it's been a rough few days, with the Yazid incident and with Noah rushing off after Nira. But she's a very robust thirteen-year-old.'

'Hmm. Much as I like having her around, how come she didn't go home? Back to Roz?'

'Things are complicated at home.'

'Poor kid. I don't mean to pry, but she seems, I don't know, tense.'

'Being a Preferred is tough. I should know, I was one for four whole years. Remember?' Stephen didn't want to have to lie to Jan, so steering the conversation away was the best thing.

But Jan was not so easily distracted. 'I remember the first time I saw Maya. When Li and I had come down just before our posting to Kirnara. She was different.' He frowned. 'Now she seems like she's carrying the world on her shoulders. Something's changed.'

'They grow fast at this age,' said Stephen neutrally.

'Maybe.' He didn't look convinced. 'Perhaps I'm just being paranoid in my current state, but I get this sneaky feeling that something else is going on, and I have a sense you know what it is.'

Stephen brushed something invisible off his arm and said carefully, 'You should know, she's been asking after you as well. She suspects something is wrong with you, and I'm having to be very creative to avoid lying to her.'

'Touché,' said Jan. He sighed. 'There's a fierceness about her that reminds me of my Li sometimes.'

'Careful there. I believe Li isn't her favourite person.'

'Does Maya know she's got a new job at the Castle?'

'I don't know. Why?'

'Li's been quite interested in Maya since she visited Kirnara. Said she asked some insightful questions.'

Stephen narrowed his eyes. 'Is it Maya she's interested in or her Watcher?'

Jan laughed. Then he fell quiet immediately. The release was always harder on the Watcher, having experienced their a'fin's entire lives, and then suddenly to be out of it.

Stephen squeezed his hand in sympathy. 'I'd give it a week or so. You'll be right as rain.'

Jan sighed again. 'Accepting that the Link is gone is part of the trick, and a really big part of me doesn't want to let go.'

'You've just lost the Link, not her.'

'I know. But it feels like something has been wrenched out of me. I feel empty.'

'I wish I could do something for you, JC.'

Jan smiled, patted Stephen's hand, and turned back towards the kitchen, where the oven was beeping. 'And I wish *I* could do something for Maya.'

~

Stephen's house made a far better meeting place than the Castle, so that's where they congregated. Chiyo spread her map out on the dining table.

'We need a plan,' she said. 'We need to be fast and efficient. If Kilyana gets the slightest hint that something is up, she will spirit him away via the Portal Road. Maya's phone's battery won't last forever, and we'll never find them.

'But this is unknown terrain, so we need to know the layout, and by that I mean not just maps, but a proper recon. We need to know how big this village—Saroye—is, how many people there are, if they have lookouts or guards, and so on.'

Maya picked up Yazid's hand-drawn map. He had marked out the house he was in, right at the edge of the village. There was some vegetation and then a river. 'Looks like we should be able to pop in from the forest here,' she said.

'It might not be as simple as that,' Jan said, studying the map on the table. 'Here—where Yazid drew the trees—there's a change in elevation, you can tell by the difference in colour. It is probably a drop into the river. If there is access, it won't be easy.'

'I see two other options,' Chiyo added. 'This one through the forest here, and this one where you double back along the river and then through here.' She turned to Jan. 'If you and Lian came with us, that would make three Linked pairs, and we could probably cover the area in under a couple of hours.'

'No!' said both Stephen and Noah in unison.

Maya stared at them, surprised at their vehemence.

'Jan has been somewhat under the weather,' Noah explained. He seemed uncomfortable, which made Maya think he knew something she didn't.

'Yes, best he didn't go,' added Stephen.

'Excuse me,' Jan pulled himself up to his not inconsiderable height. 'First of all, I'm right here. Secondly, I'm fine now, no physical symptoms. As for Li,' he hesitated, 'I can't speak for her, but I can ask. She doesn't need to know anything apart from what's necessary.'

Noah and Stephen had one of those silent conversations where they just looked at each other and 'exchanged notes'. It incensed Maya and she wanted Noah to know exactly how much, so she glared at him till he looked at her and gave a tiny apologetic nod.

'I can talk to Li,' Noah offered. 'If that's okay with you, Jan.'

'Of course, thank you,' Jan said.

'Jan, do we need any climbing equipment?' Chiyo asked. She was back studying the map like she wanted to imprint it on her mind.

'Grip-ropes might help. I think we might have some here.'

'Great. So shall we all meet back here after dinner for a final briefing?'

27

NOAH RECRUITS A NEW ALLY

Noah spotted Lian in the courtyard as soon as he got back. He told Maya to stick with Lev and Chiyo, and went up to her.

'Got a minute?'

Lian looked up and smiled a greeting. 'Of course. What's up? Haven't seen you around since the banquet.'

'I had to go away,' said Noah. 'Come with me to the Portal Road for a minute?'

Lian's eyes widened in surprised. 'I'm not sure Maya will approve, Halvard.'

Noah gave her a half smile. The day she Summoned her own a'fin and realized these jokes weren't funny couldn't come soon enough. 'I have her permission.'

'How are you?' he asked when they were at the Portal Road.

'I'm all right, considering.' She made a face. 'Jan and I have released our Link.'

'I know,' Noah admitted.

'You do? How? Stephen must have told you. Right?'

'No, he didn't,' said Noah, and feeling like he had to defend his friend, added, 'you know he wouldn't. Jan told me himself. But I've been sworn to secrecy and no one else knows.'

Lian nodded.

'Can I ask why, though?'

'What did Jan tell you?'

'Nothing. I didn't ask. You haven't been asked to Summon your Preferred, have you?'

Lian shook her head. 'No. It's just—well, we felt it was time.'

That didn't make any sense, but it was too personal to probe any further. 'It just feels like a drastic step,' he said carefully.

She leaned on her arms and stared down at the mist beyond the Portal Road. 'I just wanted to stand on my own feet before I became a full-time Watcher.' That made no sense either, but Lian continued nevertheless, 'It's been harder than I thought.'

'It's always harder than you imagine,' said Noah softly. 'But it gets better.'

'Perhaps. I'm afraid it's harder on him.'

'It probably is. It was bad for Nira when we went through it. It's always worse for the Watcher.'

She sighed. 'He's—the nearest thing I had to a father.'

'Have,' corrected Noah. 'You're not losing him.'

She took a deep breath and straightened her shoulders. 'Yes, you're right. Thank you. Is this what you got me here to talk about?'

'No, actually.' Noah was a little unsure now. Jan was far more restrained with his grief, but seeing Lian this way brought back only too sharply memories from just over a year ago, when he and Nira had had to go through the release as well. 'I was going to ask you for a favour, but now is perhaps not the right time.'

'Whatever it is, if it can take my mind off,' she gestured at herself, 'this, then please go ahead.'

Noah couldn't argue with that—he himself had plunged head-first into a week or two of gruelling physical training, until Stephen and Eidora had threatened to drag him bodily to the Dispensary and restrain him there.

Noah and Chiyo had discussed how and what to tell Lian: that Yazid had been kidnapped by his Watcher, who he suspected of being a Warrior, and was being hidden in a remote village. If she asked how they knew this, he'd tell her Yazid had managed to send them a message, which was the truth.

So that's exactly what Noah told Lian, in brief, measured sentences that he had already scripted in his head.

'*What!*' Lian cried. 'Oh my…!' She looked like she was going to choke or throw up or faint. Then she began to laugh.

'Li, are you okay? Li?'

She turned towards Noah. Tears ran down her face. So maybe she hadn't been laughing, but crying.

'I—no, I'm okay. Sands!' She walked away from him, her shoulders heaving.

Perhaps this had been a bad call. It hadn't even been thirty-six hours since her Link release, and it was insensitive to not have considered that.

He waited as she calmed down. She took some deep breaths, and then turned and walked back to him.

'I'm sorry,' Noah said. 'This was inconsiderate.'

'No, no. I just—it's a shock, that's all, to imagine a Watcher capable of such a thing. I want to help, Noah. In any way I can.'

'Are you sure?'

'Do you think I could live with myself if I didn't?'

~

They congregated at the Portal Road. Maya went with Lev and Chiyo, and Noah Tracked her there with the others. Wrapped warmly, with torches and compasses strapped to their arms, and Noah, Chiyo and Jan equipped with grip-ropes, everyone huddled around the map.

'All right, let's run through the plan once again,' said Chiyo. 'This is the closest we can get to Saroye through the Portal Road.'

The nearest point was very close to their camp on the first night of their trek in pursuit of the Key earlier that year. It was very remote, and densely covered with trees.

'From here on, we need to trek downhill about five to seven kilometres,' Chiyo continued. 'It's not steep, and we should be able to move pretty fast. At this point here, we take stock, and then split up to cover the three approaches to the village.' She turned to Jan. 'Over to you.'

'There aren't any maps more detailed than this, so we can only decide how to proceed once we get there. We've identified three probable approaches, which is perfect for the six of us. We are just there for a recon, so we stay hidden, make as little noise as possible.'

'What happens after the recon is successful?' Lian asked.

Chiyo shrugged noncommittally. 'It depends. For now, we just observe.'

Stephen's frown had been getting deeper and deeper with each passing minute. 'Be careful all of you. I'll be at home if you need me.'

He was the only one not coming along. Not only was he the odd one out, but they needed someone—someone senior enough—to stay behind, just in case anything went wrong. The Elites, if they were needed, would be most likely to listen to someone in authority.

'We'll be all right,' Jan said, patting his shoulder. 'We're basically going for a very silent walk in the mountains.'

'Is there a likelihood of security patrols?' Noah asked.

'No, but we can't rule it out. They'll have some sort of protection against wild animals, though.'

'Couldn't we hide ourselves using inverted Illusions?' Maya asked.

Everyone turned to her. Maya blinked. 'Well—it's just an idea. Lev and I can both do them.'

Noah shook his head. 'It would be too draining on us all. And wouldn't be very practical either.'

Maya wanted to ask why not, but the Halvard started talking among themselves.

~

With just a sliver of Spirit each, they trekked through the forest easily and swiftly, reaching the spot from which the route split into three different possibilities. It started to drizzle, so they huddled under an overhanging rock to talk about how to proceed.

'How far are we from the village?' Lian asked.

'Hard to say exactly,' Jan said. 'Now, who takes which path? The way through the forest is the longest path, and crossing the river will be the hardest.'

'Lev and I will go across the river to the other side,' said Chiyo. 'I don't think it'll be deep, but the currents could be tricky, and we're physically the strongest. I suggest Noah and Maya take the longest route, through the forest—they are strongest in Spirit and will be able to cover that fast.'

'Which leaves us to go on up from here,' said Jan. He unwrapped the length of grip-rope from his waist and held it out to Lev. 'Keep this, you might need it.' He turned to Chiyo: 'Try to keep out of the water and on the rocks as far as possible. If you do have to get into the water, use the ropes.'

'Right,' said Chiyo.

'All right,' said Jan, standing and pulling his hood up to cover his head. 'Be careful. We'll meet back here in one hour exactly to trade information, and decide what to do next. Good luck everyone. Come on, Li.'

Lian and Jan plunged up the hill. Lev and Chiyo turned and went the other way. Noah caught Maya's arm and pulled her through the trees.

28

A SPY COMES TO LIGHT

The moment Kilyana walked through the door, Yazid knew she knew. Not exactly what he'd been up to, but that didn't matter. To be fair, she had probably figured out he was up to something right from the moment he'd stepped on to the Portal Road, but he had planned well.

Kilyana's mistake had been to underestimate his desperation, which is what he'd been banking on. He had always been compliant—rather, she had kept a very tight hold on him right from the beginning. But distance made it harder to compel, scrape and other things like that. That she'd agreed to go on the food-gathering expedition had meant two things—she wasn't intending to leave Saroye any time soon, and she was confident of being able to control him.

The foraging team had been about a day's walk from the village when Yazid had taken off. He'd gambled that the Castle would be crowded with Raising Day—which was a remarkable piece of luck, but then, he figured, the universe owed him some luck.

By the time Kilyana would have realized something was wrong, she wouldn't be able to use the Portal Road back, not in front of the other villages. Irrespective of the situation, they wouldn't have let her go back alone either.

Yazid knew this as he had been at the planning meeting, even though he wasn't part of the expedition. Yaroslaya had stressed again and again that, 'No one walks alone.' That was when the last part of Yazid's plan had fallen into place.

So poor Kilyana would have to come back the hard way, on foot, with her companions. She could have killed and dumped them en route—she was certainly capable of that—but it would have looked suspicious, even if she did come up with a plausible story, like wild animals or an accident.

Yazid might have even got away with the whole thing pretending he'd just tried to go home to his family, but Kilyana found the mobile phone.

She didn't lay a finger on him; she only stroked his hair.

Novocha and her brother helped, while she pretended to comfort him.

She spoke to him in a low, soothing voice, but in words that only he understood.

'Do you know what they do to traitors?' she said. 'Which one of your little sisters and brothers will die first, do you think?'

Rescue wasn't coming. If it was, it wouldn't get here on time. But he didn't need rescue. He had done his part. Now all he had to do was bide his time and find the right moment.

He just had to wait.

He closed his eyes and counted his breaths.

He just had to wait until she was distracted, and she would be. Sooner or later.

Yazid just hoped it would be sooner.

~

Jan led the way.

'How are you doing?' he asked Lian.

'A few more days to go before you need to ask that, surely?'

'Just practising,' Jan said, his heart breaking a little more. 'You know I'll always be there when you need me, right?'

Lian linked her arm through his. 'Of course. There's no—' She pulled short.

'What's wrong?' Jan tensed.

'Did you hear that?'

'What? Hey—Li, what the—'

A cry. Then everything went black.

~

The forest—dense and dark—did not yield. Noah used his double-edged yent to slice through the closely growing vegetation, while Maya lit their way with muted Illusions. There were no visible paths, no way to orient themselves without the compass.

They moved slowly, as quiet as they could, in the increasingly wet ground that sucked their feet in, and kept their eyes peeled for signs of civilization ahead.

The sounds of the forest had Maya on edge—trees rustled ominously, creatures of the night slithered in the shadows, the drizzle echoed with staticky regularity.

Maya sensed Noah tensing a fraction of a second before she heard a noise that was out of whack with the wilderness. Something flashed in the trees.

Noah stopped, a hand on Maya's shoulder as warning. Her light went out instantly as he shielded it.

He put a finger on his lips. Maya hardly dared to breathe as they stood as still as the trees. Her Spirit-enhanced eyes adjusted quickly to the darkness. 'I saw a light,' she signed to Noah.

He nodded. 'Me too.'

Every sound seemed amplified. Unknown animal calls sounded like alarms. Even the rain was louder. Something squelched in the distance, like boots in mud.

'Stay,' Noah signed. He pushed Maya against a broad, mossy trunk. 'I'll check.'

'No!' Maya grabbed his sleeve. 'Don't leave me alone.'

'Just to the edge of the clearing. No point both of us trudging back through the mud. Here—keep this, but be careful.'

He thrust the yent into her hands and moved slowly and cautiously back along the path they had just cleared. Maya hunched under the tree, cursing her raincoat that seemed to be no use at all. Her feet sank into the mud.

Noah melted into the darkness. Seconds passed, then a minute. Something rustled ahead of her, another sound out of sync with the forest.

'Noah, is that you?' she called in a low voice.

No reply. But a movement, then another, the sounds too close together. Quick. Frantic. A flare of light, a burst of distress from Noah that turned to surprise, then, almost immediately, to shock.

'Noah!' Maya screamed, and surged forward.

A blaze of Illusion light beckoned her, but she let the sensation of her Watcher be her beacon. She burst into a space between a cluster of trees, and skidded to a stop.

Noah was on the ground, Lian behind him. Like some bizarre tableau.

Lian gripped him with a hand on his shoulder. Noah's head was turned to a funny, uncomfortable angle, almost like he was craning it sideways, up into the trees.

Maya's hand tightened around the yent instinctively. 'Noah, what is—'

Lian's voice cut her off. Sharp, cold, direct: 'Drop the knife.'

Maya couldn't move. She grappled with herself, frantic to make sense of what she was looking at.

'Drop the knife, Maya,' Lian repeated. 'Or he dies.'

A glint near Noah's head. Maya's vision cleared. Her heart leapt into her mouth.

The tip of a long, curved knife pushed against Noah's throat. She felt it slice through the top layers of skin.

The chill that spread through her body had nothing to with the rain, the wind, the forest. It was pure fear.

'No—don't!' She let the yent fall out of her hand.

'Good girl.'

'Let him go, please!' Her voice shook.

'You need to do one more thing for me first.'

'What?'

'Maya, don't—' Noah started to speak, but the knife pressed deeper.

Maya bit down on her lip to stop her scream.

'The Key,' said Lian. 'I want it. Now.'

29

MAYA KEEPS HER HEAD

The river was fast and unwelcoming. Chiyo tested the current with a broken branch she had picked up in the forest, and the water nearly wrenched it out of her hand.

'What now?' Lev signed. The roar of the water would have had them shouting to be heard.

'Let's walk along the river, see if we can spot the village or find an access route.'

On the other side, the river ran along a rocky, almost vertical, wall of mountain, with jutting rocks, some moss-covered, some bare, a few plants growing out at odd angles, but mostly just shadows. Spray rose high over glistening boulders rising from the river bed. Lev wasn't sure if it was the rain or the spray drenching him.

Where Lev and Chiyo stood was a rocky bank that looked like it had taken a huge bite out of the forest.

'Don't think there's any access from here,' he said to Chiyo after about ten minutes of walking.

'We'll go up to the bend,' she signed back. 'See if it eases.'

They picked their way carefully through the rocks, weaving in and out of the forest when there was no way through. As they approached the bend, Chiyo stopped and Lev bumped into her.

'What's the matter?'

Chiyo pointed ahead. Lights twinkled through the drizzle.

'Is that Saroye?' Lev asked.

'That's my guess. I think we should be able to cross here.'

The river was calmer here, the rocks larger, forming a ragged natural bridge. 'We may not need to go in the water at all,' Lev mused.

Chiyo was studying the way up. 'I think we could climb up over there. We'll need some gear, but it can be done. Are you ready to put your skills to practice?'

Lev and Chiyo had done plenty of indoor rock-climbing at the Castle's gymnasium. He knew the practice wall like the back of his hand—this one was a different cup of tea altogether.

He took a deep breath. 'I think so. Worst-case scenario—I'll fall off. But my fall-breaking skills are decent.'

'Good. Let's head back to the rendezvous point now and see what the others have to say.'

~

'Y-you want the Key? But…why? How do you know—'

Lian tsk-ed. 'I thought you were clever. Look, I can't stand here all night. I'll give you three minutes—get the Key from wherever it is. If you're not back in that time, I'm going to let the knife go right in and slice through his carotid. You know what's going to happen if I do that, right? Ready? Your time starts—'

'Wait, no!' Maya cried.

'Really, Maya, you disappoint me. I didn't think you'd want me to torture him first.'

'H-how can you do this? He's your *friend*!'

'That was a long time ago. Now, three minutes—and don't try anything funny. It's going to take me less than a second to push the knife in and he'll be dead before anyone can do anything. So if you're thinking of coming back with help—'

'Li—don't do this,' said Noah quietly. 'Put the knife down, and let's talk this through.'

'Talk?' Lian laughed. 'Sorry, the time for talk is long gone.'

Maya's fear seeped out slowly. She knew what was happening—Noah taking it out of her. She wanted to call out to him, tell him to stop. But as her mind cleared, she understood why.

Noah was starting to shake, probably from taking in her fear, and Maya was terrified anew that he would impale himself on the knife with no help from Lian. Maya took a deep breath—she had to keep her head. Noah was giving her a chance to live, because, knowing what they knew now, Lian wouldn't just let them walk away, even after she got the Key.

'Think of Jan,' Noah said, even his voice wavering now.

Maya's limbs chilled gain. Jan—where was he? What had she done to him?

'Be quiet, Noah! You are as pathetic as him. The sad part is, you didn't have to be. Maya, you're still here?'

Maya's heart was pounding, but her head was still clear, despite new fear beginning to fill in from the cracks in her being.

It was simple, really. Lian could have the Key if she wanted. All Maya wanted was for Noah to be safe.

'I have it with me,' Maya called. 'The Key.'

'I'm not playing games,' Lian said warningly.

'No! Look!' She pulled up the leg of her trousers and heard Noah's sharp intake of breath.

Amma's old mobile phone case peeped out of the top of her sock. A thick elasticated band held the whole thing in place.

'It's inside the phone case, I can show you!'

'Show me,' barked Lian. 'No tricks. No sudden movements. You don't want my hand to slip by accident.'

Slowly, her eyes on Noah and the knife, Maya bent and popped the magnetic button on the phone case. As she reached inside, the bone-deep chill of the shell spread from her fingers, coursing through her body. She lifted it out slowly, towards Lian.

~

Lian's gasp filled the space between them. The Key remained a dagger-shaped darkness in Maya's hand, even in the Illusion light that bathed all of them.

'Beautiful,' said Lian, delight dripping in her tone. Perhaps she was talking of the Key, or maybe just her luck that Maya had had it on her person. 'So much easier than I had imagined.'

'So it's you, is it?' Noah said, his voice still unsteady. 'The one given the job to retrieve the Key?'

'Ah, you're very well informed.' She sounded surprised. 'Who told you that? Actually, never mind.' Turning to Maya, she said, 'Give it to me.'

Maya pulled herself straight. 'Not so fast. Let him go first.'

'Ha, nice try. The moment I let him go, it'll be two against one.'

'Listen—' Noah began.

'You stay out of it!' Lian snapped.

'If I give you the Key, you'll kill him anyway,' Maya said, amazed that her voice was so steady, sounding so grown-up, like she was calm and in control. 'I have another idea. I'm going to walk towards you. When I'm close enough, I'll place the Key in your hand, but I'll still be holding it. You let Noah go, and I let the Key go.'

'That's not—'

Maya cut her off. 'It's your only option. If you do anything to Noah, I will kill *you*. The Key, I don't care about the Key. You can have it.'

Lian seemed to think about it. 'All right.'

Very slowly, Maya took a step forward, then another. She looked at Noah—he gave her a tiny nod, more a slow blink than a movement of the head. His eyes moved to his left.

Maya blinked back at him, deliberate, to show she understood.

Brsingr. That's what the move was called, disarming an opponent in a close-quarters melee situation. Chiyo said she had named it from a book she had been reading.

But this wasn't a practice arena. There was zero margin for error.

Maya was now close enough to reach out and touch Lian. She had deliberately moved, very slightly, towards Lian's right, giving Noah space to roll clear when he had the opportunity.

'Give it here,' said Lian, lifting her free hand from Noah's shoulder and holding it out.

Maya, still gripping the Key hard, placed its top half into Lian's hand—

And time coalesced into a single moment. Or perhaps it stretched out into eternity.

Noah rolled clear as Lian's hand closed over the Key. Maya automatically went into the opening move of Brsingr, pulling Lian's hand across her body, yanking her closer and downwards. She drove her foot into the back of Lian's knee—or at least she tried to, missed by a couple of inches and got her on the calf instead.

Lian cried out in pain, but didn't drop. She stumbled, but for a moment, and the Illusion light went out, plunging them into darkness.

30

MAYA STAKES A CLAIM

Maya flew backwards and rammed hard into a tree. Pain seared into her, furious and excruciating. She screamed, stilling the forest for a second. Then, a light flared up around them.

She slid to the forest floor, in a daze of pain, and Lian threw herself on her, grasping her shoulders, shaking her. 'Where is it? Give it to me *now*!'

The Key! Maya had been holding it a second ago. It was gone.

Lian shook her and each movement sent fresh spasms raging fire through Maya. '*Where is it?*' she said through gritted teeth. She started to search, roughly pulling aside her clothes, digging her hands into her pockets. Maya struggled ineffectually. Pain curled around her thoughts.

A sudden lightening of the weight of Lian on her. Noah and Lian grappling, rolling over and over on the ground, covered in mud and leaves. Quick, sharp, brutal movements fuelled by Spirit and desperation and rage.

Then a sudden silence. Lian grunted, struggling against Noah's arm lock.

'Li! Are you out of your mind?' he shouted through gritted teeth.

'I—just want—the Key!'

'She's a Warrior, Noah!' Maya cried, new adrenaline surging into her.

Lian's laugh, sharp, harsh. 'He knows, you stupid little pest!'

Noah's arm tightened across her.

'Where's Jan?' asked Noah roughly.

Despite her body being on fire, Maya went cold. Was Jan a Warrior too?

'Jan?' said Lian coldly. 'He's useless!' She struggled to turn her head towards Noah. 'You don't have to be part of this. I can free you, Noah—'

'Don't say it,' said Noah through clenched teeth. Maya was no longer sure what to call whatever she was sensing in him. It went way beyond anger or betrayal or hatred. 'Best if you don't say any more. You're coming back to the Castle—'

'The Key can cut through anything,' Lian raised her voice, 'I can release you from Maya—'

Noah's concentration wavered. Lian moved. And Noah was flying over her shoulder.

He landed heavily on the ground. Lian was on him and they were back to grappling. He rolled and pinned her back, but she brought him down again, shoving his head against a rock. Maya yelped, even though she couldn't actually feel anything. She could, however, sense Noah's struggle to remain conscious.

She hauled herself up. Something was poking out of her and everything was wet and sticky. But there was no time to examine it. The Key was somewhere in the mud. And she had to find it before Lian did.

She scrabbled before her, using a low Illusion light to search. Her left side felt so heavy that she could barely move it. She shuffled forward, dragging herself lopsided. If there was any pain, she didn't know—there was no time for pain.

A bright light flared in her eyes and Maya was momentarily blinded. It was only an Illusion from Lian—she had noticed Maya searching the ground, probably guessed the Key had fallen somewhere.

Maya spotted the Key as soon as her vision cleared. But it was too far to reach out to. Her resolve wavered, the pain flooding back and gripping her till she screamed in frustration. Even keeping hold of her Spirit was a chore.

Then Noah moved. Behind Lian, he rose to his feet and inched silently forward. Again, Maya's head cleared. She pulled in Spirit, gritted her teeth to brace against the pain, paused for half a second, and then lashed out fast and hard with her foot aiming for Lian's legs.

With a muffled curse, Lian fell, and Noah was on her in a flash.

A couple of seconds were all it took for Maya to shuffle closer to the Key. She reached for it—just inches to go now. She twisted to give herself better reach. The pain ripped through her again, but she got her hand around the hilt of the dagger. The chill from the Key that flowed into her was welcoming for a change. It coiled around her pain. For a moment, it felt like a friend.

When she looked up, Lian and Noah were still struggling.

Maya didn't stop to think. Lian's back was to her and she didn't see as Maya raised the Key, directed all her Spirit into it, and threw.

The chill from contact with the shell didn't leave Maya even as the Key flew through the air. The feeling changed though, drenching her in ice-cold water that seeped into every bit of her body, every cell, every atom, even the spaces in between. And it took away her pain and her fear.

Power surged through her—a feeling that she could do anything. She could squeeze the worlds together in the palms of her hands if she wanted; she could shout so loud, the echoes would be heard across the universe. The feeling tickled the back of her throat like the sweetest flavour of a delicious honey and the bitterest aftertaste of a noxious poison. She felt like she was flying, like she was being buried alive; joy and despair ripped through her body.

She couldn't—didn't want to—let go of the feeling. Its disgusting and exhilarating pull didn't want to let go of her either.

The sensations—so contradictory that it felt like being pulled apart—peaked till she could bear it no more. Screams rent the air—maybe hers, maybe others'. Then, as quickly as they had flared, the feelings faded and finally winked out completely. Only Maya remained, gasping on the floor, drenched in pain and sweat, and hopelessness. And a weakness that left her immobile.

There was nothing else but the pain in her side.

The Key had struck Lian in the back of her thigh. She gasped, staggered around in horror, opened her mouth to scream, but no sound came.

She crumpled to the ground and didn't move again.

Maya's strength died and she sank down. The pain was worse than before, and it jumbled everything up in her head.

Who had screamed?

When did Noah reach her?

Who was holding her?

Why was she so cold?

Why was she sticky?

Who was shouting and running?

Where was the light coming from?

'What the hell! What happened?'

How did Chiyo get here?

'She's been stabbed.' Noah's voice.

That's my fault! I threw the Key at her.

'I'm sorry!' gasped Maya. 'I had to—with the Key—she wanted—'

Someone tickled her with a probe.

'Shit.' Chiyo again 'How did this happen?'

'Lian attacked us. She tried to get the Key.'

'Jan—' said Maya.

Jan is in danger!

'We'll find him.' Noah's voice.

'Jan—' said Maya again.

So much to say, but darkness came instead.

31

LEV BREAKS A FALL

Noah was so pale, he was almost translucent, his eyes dark beads against the ghostly pallor. Lev's knee jiggled nervously and he pressed a hand on it to keep it still. Some part of him wished he could have Noah's knowledge of what Maya was going through. But another part was sure that knowing would probably kill him. His worry was almost a physical thing, a hard, painful knot in his chest that wouldn't shift.

If Noah's sitting here so calmly, she must be okay.

A small dressing on the top of Noah's head gave him a weird lopsided look. He had other scrapes, including the cut on the side of his neck, below the ear. He was still wearing his blood-stained clothes.

There had been so much blood.

Maya had been stabbed deep by Lian's knife. It was a serious wound, damaging her intestines, kidney and ovary. She was being Healed as they spoke.

Lev breathed in deeply and out again through his mouth. It came out in a strangled half-sob. If anything happened to Maya—

Chiyo's hand folded over his wrist.

Noah looked at him. 'She'll be okay,' he said.

He shouldn't be having to comfort me. Lev nodded, grateful nonetheless. 'Thank you.'

He hadn't even been paying attention to what Noah and Chiyo were discussing. He only checked back in when Chiyo said, 'I think we should go back.'

Noah replied: 'You can't go back by yourselves.'

'There's no choice, Noah. You can't leave Maya, and after everything that just happened, I don't want to wait. It shouldn't be hard—there are no signs of patrols, it's the dead of the night. I can handle Kilyana, and Lev will move out with Yazid.'

'If you're sure,' Noah said. He looked as impassive as usual, but Lev was sure there must be complicated emotions running through him. 'The sooner he's separated from Kilyana, the better.'

The door swung open, and Stephen came out of the operating area. His face was tense, like he was clenching his jaw, like he was either very angry or holding some very intense emotion back. He toyed with a Healing shell on his fingers.

Noah sprang up, even though he had already told them all that Maya would be fine. Stephen nodded at him, grasped his arm like he was going to support him. 'All good. She'll sleep for a while now. I'll fill you in on the details later.'

Stephen sat down, Noah next to him. 'I want to know everything.'

Lev had never seen him so stern.

'Noah will catch you up,' said Chiyo, standing. 'We have to go back and get Yazid out of there as soon as possible.'

Stephen stared at them as if he hadn't noticed they were in the room.

'I'm sorry, I don't like leaving you—' Chiyo started to say.

'We're okay,' Stephen interrupted. 'You're right. You have to go back. Yazid's life could depend on it.'

~

Lev remembered little of crossing the river and climbing up to Saroye. He just relished the physical labour that kept his mind from wandering over to Maya.

The village spread out between the trees, the entire area in a sort of dip on the mountain. The location probably protected them from cold winds.

Large boulders formed a natural semi-circular boundary between the village and the mountain edge. He and Chiyo crouched behind one of them to discuss how to approach. Ahead, lay a couple of houses. From Yazid's map, they already knew that the one closest to the edge was his and Kilyana's. A dim light shone from one window, but the village looked dead otherwise.

'That must be the back door,' Chiyo signed, not wanting to risk the breeze carrying sounds towards the village. 'I'm going to go round the front and distract Kilyana. When you hear me inside, you go in from the back, grab Yazid and retreat to the Portal Road. I'll deal with Kilyana and join you there.'

'What if the door is locked—' He stopped when he saw the expression on Chiyo's face. 'All right, all right, but what if she sends Yazid to check it out?'

'Then I'll grab him and run. If you sense me making for the Portal Road, abandon everything and follow me.'

'But Kilyana? She'll run away to the Portal Road and we'll never find her.'

'She's not the priority. Yazid is.'

'Fair enough, but Kilyana is dangerous. Shouldn't we stick together?'

'I've been in worse situations, handled more dangerous people.'

'I don't like this, Chiyo.'

'Your objections have been noted. We'll argue about it later. Now, can I depend on you to take Yazid to safety?'

Lev agreed grudgingly. They climbed over the rocks and crept forward until they were standing next to a low fence penning in a small vegetable garden. Chiyo gave a thumbs-up sign and they separated.

Chiyo crouched down to stay below the level of the window and ran soundlessly along the side of the house. Lev darted towards the back, pulling in Spirit so that—

'Stop!'

Lev plastered himself against the side of the house, his heart racing. Footsteps shuffled. He peered carefully around the corner.

Two people—tall and well-built—teenagers from the look of them, raced up towards Chiyo. One brandished a butcher's knife and the other had a long, thick stick.

'Who are you?' one of them challenged. It sounded like a girl, speaking in accented standard Proto. 'This village is out of bounds to strangers.'

'I mean you no harm,' said Chiyo, raising her hands to show she was unarmed, her voice low. 'They are not who you think they are. They can hold Spirit. I have come to take them back.'

'Then the High Council have sent you,' the other one said. 'Well, you can go back. We don't have anything to do with your kind of people.'

'Shit, shit, shit,' muttered Lev. He hesitated. What should he do?

But he already knew the answer. Chiyo could handle a couple of teens. He turned, kicked the back door down, and rushed into the house.

~

When Yazid heard the shouts from outside, he knew it was going to be over soon. An indescribable calm came over him. He smiled, turning away so Kilyana wouldn't see his face.

A crash. Yazid jumped. The back door of their shack was hanging from a hinge. A figure stood framed in the doorway, something vaguely familiar about it.

Kilyana gave a low cry of rage. Something bright yellow shot from her hand, but it winked ineffectually out before it reached the person in the door.

Was that...*Lev*?

Something else burst from Kilyana, at immense speed, but Lev ducked, rolled and was on his feet in seconds.

Kilyana had an arm bolt on one wrist, and she aimed it at Lev. Yazid would have shouted a warning, but it was all happening too fast.

With a tiny *shtick*, the bolt discharged again, and Lev ducked again. But this time, Kilyana was prepared—she shot another bolt, this one low, just where Lev's momentum would take him. Yazid tensed.

But things didn't go as he feared.

Lev's arm snapped forward, and something hard tied to his wrist deflected the bolt. It thwacked into the wall, as Lev leapt up and closed the distance between them. And then he was flying.

Kilyana cursed again, as another of her Illusions shattered harmlessly against Lev's shield. His body twisted in the air, one foot struck the bolt, breaking the wooden frame into two. Yazid felt it slicing into the flesh of Kilyana's forearm.

The second kick smashed into her other hand with the snap of a breaking bone. Lev—magically—landed back on his feet, but as he was getting his balance back, Kilyana delivered a savage kick to his abdomen.

Or almost did. Lev caught her foot and pulled, bringing Kilyana down. She put out her hand to break the fall, but she had forgotten about her broken arm bolt dangling from her wrist. She landed awkwardly.

Lev landed on her, his hand on her neck. He pressed down.

Kilyana's consciousness flickered and died, and the tight hold in the middle of Yazid's torso loosened.

This was it! The chance he had been waiting for. The chance to end it on his own terms.

He pushed himself up and ran as fast as his weakened legs would allow.

A shout from behind him. He didn't stop running.

He reached the rocks and scrambled over them. He was used to them, he knew the friendly handholds that took him to the top. He slid down the other side, got up, and ran again.

'Hey! Yazid, stop!'

That was Lev. A pounding of feet—he was giving chase. At the edge of the mountain, Yazid stopped for a second.

'I am sorry,' he whispered to the family he would never see again. 'I let you down.'

Then he jumped. As he did, a hand closed on the cloth of his shirt.

But it was too late.

The wind rushed into his flushed face, cool and welcome. He hoped those sharp rocks under him would be every bit as painful as he deserved.

He closed his eyes and braced for impact.

His life didn't flash before him. He only saw his sister. She was smiling.

Then something closed around him tightly, almost like a hug. A second later, something else hard and solid slammed into him.

~

Lev emptied his entire vocabulary of swear words into the silence of the Portal Road. He rolled off Yazid, clutching his shoulder.

'What the hell?' he yelled at Yazid. 'You jumped off the flaming *mountain*?'

The other boy stared back at him, still lying on the ground, eyes round in shock. His chest rose and fell fast.

For the first time, Lev had a chance to study Yazid. Maya had described him as shrunken, and that was about right. He looked withered and sick. He stared back at Lev with those weird double-coloured eyes, and Lev's anger melted away.

'You okay?' he asked.

Yazid continued to stare for another second or two. 'You—what—how did I get here?'

Lev pressed his eyes shut. 'Listen, please don't *ever* do that to me again.'

'You brought me here? How?'

‘It’s called fall-breaking, it’s a techni—oh forget it. Yes, I brought you here. Are you really okay?’

Yazid appeared surprised at the question. He stared into space for a few moments. ‘I…yes, I am. I’m no longer in—’ He touched the hollow of his stomach gingerly. ‘She’s not controlling me anymore.’ His eyes flicked back to Lev. ‘Thank you.’

Lev held his head. He couldn’t even.

32

MAYA HAS MANY QUESTIONS

When Maya woke, she had no sense of time having passed. She was just so tired. Her throat was dry and everything hurt. Then the events of the night rushed back, consuming her like a tidal wave, knocking her flat, even though she was already lying down.

Something clutched her hand. She turned and saw Noah watching her. He gave her a small smile.

They didn't speak. He adjusted her bed so she could recline upright, handed her a cup of water in a spill-proof cup and held it as she drank. She was panting when she finished.

Noah set the cup down and looked at her. She looked back. Grief and betrayal tore deep into him. He took her hand again.

'It will be all right,' he said softly. 'Yazid is okay. Lev and Chiyo got him. Kilyana is in custody.'

Maya closed her eyes, trying to feel relieved.

'What'll happen now?' she said, her voice a hoarse whisper.

'I don't know.'

He climbed on to the bed beside her and tucked his arm under her. Maya rested against his shoulder, grunting at a sharp pain in her middle.

'What happened to me?'

'Lian stabbed you. You lost a lot of blood and had some serious injuries. But you've got a lot of Healing and you'll recover.'

'I am sorry. I didn't want it to turn out this way.'

'Neither did I.'

'She's your friend.'

Noah's arm, the one he was holding her with, tightened. 'A long, long time ago. But a lot of things changed since. More than I realized.'

His face was expressionless as usual, but Maya knew better. 'I wish it didn't hurt you so much.'

He nodded. 'I know you do. But Maya, I need to know—why did you have the Key with you?'

Maya bit her lower lip. 'You'll think I'm stupid.'

'You saved our lives. I know you are not stupid.'

She sighed. 'I thought…if things went wrong, then maybe we could give Kilyana the Key in exchange for Yazid.' When Noah didn't reply, she added, 'See? Stupid, right?'

Noah still didn't speak. He didn't really need to reply. He just pressed his cheek to the top of her head.

It puzzled Maya, though. Noah didn't go in much for overt gestures of affection. He preferred to communicate with well-placed nods.

'But I know I did something bad. Didn't I? With the Key?'

'Maya.' Noah's voice was soft, but Maya wasn't fooled.

'What? What did I do?'

'Not you. It's Lian—she died.'

Maya gasped. 'I killed her, didn't I?' Tears began to run down her face. 'The Key.'

Noah hugged her tighter. 'The Key struck her, and she died. I don't know how it happened.'

'I knew it! I'm evil, a murderer!'

'Maya, she was going to kill us both once she got the Key. You knew that, right? You didn't kill her, you couldn't have—the Key got her in the leg, there was barely a scratch.'

'But I threw the Key, and it…oh Noah, it…it *did* things. I could feel its power. Lian said it could cut anything—I cut off her life!'

'You saved our lives. In fact, this is the second time you've saved my life.'

Maya tried to push him away. 'No, no, let me go. I'm evil! I killed Jan too, didn't I? He was my friend. Oh, please, tell me he wasn't a Warrior!'

'Maya, Maya!' Noah held her hands to stop her from struggling. 'Careful, you'll pull out your staples. Listen to me—Jan is not dead. And he's not a Warrior.'

Relief coursed through her. She sagged against Noah again. 'But—how?'

When their a'fin were close to death, Watchers automatically transferred every bit of their strength to them in case it might help them survive. If Lian was dead, how could it be that Jan wasn't?

'Li and Jan had had a release procedure a day ago,' Noah explained. 'But the Link doesn't just snap, it fades. She had stabbed him too, and left him for dead, but because they weren't fully Linked, the life transfer didn't happen.' Noah paused. 'He would have died if Li had lived, because she would have drained his strength.'

'Where is he? Is he okay?'

'He's very weak. They've kept him on life-aid to let his body heal.'

Whether it was relief or fear or just being overwhelmed, sobs wracked Maya's body. They came without warning and there was nothing she could do except let Noah hold her.

~

The news of Yazid's rescue and Kilyana's capture spread like wildfire through the Halvard Castle. There was an emergency hearing first thing in the morning with the High Councillor, the First Commander of the Elite Guards, and his deputy. Chiyo and Lev, joined by Noah, and later by Stephen, narrated the entire story—leaving out any mention of the Prophecy.

Noah told them about Yazid's appearance in Maya's room and the drawings, and explained why they hadn't reported it. He didn't volunteer information on Nira's role, saying that Yazid had let them know where he was. Of course, he also had to be selective with the truth when it came to Lian's involvement. He said that they had included her in their plans, but being a Warrior, she had tried to stop them. Chiyo and Lev told their part of the story.

The First Commander of the Elite Guards, Halvard Arjun, wanted to talk to Maya as soon as she was awake, but Noah put his foot down. As per Olaman laws, Maya was too young to be required to give evidence, and as her guardian, he told Halvard Arjun, he wasn't allowing it. Arjun gave him a cold glare that Noah returned with a colder one.

They, in turn, were briefed about what was to be made public—a very different version from the truth—'in the interests of the people at large, so as not to cause unnecessary panic', according to Halvard Jiro, Arjun's second-in-command.

There was to be no mention of the Warriors. Kilyana had apparently kidnapped Yazid for ransom, and Jan, Maya and Lian were injured in a brave attempt to rescue him.

Chiyo had to keep a very tight rein on Lev's temper, and Noah counted his blessings that Maya was asleep.

~

Lev nearly wept with frustration and rage. 'How can they do this? Lian sounds like a…a hero, for Sands' sake!'

'We have to choose our battles,' Chiyo told him. 'However small they might be, they are no less important.'

'What battles?' said Lev angrily. 'What's the point of capturing a Warrior if they won't even acknowledge it? For all everyone knows, Kilyana was just a common kidnapper. And Lian—she tried to kill Maya.' His voice quivered. 'Not to mention *her own Watcher*! We are back to where we started—the Warriors are still out there, just like they always have been and will be.'

'You're wrong about that,' Chiyo said. 'There are two Warriors less out there. And one less victim. Little drops of water, little grains of sand—you know what I'm saying?'

He still seethed with helpless fury for a few minutes. 'I'm going to the Dispensary. Maybe they'll let me sit with Maya.' Even though he knew they wouldn't.

'You'll be the first to know when you can go to her,' Chiyo reminded him. 'Noah is with her now, so you needn't worry. You should go get some sleep.'

'I'll sleep in the visitors' hall then,' said Lev, feeling mutinous. At least something should be in his control.

33

CHIYO AND NOAH DELIVER AN APOLOGY

'I have so many questions, my head is going to burst.'

'How about you ask me one by one,' Noah suggested.

'Okay,' said Maya. 'First of all, tell me how this works—how could Lian have been a Warrior without Jan finding out?'

'It's not as impossible as it sounds. A'fin are still individuals, each with their own lives and beliefs and so on. Jan couldn't have known every possible thing about Lian, what she was doing every minute of the day, who she was friends with, where she went, what she thought. Now that we know her to be a Warrior, it makes sense she would want the Link released.'

'But wouldn't Jan have known *some*thing?'

Noah shrugged. 'People are allowed secrets, even a'fin. That's why trust is essential between Linked pairs. Look at it this way—Nira and I, even before I had to Summon you, had to have secrets between us. It was part of her job, she had to deal with classified information that I did not have access to. This included her having to handle stuff related to the Warriors. She even had contacts who were Warriors or connected to them—we already know that, right? That's how she's been getting us information, after all.

'It's the same with Rafa and Chiyo—he's been an Elite Guard for a while. Even before she had to Summon Lev, Chiyo had no idea what he was up to, or where he was, half the time. He just turned up for her training and whenever she needed him. Both Nira and Rafa could easily have been Warriors with us being none the wiser.'

Maya digested all that. 'I suppose, if Jan had been a Warrior, Lian would have had no reason to harm him.'

'Exactly.'

She didn't like thinking of Lian, though, because it always took her around to whatever the Key had done. Whatever *she* herself had done with the Key.

'There's a secret I've been keeping from you,' said Maya, sighing. 'About the,' she lowered her voice, 'Key.'

Noah nodded slowly. 'I had a feeling, but I also had a feeling you would tell me when you're ready.'

Maya studied him. His head wound was healing fine and the bandage was gone. He had a bald patch, but his scalp was as pale as his hair, so it was barely visible. She couldn't tell if he actually looked tired and strained, or she just thought he did because she knew he was.

'Where is it?' she asked.

'Safe.'

That's all he was going to say now, so Maya took a deep breath. 'Something happened when I used it. Something—I don't know how to describe it—like an overwhelming joy, but not really joy, and it was somehow also bad, like, really terrible. But I wanted to hold on to the feeling, it was like a magnet, and I was the opposite pole, and it was like I just couldn't let it go. And I also felt really, seriously powerful. Then this whole feeling of happiness and horrible sickness got too much and it just…went, and I felt—I felt, like, there was nothing left in my life. Like a million times worse than just feeling sad.'

She watched Noah's impassive face for a moment. 'That sounds crazy, doesn't it?'

'No, actually, it doesn't. I think it's what that thing does, what it is capable of. I knew something was wrong. Well, I can't say *wrong* exactly, but I had a sense something extreme was happening with you, not physically, but otherwise.'

They had no chance to discuss it any further, because someone knocked and Stephen came in. He looked pretty awful himself, but he smiled and tried to lighten the atmosphere.

'Look at you two, like what's left over after a pitch brawl on derby day.'

'Sorry, what?' asked a bewildered Noah.

Maya tried to smile, if only for Stephen. 'Don't worry, that wasn't for you,' she said to Noah. To Stephen, she added: 'How's Jan?'

'Stable. Now, let's check you over. And after that, are you ready for some visitors?'

~

Maya had already heard from Lev about his dramatic midair rescue of Yazid, and she was now waiting for Yazid himself to tell his story. But when Stephen led him into the room, she could hardly believe her eyes.

Even in a shapeless Dispensary robe, he looked completely changed from the boy she'd found in her cubicle just days ago. Oh, he was still very thin, and his hair still flowed down to his shoulders, but his face was brighter, his eyes clear. The worry lines had gone from his forehead.

But the biggest change was something that neither she nor Lev, when they compared notes later on, could put a finger on. It was in the way he held himself, some kind of loosening, a sort of relaxing that she found hard to reconcile with the tense, serious, almost formal Preferred she had once known and tried so hard to be friends with. Even the way he spoke was different.

'Hi,' he said to Maya. 'You all right?'

'Yeah, I'm okay. What about you?'

'I'm okay too.'

Lev and Chiyo were already there, sitting on a bench by the wall. Noah pulled up a chair for Yazid, while he loomed next to Maya's bed. Stephen stood by the door, like a sentry.

'What's going to happen to Kilyana?' Maya asked.

'Her trial is pending,' Yazid said casually, staring at his hands. 'They made us release our Link.'

A silence followed—so loud that it filled the room. It was broken by both Noah and Chiyo speaking.

'We wanted—' said Noah.

At the same time, Chiyo said, 'Yazid—'

'Let me,' said Chiyo quietly to Noah, who nodded. 'I speak for both of us, but I take primary responsibility because I was the one who witnessed what Kilyana was doing. I should have reported it, should have trusted my instincts. I should have stopped it—'

'*We* should have stopped it,' Noah interrupted.

'Yes. I am—we are—so very sorry, Yazid, for what you have had to go through. It was unforgivable. And the fact that we did nothing was unforgivable too.'

Maya caught Lev's eye. He was looking as sombre as she felt.

Yazid continued to stare at his hands. When he spoke, his voice stayed quiet. 'Please don't apologize for what Kilyana did. Whatever happened is on her, not on you. She had been controlling me, forcing me to do things, believe things, right from the time I met her. Maybe even before that, who knows. I didn't even know the extent of her control until it was too late. But I'm free now, thanks to all of you. I'm still getting used to the new me, getting used to having free will again, and I know I will be okay.' He looked up, looked at all of them in turn, unblinking. His voice was steady. 'Thank you for not giving up on me. I hadn't realized how much I wanted to live.'

Lev was already wiping his eyes. Maya had a giant boulder in her throat. She looked around for something to clutch, and the nearest thing was Noah's hand.

'You're right about one thing,' Stephen said, when the sombre silence was getting too much. 'You will be okay. I'm not an expert in this, but I do know theoretically that a Link has to be nurtured. It deteriorates with misuse, and because of that, your release was quick and easy, with no lingering side effects.'

34

YAZID TIES UP SOME LOOSE ENDS

It was still another full day before they were able to get together in a place they could talk freely. Maya had been discharged from the Dispensary—with strict instructions of no physical activity—and back to her room, which, thankfully, she had all to herself. Mingmei was taking a break for about week, and their new roommate, Arian, hadn't moved in yet.

But it was in Chiyo's room that they met—because she had loads of floor cushions to sit on, and very little chance of anyone barging in.

'What does the Key do?' Maya got in the first question to Yazid before they had even settled properly. This had been bothering her for days, and she wanted to know how the Key had killed Lian by just grazing her leg.

'All I know,' he replied, 'is that the Key makes the Shadow. It is a powerful instrument that can only be used by someone who claims it.'

'Powerful enough to destroy the Sands?' Lev asked.

'Not destroy it—control it,' said Yazid, his eyes wide. 'That's what the Warriors want, didn't you know that?'

'Most of what we know is conjecture,' Noah put in. 'I'm sure you know far more than we do.'

'I'm not sure I do,' Yazid said. 'Kilyana used to say I was on a need-to-know basis. Like I said the other day, she kept such a tight hold on me, half the time I never even realized I could ask anything. Before I was inducted as Preferred, she taught me Proto and English, she taught me how to hold Spirit, and I truly believed that I had some kind of Power that was special.

'In the beginning, she told me that every Halvard was secretly trying to gain power to control the Sands, but only the Warriors had the means to achieve that. When I started to train and saw that there were others like me, Kilyana would tell me that I was still different. She made me believe that nobody trusted anyone, and every Watcher was training their Preferred to be the Shadow. But the Warriors had chosen *me* to be their saviour. She said I had a bigger task, to free the world—worlds—from the limiting control of the Sands. For that, I would need to claim the Key.'

'I think we already figured some of this out,' Chiyo said, 'from whatever little we could read of the Prophecy and from everything that went down. What we don't know is what the Key does?'

'It's a shell, but you already know that too. It was forged many years—actually centuries—ago, though I don't know who made it or how. It's a very powerful shell, which is to say, the Spirit threshold is very high—so high that it would need someone unusually strong to wield it.'

He looked at Maya and then Lev. 'They made us, you know.'

'Who made us?' asked Lev. 'The Warriors?'

'Yes. They believe that the total amount of Spirit available in the worlds, among all Halvard and other people who are not Halvard but can control their Spirit, is directly proportional to the instability of the Sands. Is that,' Yazid looked to Chiyo and Noah for confirmation, 'a proven fact, or commonly held theory?'

Chiyo nodded. 'Anecdotal evidence shows that harder times result in more people being Summoned in the next generation or so.'

'They've been trying for years to start a global pandemic,' Yazid said. 'Large-scale disasters are best for producing stronger Halvard.' He trailed off into silence.

'But,' began Maya, frowning, 'we're already here. Now. The result of the pandemic producing super-strong Halvard will only be felt some fifteen, twenty years from now. So what's the point?'

'An unstable Sands is going to be easier to control,' Yazid said. 'In any case, until they can fulfil the Prophecy, the Warriors won't stop. I may have failed, but they haven't stopped preparing for the next Shadow.'

'But they no longer have the Key. We do.'

'That's why they wanted it back.'

'Even though you don't know what the Key does, do you know anything that can explain how it killed Lian?'

Yazid's eyes widened. 'What do you mean it killed her?'

'I, um.' Maya swallowed. She hadn't expected to have to relive it again, before so many people. 'I threw it at her, and I—I think it cut off her life. Lian said it can cut through anything.'

Yazid was staring at her open-mouthed. 'You used the Key? You mean, you used it like a…like a shell? Directed Spirit into it?'

'Er, yes.' Why was he being so weird?

He wasn't done being weird. He jumped up and grabbed Maya's hands. He studied them for a second and dropped them. 'I—er, sorry!' He sat down again.

'Yeah. Well, the Key,' he paused for a few seconds. 'The way I understand it, it is like a real key, it opens things. So you could say, in way, that it can cut through anything, even things you can't see or feel.' He hunched his shoulders for a moment. 'I don't know how that helps, what it means to the Shadow, or how they're supposed to use it to control the Sands.

'But yes, it is a very powerful shell, so it has a powerful reaction. Kilyana told me that it would diminish my weaknesses and magnify my strength, but only if I had the power to control it.' He looked at Maya. 'Does any of that that make any sense?'

Unfortunately, it did.

'I felt really powerful,' said Maya flatly. She didn't feel like going into it again. 'And I didn't want to let go. Or maybe it didn't want to let go of me.'

'And then?' Yazid leaned forward, as if Maya had been the one telling the interesting story. 'How did it end?'

Maya shrugged. 'It—well, I didn't just feel powerful, I also felt, I don't know, like something disgusting was inside me. It got so overwhelming, that I had to let go.'

'You let go?' He repeated her words slowly.

'Yes. But some part of me didn't want to.'

Yazid sat back, apparently satisfied. 'That's what Kilyana said: if you use the Key often, all your weaknesses will get consumed. Subsumed? And all you'll be left with is power.'

Noah seemed to be the only one who was following Yazid's train of thought. 'I've heard of these kind of shells, but only in the most speculative terms,' he said. 'Shells' abilities to behave this way was one of the reasons they were banned.'

'Behave what way?' Lev asked. 'I'm very confused.'

'The Key,' said Noah, 'seems to be a shell that, by way of a reaction, almost behaves like a drug. It gives you a feeling of power and control. It's addictive.'

'But…' said Lev, 'then how come we can use Healing shells without getting addicted?'

'Healing shells require relatively small amounts of Spirit,' added Stephen. Maya had almost forgotten he was in the room. 'Even relatively weaker Halvard can use most Healing shells, and even then, their reactions are usually mild or harmless.'

'The way Kilyana explained, I actually thought the Key was a magical thing,' Yazid said. 'But if it is just an object, how will it make the Shadow?'

'I suppose the feeling of power, the addiction to it, could eventually impair your ability to make sound judgements,' Noah said. 'That, combined with brainwashing—that's a potent formula to control a powerful Halvard.'

Maya shuddered. 'There's one thing I don't understand, though,' she said to Yazid. 'How did the Key burn you if it's just a shell? How come you couldn't handle it, but I could?'

'I did handle the Key,' said Yazid. 'It only started to hurt me when I directed Spirit into it. You need to feed it an immense amount of Spirit. Obviously, Kilyana never accounted for the fact that all her brainwashing also made me an overconfident ass at times. I didn't feed it enough Spirit.'

Maya's head reeled. 'So...wait. That means I am not evil. It was just...just chance that I picked up the Key without using Spirit?'

Yazid looked puzzled. 'You thought you were evil?'

'Because I am the Shadow.' She frowned. 'Am I the Shadow or not?'

Yazid stared at Maya. 'Don't you get it? Everything that I've just being saying—that the Prophecy describes a Halvard who is strong enough to handle the Key. It could have been me or you or Lev. Or someone else, even. But that's only the beginning. The Key *makes* the Shadow, and that is the person who claims the Key.'

'What he's trying to say, I think,' said Stephen, 'that this is more than an *Arabian Nights* tale where you pull the sword out of the rock and become king.'

'You have your mythology mixed up a bit, but yes, that's basically it,' Chiyo said. 'We knew that the Oparian window had all of you in it, but with Kilyana being a Warrior, they had picked you, Yazid, to make you the Shadow, right? They planned to let you take the Key and teach you to use it.'

'Yes,' said Yazid. 'That's why Kilyana wanted it back, because without the Key, she would have been useless to the Warriors. But they weren't sure if you had claimed it, Maya, because once the Key has been used by someone, it cannot be used by anyone else.'

'And by *claim* it, I suppose you mean, tried to direct Spirit into it and survived?' asked Maya.

Yazid grimaced. 'Yes. I'm sorry, but also in a way, I'm not. You see, if I had not directed Spirit into the Key, it would not have hurt me. I would have taken it and god knows what might have happened once Kilyana made me claim it and taught me to use it. But now it's bound to you, and you won't use it to harm the Sands.'

'Does this mean the Prophecy has effectively been rendered useless?' Stephen said.

'Not till the Key is destroyed, I should think,' said Noah, a thoughtful frown furrowing his forehead.

'But how do you destroy a shell?' Maya asked.

No one had an answer to that.

Then Chiyo sighed noisily. 'The best laid plans,' she said.

'Sorry, what?' Lev asked.

She grimaced. 'The Warriors thought they had everything planned out for centuries. Then a young boy got a bit excited and tipped the scales.'

The weight that had started to lift from Maya's shoulders settled back down. 'So, all this time I had been thinking I was the Shadow,' she said, 'I was not. But when I killed Lian, I actually became it.'

'Is this what you call irony?' asked Lev, but no one answered him.

35

MAYA PAYS A VISIT

'Come on in,' said Stephen, opening the door and standing aside for Maya to enter. When she hesitated, he added, 'It's okay, come.'

She stepped in silently, tentative, scared of what she might find.

Halvard Eidora and Halvard Gurjeet, two of the senior-most Healers in the dispensary after Stephen, looked up as she came in.

'Just finishing up here,' said Gurjeet. He fiddled with some tubes, while Eidora added a signature to one of the screens on the wall. The two Healers picked up their things, nodded to Stephen and Maya, and left.

It was only then that she allowed herself to look at the person they had been tending to.

Jan was on his back, his bed inclined up. His hands lay by his side, on top of the covers pulled up to his chest. He wore the Dispensary's light green gown with thin black stripes. A mask covered his nose and mouth, and wires and tubes ran in and out of him.

The screens and panels at the head of his bed whirred and clicked, breathing for him, pumping his heart, and keeping him hydrated and fed—life-aid instruments that kept his body functioning even as his brain decided if it was up to living.

Maya took a moment to read the screens. Everything said he was stable, but that was because the machines were keeping him that way.

She shifted her focus reluctantly to Jan's face. He looked so calm and peaceful that Maya felt her own tension ebbing. A faint stubble shadowed his cheeks and chin, though his scalp remained smooth as ever. His eyes were closed, and his nose sported a scratch. His chest rose and fell rhythmically. He looked like he was taking a nap.

'It's all right.' Stephen touched her elbow lightly. 'Come, let's go say hi.'

He stepped up to the bed and touched Jan's hand. 'Hey, JC. You've got another visitor.' Aren't you popular today?'

To Maya, he explained: 'Nira was in to see him earlier.'

He spoke so normally that Maya almost expected Jan to open his eyes. 'Can he hear us?' she asked.

'Probably not. But just in case.'

Maya nodded. She lifted her hand tentatively, but put it down again.

'Go on, touch him if you want,' said Stephen. 'Just remember not to Probe.'

'I know,' said Maya. Probing or Healing while one was on life-aid machines could cause electrical imbalances in the body. She touched Jan's hand. It was warm, soft, comforting. She held it for a while, and then gently put it back.

Please don't die. Please wake up.

Lian had stabbed him. She shivered involuntarily—she couldn't ever imagine hurting Noah like that. She swallowed.

'How come he's got a stubble on his face, but nothing on his head?' she asked.

'Because he's bald. He'd started going bald since before I knew him.' He scrolled one of the screens with a stylus. 'He wasn't bad looking when he had some hair.'

'I think he looks just fine now.'

That made Stephen smile. 'Hear that, JC? Just the kind of compliment that should wake you up in a flash.'

Maya stared at Stephen, confused. 'How can you do this?' she burst out. 'Talk to him…pretend that it's all right?'

She turned away and walked towards the single window in the room. She gripped the sill hard.

'Because if I lose hope, I won't have anything to hold on to,' Stephen said quietly.

'I'm sorry,' said Maya, addressing the window. 'It's just…it's not *fair*. Why him? If he d-doesn't make it, I'll…I thought he was… If he dies, I swear I'll never forgive myself!'

'It's not your fault. JC won't want you to think that way either.'

'But it *is* my fault,' said Maya fiercely. 'We should have never taken him along.'

Stephen walked towards her and sat on the window sill. He took Maya's hand. 'It was his decision to go along, Maya, not yours, not Noah's, not mine.'

Maya swallowed hard.

'He's Halvard, and that's important to him,' Stephen continued. 'He was doing what he thought was the right thing. And even though he could no longer pass his life to save Lian, he couldn't let her go without trying to save her, even though she had…hurt him. He loved her like his own daughter.'

'He will hate me, won't he?' said Maya, her voice small like a mouse.

Stephen shook his head. 'You had to save your own life and Noah's. That's logical. He's a Logician, too. Did you know that?'

Maya nodded.

'Look, JC is the warmest, gentlest, kindest person I have ever known. If he doesn't make it—'

'No!'

'Listen to me, Maya.' Stephen gripped her hand harder. 'He was stabbed and left for dead by his own a'fin. Yet he tried to save her. That's the kind of person he is. If he doesn't wake up, that's how I want him remembered, as having given his life trying to save someone else's. I know you are his friend and you care about him. You should be proud of him. I know I am.'

'How could Lian do this to him?' Maya whispered.

Stephen looked down at the floor. 'I don't know.' He ran a thumb and forefinger across his eyes under his glasses, coming together to pinch the bridge of his nose. 'If he doesn't wake up, at least he won't have to deal with that.'

Maya had to turn away. She pressed her face against the curtain until the unyielding surface of the windowpane pushed back against her.

When she looked back towards Jan, Stephen was adjusting a pair of headphones on him.

'What's that?' she asked, trying to keep her voice steady.

'Some sleep music that he likes,' Stephen replied, a little too brightly. 'He's into all this wellness woo.'

'Right.' Maya's eyes fell on some periodicals on a table near the window. 'Do you read to him?'

'I intend to. If he wakes up and finds he's not up to date with all that's happening, he's going to get really cranky.'

Maya smiled at the thought. 'Maybe you should get him some football magazines. He'll wake up all crazy about football.'

'Hmm, not a bad idea.' He gave her a crooked smile back.

'Do you think, I could—I mean, if it's okay with you—come and visit him sometimes? Or read to him?'

Stephen turned towards Jan. 'What do you say, JC? What's that? Well, how rude.' He looked back at Maya. 'He says he'd much rather have you read to him than listen to a boring old man going on and on about boring old things.'

Maya smiled. 'You're not old.' She faced Jan and said, 'Don't call him old. He'll get cranky.'

'Thank you for coming,' Stephen told her. 'I know Jan would appreciate it, and I do too.'

'Could I, um, say something to him right now?'

'Of course, go ahead,' said Stephen. 'Oh, you mean, in private? Certainly. I'll be by the door.' He adjusted the covers, and bent down and lightly kissed Jan's forehead. 'Be good, JC. I'll look in again later.'

The lump came back and rammed itself in Maya's throat. She took Jan's hand again and studied his face for a while.

What could she even say to him that wouldn't feel completely useless?

'I'm really sorry,' she whispered finally. 'I don't care if you hate me, but please wake up.'

36

STEPHEN MAKES A DECISION

Maya couldn't bear the thought of returning to the main wing of the Castle, not even to the comforting presence of Noah or the supporting one of Lev. She found an empty bench in quiet corner of the Dispensary's lawns, and claimed it. She pulled her legs up and hugged them, resting her head on her knees, keeping her eyes tightly shut.

Skin was waterproof, wasn't it? Maybe if she kept her eyelids firmly closed, the tears wouldn't leak out.

But of course it didn't work that way.

She felt as though she would break if she thought about the number of people who were hurting right now. Noah. Stephen. Jan—at least he would when he woke up. Yazid. And it was all because of her. Because—

'Hey, are you all right?'

Maya jumped. She turned her head to find Yazid staring down at her.

'You…I…I saw you from there,' he made a vague gesture, 'and you looked—I'm sorry, I just wanted to check—I'll go. I don't want to intrude.'

'Don't go,' said Maya, surprising herself.

'Are you sure?'

'Yeah.' She shifted on the bench, making space for him, and while he sat, surreptitiously wiped her eyes. 'Have you got your all-clear from the Dispensary?'

'Not yet,' he said. 'I don't have to stay, but I have to have checks every day. They say I'll be fine. You?'

Maya touched the lower left part of her abdomen. 'It's healing, but I still have a bandage, so I can't go home just yet.'

'That's good.' Then he added hurriedly, 'I mean, about healing, not about not being able to go home.'

'I got that,' she said, smiling faintly.

Silence.

'What will happen to Kilyana? Sorry, is it okay to ask?'

'Yes, it's fine. I don't know. There's a death penalty for conspiracy against the Sands, so—' He left it hanging. He looked away. 'I am not a bad person. I don't want you to think that.'

'Why would I think that?' Maya asked, surprised. 'I think—Lev and I both—we think you're very brave. I saw you trying to resist Kilyana so many times—I remember how you tried to warn me at the cave, the way you were fighting her control. And you risked your life to come and warn us. I think you might be the bravest person I know.'

He gave a sudden laugh, but Maya could see he wasn't amused. 'You wouldn't talk of courage if you knew how afraid I am now.'

'Courage has nothing to do with how scared you are.' Noah had said those words to her an age ago, but they hadn't meant much to her back then. She understood now. 'What is it you're afraid of?'

Yazid shrugged. 'I don't know. Everything. Kilyana always kept such a tight hold on me. What I could do, what I could say, who I could talk to. There were times when I didn't know what I was doing or why. Now I'm free, but I don't know what to do with the freedom. Do you understand what I'm trying to say?'

Maya thought about simplifying matters by saying she did, but changed her mind. 'I'm not sure.'

'I thought not.'

They lapsed into silence.

'Lev was so amazing, the way he fought Kilyana,' Yazid said. 'I was so afraid for him.'

'He was the Raising Day duellist,' said Maya, feeling a spark of pride for her friend.

Yazid nodded, as if to say that that made sense.

'Sometimes, people say everything happens for the best, but I don't know,' he said. He stared ahead, into the trees for a while before continuing. 'Halvard Jan, will he be all right?'

'I don't know. I hope so.' She looked away.

More silence.

'Yazid, how long have you been here? Without returning home in Roz, that is?'

He didn't respond for a long time. He seemed to have folded in on himself. 'Almost half a year,' he said finally. He added after a pause. 'Halvard Stephen said my eyesight is getting weaker as a result.'

'No!' said Maya, horrified. 'You should go back. As soon as you can.'

'Go back where?'

'Home. To your family.'

'It's too late to reverse the damage now. And anyway, I can't go back.'

'Why not?'

He leaned down, looking at the space between his feet. 'When Kilyana came to get me, she told my family that she was taking me some place where I'd be powerful and famous and rich. And then I'd come and get them.' He paused. 'And they believed her. I believed her. I don't think I could go back and face them. Tell them that she had taken me to destroy the worlds. They wouldn't understand why I stayed so long.'

'What are you saying? That you'll never go back?'

He shook his head. 'Not never, just not yet. When I'm not so ashamed any more. When I can keep my promise and give them a better life.'

'But don't you miss them?'

He didn't answer.

'I'm sorry,' said Maya quietly. She was saying that a lot these days. 'For everything that happened, for what Kilyana did.'

'Don't be,' he said. 'Don't waste your time thinking about her. I don't think she had any affection for me or trusted me much. She only wanted—' he shrugged. 'Well, you know.' He stood. 'I'll go now. I have to see Halvard Ariba. They're assigning me a new Watcher.'

As he was leaving, Maya got up from the bench as well. She called out to him again. 'Hey, Yazid.'

He turned. Maya was struck anew at how different he looked. He used to be rather big and sturdy for his age. He looked diminished now. Plus, she had grown taller, and had caught up with him.

'Don't be a stranger.'

He smiled at her and nodded.

~

With physical activity restricted over the next few days because of her injury, Maya spent a lot of time on her other work. She and Lev stayed close together, generally avoiding everyone else, even as their Watchers warded off the curious. Yazid joined them sometimes, but he was mostly busy with his reintegration, adjusting to having an a'lef—or unLinked—Watcher.

Halvard Roh-Ahn had been assigned to him, a Lam native from Snowce, and the single braid hanging down behind her right ear, separate from her long, dark hair, identified her as an Ing. She was older than Noah and Chiyo—in fact, she had been raised with Stephen—and specialized in training a'lef Preferred. She was a woman of few words, with calm, grey eyes that spoke of patient understanding.

Maya had gone back home, once her bandages were off and her injury healed, much to the relief of Amma and Appa. She still had an ugly scar, but that was fine because nobody was going to see it anyway. She went back to doing double-duty as a school student by day and a Preferred by night, and the familiar routine was something of a relief.

About a week after she had returned home, one afternoon, she found herself with Stephen and Noah, walking through the gardens of the Castle.

'Where are we going?' she asked, slightly puzzled and definitely uneasy, mainly because Noah had also excused her from classes that day. He seemed suspiciously restrained as well. Plus, Stephen was far too busy to be taking walks in the middle of the day.

'I wanted to speak to you,' said Stephen.

That did nothing to allay her fears, but she didn't probe any further. They walked in silence through the gardens and came to a small courtyard, the one with the fountain in a chipped stone statue, a place she had discovered months ago.

'I'll wait here,' said Noah, sitting down on a dusty wooden bench just off the path.

'What's going on?' said Maya, her disquiet peaking into full-blown anxiety.

'Come on, let's walk to the lake,' Stephen said.

Maya wanted to turn around and run as fast and as far as she could. Instead, she let Stephen guide her up the hill and on to the stone-and-wood walkway that spanned the lake.

For the first time, she didn't even stop to look around and marvel at her favourite place in the Castle.

Finally, she couldn't bear it any more. 'It's about Jan, isn't it?'

Stephen stopped in the middle of the walkway. 'Yes.'

A flicker of alarm went through Maya. 'What about him?'

Stephen leaned on the railing and stared at the surface of the lake. 'JC will have been on life-aid for ten days tonight.' He spoke mechanically, like he was reading from a textbook. 'So far, he has shown no signs of breathing on his own. It's time to decide whether to take him off the machines.'

Maya was already backing away before he had finished. 'No! You can't!'

Stephen reached out and caught her arm. But his hold was light—not like he wanted to stop her, but more like he was asking her to stay.

'He wanted it this way, Maya.'

'How do you know he's strong enough to be taken off life-aid?'

'I don't. But it is what he wanted. He always said that if the situation ever arose, he wanted to be taken off. He signed the paperwork. This is a decision he made for himself, and he trusted me to carry it out.'

'No, no, *no*! Stop talking about him in past tense! This is not right! He can't want this. He *can't*. How can you do this to him? How can *you* do this to him?'

'I am so sorry, Maya. I so wish I didn't have to.'

He had splintered into pieces. Tears ran unchecked down his face. Maya grabbed his sleeve—the same arm that was still holding her. Though it was hard to say who was holding whom.

With her other hand, Maya clutched the front of his jacket. She wanted to shake him and push him into the lake so he couldn't do what he was talking about. But she also wanted to hold him and put the little pieces back to mend him.

'Then don't,' she pleaded. 'Please, Stephen. *Please*. Please don't do this.'

'I don't want to. If he doesn't make it, I cannot put into words how much I'll miss him. But I love him too much not to do for him what he trusts me to.'

'Please,' whispered Maya again. 'I'll do anything you want me to—' But she was sobbing too hard to continue.

Stephen caught her face with his hands. 'I have to,' he said, almost yearning. 'It's important to me that you understand why.'

An inhuman wail filled her ears. It took a moment for Maya to realize it came from her. She wrenched out of Stephen's grasp and punched a pillar on the walkway. Pain shot up her arm, and she welcomed it.

She bunched her fist again, but Stephen caught her, firmly this time. He pulled her into his arms, but he was the one who seemed to need comforting.

37

ENOL GIVES SOME ADVICE

'Good morning.'

Maya looked up to Councillor Enol walking towards her.

'Good morning, Councillor,' she replied.

'Got a few minutes for a chat?'

She hesitated. But he wasn't really making a request. 'Yes, Councillor. But, um, should I get my Watcher?'

'Oh, no. Just a friendly talk. You've been under a bit of stress. I wanted to see for myself that you were okay.'

'I'm fine,' said Maya, hoping that would be enough.

'Good. Good. Come on, let's go to my office. You like coffee?'

There was no way she was getting out of this. She sensed Noah coming closer—just around the next bend.

'Ah, Noah,' said Enol pleasantly. 'May I borrow your Preferred for a little while?'

'Of course, Councillor,' said Noah. 'Though her next class is in less than an hour from now.'

'I'll have her back in good time.'

Noah gave her a slight nod. 'I'll be in the courtyard.'

Enol had coffee and buns waiting in his office. He asked her to help herself, and she didn't know how to refuse, but the Castle's usually excellent fruit buns tasted like cardboard.

'How is Halvard Jan?' Enol asked. 'I believe you are close to him?'

How does he know that? Of course he knows that, he's a COUNCILLOR.

'He came off life-aid yesterday, but he hasn't woken up. He's in a coma.'

'I am very sorry. I hope he recovers.'

Could he be the Warrior? Had one of his people hurt Jan?

'Thank you, Councillor.'

'You were very brave to go and try to rescue Yazid,' said Enol.

Every cell in Maya's body sprang to attention. 'I would say he was the one who was brave.'

Enol bent his head in acknowledgement. Maya braced for a question about Lian's death, about an indirect question about the Key, but none came. Instead, what he asked was: 'Do you ever wonder about the future?'

The question threw her. 'Depends on what you mean, Councillor. My future specifically or of the worlds?'

'Well, both. After all, you'll be a Halvard one day.' Smile. 'Your future may have a major impact on the worlds' future.'

'Well, yes, I do wonder sometimes,' said Maya. That was the truth, after all.

'Halvard of the future have an immense responsibility. See how Roz has failed to sustain itself. How we have failed, and now your generation must find a way out of the mess.

Tell me, if you had the power, what is the one thing that you would fix?'

'Oh.' This line of questioning was turning out to be very unexpected. 'I—well, I think climate change.'

Enol's bushy eyebrows rose. 'Interesting. Very interesting.' He suddenly changed tracks. 'Maya, what would you say is the best part of being a Halvard?'

This she didn't have to think about at all. 'The ability to do things in the worlds in ways it wouldn't have been possible otherwise.'

Enol smiled and nodded, as if she had passed some test. He swung his swivel chair around to face the window—rather Illusion art that pretended to be a window. 'Suppose you could choose to use your abilities in a way that could have a profound impact on the world we live in. Salvage Roz, solve the climate crisis, end war and hunger, start over from scratch. Would you go for it?'

Maya frowned. 'I don't know if I understand, Councillor. Are you asking that if I could fix Roz, would I do it?'

'You do have a way with words. Yes, that is exactly what I am asking.'

'Of course,' said Maya.

Enol nodded. He smiled at her. 'I always like to hear young Preferred say that. It gives me hope. Have another bun.'

'No, thank you,' said Maya politely.

Enol poured himself some more coffee. 'What do you do in your free time?'

Maya was starting to get used to the sudden changes in subject. 'Um, I don't have much free time these days because of school and Preferred training. Mostly, when I do, I go and read to Halvard Jan. I am reading a lot these days, mostly about the Powers and for lessons.'

'I like to read, too,' said Enol. 'Ancient texts. I was raised as a Guide. I am fascinated by old books and artefacts.'

It didn't sound very interesting to Maya. She said diplomatically, 'Oh. Is that—fun?'

'It's fascinating,' said Enol. He got up and took a book from his shelf. It was a slim volume, with a soft binding. 'This is actually the very book that got me hooked. We found this text at an Inshai excavation site many decades ago. Of course, this isn't the original, but I had it scanned and copied.' He handed it to Maya.

'*The Powers and Us*,' read Maya. 'I read this when I was a new Preferred.'

Enol shook his head. 'You read a different version. This is the original text, dating back to over a thousand years. I was amazed to find that so much we can do with the Power has been lost to us.'

'What do you mean lost, Councillor?' asked Maya, fascinated despite herself.

Enol smiled. 'Being a member of the High Council and responsible for passing laws in this land, I shouldn't tell you this, but I trust you're sensible enough to understand. The thing is, we don't teach our Preferred everything. We tell them the limit of their ability and they take our word for it. The truth is, no one knows what the limit of anyone's ability is.'

He paused. Maya was hooked.

'What is the first lesson in Healing you learn? That you cannot Heal yourself, right? But how do you know it's true? Have you ever tried?'

Maya shook her head. She remembered something else. When she was studying about the Link, she had been told how one could draw Spirit from one's a'fin, but not give them Spirit. Yet she had done so. She had saved Noah's life that way.

'There, you see,' said Enol, watching her carefully. He got up again and took a plain wooden box from a cupboard. He set it down on his table and regarded Maya.

'I'm wondering if I should show you this.'

'What is it?'

'Other things I found at the same Inshai site. They said these were useless and threw them away, but I kept them. I wanted to study them.'

'What sort of things?' Maya asked.

Enol opened the box and Maya peered in. There were six small objects, all different shapes—a ring, a flat disc, a cube, a hollow cylinder, something shaped like a crudely cut Healer's symbol (the tree of life), and something that just looked like a pebble. They were all metal, silvery-grey, black or rusty brown.

'Go on. Touch them.'

Maya picked up the one that looked like the Healer's symbol. She drew in a breath.

'Are they all shells?'

Enol's eyes gleamed. 'Yes, well done. It took me three years to figure that out.'

It had been a test!

'What do they do?' she asked, trying to keep her face neutral and voice steady. 'Are they Healing shells? Are they harmful?'

'No, not so far as I've been able to ascertain. They do different things. The one you're holding is a Healing shell of sorts.'

She wanted to ask more questions, but Enol looked at the clock on the wall. 'It's time you went back, Maya.

Once again, it was a pleasure talking to you. I often call in Preferred to chat with them, but not too many of them show any interest in my old books and shells. Will you come again?'

Maya swallowed and said the only thing she could: 'Of course, Councillor.'

He stood and walked with her to the door. 'There's one bit of advice I have for you. You have a lot of Spirit in you. You may be able to do things others can't. Remember that.'

~

Maya gripped the cold metal of the fence that bound the Portal Road as she considered her Watcher's question.

'I don't know what I think,' she said at long last. 'It was so *stupid* of me to let him know about the shell. He was testing me, wasn't he?'

'Perhaps. It's all conjecture.'

'I don't like it. I don't want to talk to him. The next time he calls me, I won't go.'

'That's not an option,' Noah reminded her.

'But you are the one who thinks he's a Warrior.'

'That's still guesswork. It doesn't make it true.' He took a deep breath. 'But it's besides the point. Nothing has changed. We have the Key, the Warriors want it back. We can't trust anyone. Not Enol, not Ryder. Not even the High Councillor.'

EPILOGUE

Halvard Jiro of the Elite Guards read the report laid out on his screen with a tiny frown. Then he read it again.

'Karlize,' he called, and his colleague tapping on the plasma screen at the other end of the room turned to him. 'Have you seen the Lian Yeo autopsy reports?'

'No.' She came over and stood at his shoulder. 'I thought you should read them first.'

'This doesn't make sense to me.' He turned his screen towards her.

She read through quickly. 'It's incomplete. Where's the cause of death?'

'That's what I want to know as well. All her injuries are superficial, corresponding to the struggle Noah reported. But otherwise, she was perfectly healthy, until she was not.'

A deep furrow bisected Karlize's forehead. 'She couldn't have just dropped dead.'

'No.' He paused. 'Noah won't let his a'fin talk to us. I have a feeling she holds the key to this puzzle.'

COMING SOON

SANDS *of* TIME
BOOK THREE

THE SHADOW

PAYAL DHAR

Speaking Tiger
YOUNG ADULT